WAKING

A Novel

by

Celia Gilbert

Copyright Notice: Copyright ©2021 by Celia Gilbert

Cover art by Celia Gilbert

Table of Contents

Chapter I	7
Chapter II	31
Chapter III	47
Chapter IV	63
Chapter V	89
Chapter VI	107
Chapter VII	131
Chapter VIII	141
Chapter IX	165
Chapter X	199

Chapter I

Waking. But not because of the light. A drill was gnawing the street, footsteps were ringing against the pavement, and far off there was a slow murmur that advanced and receded but grew steadily stronger on its way to some inevitable crescendo.

She opened her eyes to the dark, the deep green dark of moss in the depth of the forest, the dark of velvet curtains which draped the high wide French windows with a voluptuous serenity. It was a green unique to the nineteenth century, and it troubled and amazed. Like the head of Nefertiti, lifted from the sands of Amarna, it was witness to a vanished life.

Today was their ninth day in Paris and her birthday. She was thirty-six. Was that the excitement – the age old excitement of one's own, one's special day – or was it the thought of Paris, after so many years, waiting again to be discovered behind the window? In the other bed Tommy began to stretch and to reach out an arm to pull her in, but Diana jumped out of bed and, slipping on the polished floor, ran to let in the light. First the underwater green pulled away, then the white diaphanous under-curtains. There was sun, and she leaned out feeling it warm her before it warmed the little narrow street along which people were briskly passing. It meant so much to feel the sun. . .

"Come back to bed, let's snuggle," said Tommy.

"Mommy, mommy, I'm sick." It was Kit's voice, weak and

anxious from the next room.

Diana's heart began to race. "Please God, don't let her throw up all over Sylvia's things," she whispered to herself. Running out of the bedroom she encountered Kitty hopping to the bathroom. She had already thrown up a bit on the rug but was doing her best to get to the toilet in time. Diana followed her, gathering back her hair while she leaned over the bowl. Afterwards, Diana wet small mounds of toilet paper and started cleaning up the little heaps on the rug. Kitty lay back greenly on the pillows.

"I think I feel a little better now," she said hopefully.

"It's my birthday," remarked Diana, feeling sorry for herself.

"Happy Birthday," Kitty replied, politely

Diana felt guilty. "So yours," she went on trying to pretend that what was coming was the statement that had been meant all along, "is coming up in just nine more days, and you'll be eight years old."

Kit smiled feebly.

Most of the vomit was gone but a sour odor lingered over the damp spots. Diana went back to the bathroom, rubbed soap on paper, rubbed paper on the spots. The paper rubbed down to little crumbs, and she began laboriously picking up the little crumbs, when suddenly the phone rang. It frightened her with its shrill hysterical ring, and because she was frightened, it made her angry, and she, of course, was the only one who could answer it, because she was the only one who could speak French. In one way it was amusing to see the look of amazement on the children's faces, and pleasure on Tommy's, when she would rattle away; in another way it was exhausting like being the leader of a tour group, responsible for everyone's coming and going and well-being. She had been going for a long time on an energy which wasn't there.

The front hall was dark, and for a moment she forgot where the phone was. It rang once more, and she snatched it from its high old fashioned cradle and shrieked "Allô." There was complete silence, and then a voice, a man's voice, an American voice said, "Diana? It's Ronald. I'm on my way back from Copenhagen, leaving tomorrow. Can I come and see you tonight? Why don't we go out to dinner?"

Her hands were like ice. She loved him, but how could she bear to see him? How would it affect the children? She stared out into the kitchen courtyard. All around the courtyard other apartments repeated the shape of their own, other footsteps, other voices. It was ten years since they had lived in an apartment house. She turned her eyes from the courtyard and stared at the huge polished oak doors with its array of locks and bolts.

"That will be great," Diana said. "We're all a bit queasy now, but some of us should be up to dinner, so come at 7:30." And she gave him directions.

His name wasn't Ronald, of course, it was something more slavic, but Ronald was *echt* Bronx for the thirteen-year old, who arrived there from Bucharest via Paris and Lisbon in the 1940s. He and his parents were the lucky ones. On both sides there was nothing left of his relatives.

At twenty-one he had his Ph. D. in chemistry and was doing post-graduate work when he met and married Nora, a graduate student in social work. Together in the same department at the university, Ronald and Tommy had become good friends, and they had all been close without being intimate. Diana had always been fond of Ronald for his wit and warmth, and she admired Nora. Of mixed Scandinavian ancestry, Nora was loving and reserved. She was at home in her home with her children and Ronald. Around her things harmonized, children flourished, rooms displayed subtle and delicate colors, life had an order which was sensuous rather than spartan. And Diana whose household life always seemed to her chaotic and makeshift longed for a kind of serenity she thought Nora possessed. She and Tommy named their third child, a girl, for Nora.

Now the shadow of that child's death lay over all their lives. Into the circle of death they had drawn Nora and Ronald, the wrong magic had prevailed. Diana had seen her last the day before Nora died. What did she think when she came, bearing a strawberry and a book for her namesake, once golden haired and radiant, then hollowed to the bone, yellowed and shrunken by the cancer? A six year old whose skeleton was propped on the pillows. Death in April. Diana telephoned. There was no funeral. Did the child wait for the long promised visit of her godmother? She was a child of decorum and grace. How did Nora tell her four daughters, the oldest a year older than Nick, the Field's son, the youngest two years younger than Nora was. How to tell that they had no power to protect, ward off danger, that the good they wished for them and bought for them and themselves was as frail as paper.

Shivering because the high ceilinged apartment never warmed up, Diana returned to the bedroom and found Tommy standing naked in the middle of the floor, slowly picking his ear with a bobby pin carried especially for that purpose in his wallet.

"Happy Birthday, darling, he said tenderly.

Diana went to him to be hugged and be warm. He was always warm, that's why she loved him. Immediately he started to push her on to a bed. His cock rose.

"Oh, no," she hissed, "I'm starving, Kit's throwing up, and Ronald just called and is coming by to have dinner with us tonight, and we've got to find an apartment, remember?" He kissed her. "That's nice," he said, meaning Ronald. A slam of the front door made both of them jump. Then Nick's voice, followed by a discrete knock at their door,

"Mom, I've got the *croissants* and a *baguette* and three *brioche* because Kit doesn't like them."

Diana sighed. He was amazing to her, he always had been. "We'll be there in a minute," she called. The mysterious substance arrived at through one's agency, totally out of one's control. Everything was there, the feelings of trust, fear, their world as they are going to perceive it waiting to open like a Japanese paper flower when dropped into the solution of their lives. They had named him Nicholas Taylor Field, the Taylor for Tom's father, and from the beginning he was like the Field side of the family, loving, sensitive to others, intuitively knowing how the world was put together. Afraid, like everyone, he had better ways than most of controlling that fear.

Diana turned away from Tom, angry, because she had really wanted breakfast in bed, and he knew that's what she loved more than anything. He never did anything he didn't want to do.

Tommy remained on the bed, reaching for the book he had been reading the night before, He detached himself from bed with infinite slowness, always unaware of Diana's envy, an envy she was scarcely aware of, more often masked as scorn. How he could lie there scratching or reading. She dressed quickly, staring curiously at herself in the graceful mahogany glace a cheval. How many times in the last year she had noted with astonishment that she still had a face. Small, no more than five feet, she had grown thin, her cheeks always round and rosy, had hollowed. Her black leather belt was in its last hole but she easily could pass for someone in their twenties. Apparently even death, like loss of virginity, leaves no traces. Ten months to die. Six months later was not a measure of time, it was merely waking and sleeping.

She tied her shoes. "Come on," she said to Tom, "I'm hungry."

She peered into Kitty's room. "If you feel like eating, Nick's brought back some *croissant*." Kit's long hair was fanned out over the pillow. A bit of color had come back to her cheeks. "Maybe," she murmured. There was a book on her raised knees, like her father, she was only half in this world.

Diana passed through the dark hallway into the dining room, gloomy in the daytime because its windows gave on the inner courtyard. She stroked the antique table, admired the small porcelain chemine e, the delicately articulated chandelier, and small sideboard with its huge terracotta soup tureen. She moved down the narrow corridor which snaked its way to the kitchen. On the left was Nick's room, a dim maid's room of the past, now fixed as a room for cousin Sylvia, who in best French style reserved it for herself when she rented out the apartment, but came in from Switzerland where she and cousin Ed lived.

High on the kitchen walls hung a series of botanical drawings of fruits and vegetables. They presided over the sepia-walled temple, where bottles of fruit syrups were neatly arranged on the shelves, and in their homey Mason jars preserved fruits swam in liquid matrices whose colors rivaled stained glass windows.

Diana put the light under the water for coffee, and kissed Nick who was seated at a small green table ecstatically munching a *baguette*. His cheek of a ten year old was firm and red. His brown eyes shone benevolently behind his glasses.

"It was wonderful of you to get the bread," said Diana, "It's my birthday today."

"Happy Birthday, Mom," Nick replied obligingly.

Diana began to grind the coffee beans in the small electric grinder. When the plastic dome was taken off, there was a brown hemisphere with its sharp scent of mocha and chicory. She was warming the milk when Tommy appeared, dressed, beaming, ready to be fed. She reached for the huge breakfast cups and filled them with the dark coffee and foaming milk. The sight of those cups brought back those cold winter mornings of her junior year in Paris at the Freilanders, when *Monsieur* Freilander would knock like thunder on their door and she would rise and bring in the breakfast tray for herself and Jessica, quickly taking a great gulp of café au lait before it cooled off to try to stabilize herself before the onslaught of a French winter school day. It was so vivid, that memory, that she stared across it as from a vast distance at Tom and Nick, two strangers.

Tommy was reading a guidebook. Nick was smiling at Tommy. From his first weeks of life he had sensed the difference between his mother and his father. When Tom held him over his shoulder to pat him and bring up gas, he would lie, muscles tensed, his cheek against the tweed fabric, smelling the odor of tobacco and man flesh, twisting his head just a bit from side to side to investigate this new universe without softness, without contours, without smell of wet milk. He accepted me, Diana thought looking at them, the two profiles so similar, but he has always cherished Tom, as though he were the father and Tom the son. And Tom loves him in that man way, deeply, but always with that withholding of men who love their women best and resent any distraction in that relation. Or are all men only the siblings never the parents of their children?

I refused to let you suck from me when I nursed the children, Diana thought, looking at Tom. I never wanted to mother a man. I wanted to mother my children. And to be mothered. Suddenly she wanted to burst out of the kitchen.

"Where shall we go today?" she asked. "It's such beautiful weather and it's getting late." She grew tense at the thought that it was getting near eleven, she hated eleven and desperately coveted the early morning hours. Tommy looked up from his book. "Is Kit well enough to come with us?"

"If she isn't, she can stay with *Mme. Rennet*. We should get the paper and call up the agents," Diana added. Cousin Sylvia's elegant haven was not theirs forever. Suddenly she remembered that she had put the *croissants* in the oven to warm. "Just in time," said Nick cheerfully, as he watched her rush to rescue them.

She set out the good pale creamy French butter, and reached for the shelf where the jams were to take down her favorite, the morello cherries, labeled in Sylvia's bold artist's hand. A bit of butter on one end of the *croissant*, a large cherry on top and, crisp and soft, fruit and fat were consummated in her mouth. She held the cup in her two hands, the warmth entered her palms, and she inhaled the fragrance of the coffee while she swallowed its bitterness letting it marry the sweet.

Tom was gulping, had gulped, had finished his coffee. He swallowed neatly, like a person folding paper. He ate with rapidity, faster even than Diana's father.

We're going to look at that apartment on the *Rue de Grenelle* at one thirty, so we'll be near Napoleon's tomb, and we can go and look at that.

Was it odd, Diana wondered continuing to sip and eat slowly, was it odd to have lived in Paris for a whole school year and never have visited Napoleon's tomb, or indeed a host of places? She viewed herself again through that far end of the telescope, nineteen years old, fantasies of being a great writer competing with those of marrying the most perfect man in the world. Faceless, nameless, he was powerful, famous and she at his side was envied and sought after as his wife, the woman he passionately adored. Why hadn't she done more that year she wondered, remembering how often she had been sick, how inadequate she felt compared to her friends who biked down the Champs Elysées, got better grades, spoke French more fluently.

Soft footsteps creaked in the kitchen corridor. Kitty appeared, very small in the high door frame, a green quilted robe over her ski pajamas. With her dark rosy skin, dark the way the colors of pansies are dark, her long straight brown hair, her full pouting lips and her brown eyes, like two fishes in her face, she was already voluptuous, a young odalisque. When she was born they had called her "rosebud." Diana marveled at the way her nose was graceful, slightly tilted at the end, the nose she had always wished for herself, and she loved her for gratifying her by having it. Kitty shuffled across the floor with her odd gait. One foot still turned in, although years ago the orthopedist had assured Diana that it was a condition which would eventually correct itself.

"Put inner wedges, one quarter of an inch in the left shoe and every morning and every night hold her feet and gently rotate the leg outward thirty times." He had looked at her seriously as he said that. He had the bland neat mask face of many doctors. His name was Randell. He was the head of orthopedics at that hospital and all the pediatricians sent their patients to him. Diana had fought with the X-ray technician, refusing to let them x-ray Kitty until they had covered her with a rubber sheet. Randell rebuked her for this coldly. "There is no amount of radiation that could hurt her at the speed we use," he said. Diana said, "My husband is a scientist and he says you cannot be too careful." Citing authority against his, having none of her own.

When they had left the hospital, she held Kitty close. She had hated doctors, even then. For a few weeks she tried following his advice, and then it had seemed ridiculous. There was no time in her life to do anything with regularity. There were the demands of Tom and Nick, then three, and the house and entertaining. She rose early with the children and went to bed late with Tom.

"You must take naps," Tom would say authoritatively when she complained that she was tired. He had read an article in a woman's magazine she brought home where a sympathetic woman psychoanalyst noted that many young mothers were tired and suggested that the way to get around the whole problem was to nap in the day. Diana hated naps then. She hated regularity. When she thought about Dr. Randell's advice it seemed mad. For what would Kitty think at her impressionable twenty months about being stretched on the diaper table having her foot turned outward, what would she think about Diana and herself? Perhaps it would make her feel strange about her feet, and that would be a bad thing concluded Diana.

But now looking at Kitty, like a fortune teller reading her pack, or a medium reading the tea leaves she saw how it had been Kit's lot to have been loved because her nose was a desirable shape and because her foot turned in, to fall a good deal of the time. And this falling reinforced some of the feeling that Kitty had that the world was a difficult place, full of an unexpected bad which lay in wait often at the moment of one's most spontaneous joy. One would be brought low, there would be tears.

There were dark shadows under Kitty's eyes, but she seemed cheerful. "Cousin Sylvia must be a very remarkable woman," she announced. "I wonder if we'll ever find an apartment as nice as this one," Nick said. He always kept his mind on the realities of the situation.

Cousin Sylvia. Apartments. The children had never lived in an apartment before. There was so much for the ear to take in; sounds of running feet going up and down the wooden stairs, the clank of the heavy elevator, the ring of other doorbells, voices in the courtyard, the small bubbles of salutation arising from the concierge's aquarium, *"Bonjour Madame, Monsieur,"* the heavy slam of the great front door. Cousin Sylvia. The way the children spoke of her made Diana and Tom laugh. Her presence lay over all of them. In a family outstanding for its generosity Sylvia was noted for her legendary penny pinching. But seeing her through the children's eyes, the children who had never known her, Diana received another impression. For it was Sylvia who had made the jams that they sighed over each morning, and it was Sylvia who had made the gilded frames which so charmingly held the series of eighteenth century prints in the little library, and it was Sylvia who was slowly antiquing the moldings in the little salon, and it was Sylvia who had upholstered the headboards of the two twin beds in the master bedroom so that Diana was afraid to push them together because the first night when they arrived they had tried doing that and one of the headboards had fallen down. Diana had visions of something happening to the apartment during their tenancy and being forced to scrub for the rest of their lives to pay for the damages.

But most compelling of all was Sylvia's latest interest – her shell collection. In wide old glassed-in bookshelves, on open shelves in the library, in the bedroom, elevated on round plexiglass forms (which Sylvia had made) were the shells. Each one was a marvel from the ivory fragility of the Venus Comb, to the gaping conches, cunt and labia, sea urchins' puffy cushions, sinister smooth razorbacks, periwinkles, turbans of mother of pearl. There was one perfect chambered nautilus. All of the shells were lit from behind, and at night the family went about illuminating them, peering at a magical world they had never thought of before, lacy coral fans, heavy involuted brain coral.

Sylvia was not a person one could like, but the children didn't know that, and Diana felt a twinge of jealousy at their admiration for her, for her "doing." Their mother was not a doer. It was Tom who was good with his hands, could fix things and build things.

Kitty shuffled over in her furry slippers to Tommy and put her head on his shoulder. Odd, Nick looked just like Tom and the Field side of the family, the square jaw, the habit of sticking out a lower lip in concentration, the strong curved nose, yet Kitty, too, who was so much more like Diana, resembled Tom. It was something brown around the eyes and round and full about the mouth.

Tom put his arm around Kit. "Feeling better?" he asked. She nodded and sat down. To her and to Diana Tom gave off a necessary reassurance.

Nora had looked most of all like Tom. She had exactly the set of his eyes, her brow, and her delicate eyebrows were shaped like his.

The old wives' tale says that the one who is loved the most is the one the children resemble, remembered Diana. And she recalled at that moment the Field cousin who, looking at Nick as a toddler remarked to her, "It looks as though they rented you for nine months.

"O. K." said Diana, restless or rather restive under the weight of moving them all out. "So we're going to the apartment and then to Napoleon's Tomb. Kitty, do you want to come? If you don't, you can stay here with *Mme. Rennet*."

"Yes, I want to stay and read."

It was just as well, Diana thought. Kitty had a way of suddenly caving in which was very disconcerting. In crowds she immediately began to yawn like someone whose oxygen supply has been cut off. And she was usually assailed by unquenchable thirst as well.

Nick finished off the last of the bread. Diana made Kitty a cup of tea, something which she had discovered she loved coming over on the plane. She watched her nibble daintily at a *croissant*. Diana was beginning to feel queasy herself but decided to ignore it.

"Ronald is coming tonight," Diana said as casually as possible. The children smiled. They had only vague memories of him and a visit to the Cohens' house. But did they think of Nora? It made Diana wince. She would never know what they were really thinking, what they were suppressing from themselves, from her.

"I'll bet he'll be amazed when he sees this apartment," Nick said with satisfaction. It made Diana smile. She knew that he was impressed, but she hadn't realized how much he loved the beauty of this place, how utterly responsive he was to all the elements around him. But shouldn't she have known? Hadn't he always revealed how much he understood? She knew that in particular he loved the massive black Bechstein in the grand salon. It filled him with a sense of awe, and yet familiarity because there was one like it in the house of his German-Jewish refugee pediatrician, and on the wall alongside it was a little engraving of the fat, jolly Brahms playing one, and now to his intense pleasure he lived in a house with one. But none of them could play the piano, and that made him unhappy. Kitty, when she saw it, sat down instantly and began to play chords pretending she could play. She yearned to play the piano. Diana promised her lessons when they got home.

And Diana smiled too, because Nick expressed her feeling about Ronald. She, too, thought he would be impressed, and Ronald always made one want to score points. He was the most overtly catty man she knew, always probing for one's weak spot, always displaying his good in contrast to your bad. He did it so effectively that she often had to remind herself that in the world he and Tom lived and competed in it was really Tom who had gone further than Ronald, the prodigy whom they had met so many years ago.

The locks of the front door were heard, all three of them, noisily opening. *Mme. Rennet* had arrived. Diana began to shoo them out of the kitchen and pile the dishes, somewhat guiltily into the sink. She was disturbed by the social uncertainties. *Mme. Rennet* was expected to do work for Sylvia, but on the other hand she would surely expect a tip for the extra work they made for her anyway. She would of course have nothing to do but light dusting, but Diana knew that Sylvia always got the last drop out of anyone who worked for her and was sure that there were tasks left for her to do. Money and the French! If only she could lose the notions of her upbringing, that money was a dirty word, and that people must do things for love, that payment degraded the giver as much as the receiver. Diana knew that was not the French way, but what good did it do to know a thing if one still went hot and cold and felt queasy for days beforehand, knowing one was expected to pay (but how much and when?) for services, that is personal relationships of services rendered. And the knowledge that smiles were the smiles of expectation of payment. Worse, that all relationships were personal, that is the concierge expected something by virtue of their having entered her sphere of influence, even if she did nothing for them, they were now included in her omniscient nodding. That was enough.

"Bonjour Madame, Monsieur, les enfants," sang out *Mme. Rennet*. She beamed approvingly at the children, She had one, Paolo, a boy of three, whom she worshipped. It was clear to Diana that *Mme. Rennet* admired her for having two. *Mme. Rennet* was Spanish, dark, wiry, neat, in her late twenties. Sylvia had always had a Spanish bonne-à-tout-faire. They were paid less, and they worked more. Last week Diana had seen her leaving with a yellow backed novel in her hand, and, out of curiosity, asked her what she was reading" Without a word *Mme. Rennet* revealed the cover: Balzac's *"Le Lys Dans La Vallée."* Diana was startled. Suddenly she was back in her parent's bedroom

searching the bookshelves for something to read. She was no older than Nick was now, and she had taken down from the many volumes of The Human Comedy the one called "The Lily of the Valley" and had stared for a long time at the old-fashioned engraving, which showed a man in cape and riding breeches standing alone before the terrace of a French chateau. Then years later she found herself staying at Sache with Caroline Richardson not far from that very chateau.

"Bonjour, Madame Rennet," Diana heard her voice ring out, hitting the right note, amazing herself and the others. A mother, so habitual, to do something so clever as to speak another language!

Tom looked at her with admiration. In the first years of their marriage when they had traveled Diana had always been the one to speak, to arrange, to manage. Tom was shy with strangers and terrified of telephones. In that very kitchen Diana had wept on their first anniversary because he had seemed so dull, inept, lack-luster. She had poked and prodded to get him out of the apartment. When one marries one expects to be marrying one's father, after all.

Diana explained to *Mme. Rennet* that they were leaving Kitty with her. She nodded sympathetically when told Kitty was feeling unwell from all the traveling. *"La pauvre,"* she murmured. Last week Diana had heard the story of her child and his visit to the clinic for a *"bronchite."* It was a long story of alarming fevers, hours in the waiting rooms, and finally partial reassurance that the child would recover. Their lingua franca, their common culture, the child: to be watched over, worried over, the essentials.

Together they got out the children's new school uniforms, the first they had ever worn, and the labels to be sewn in them. *Mme. Rennet* grimaced as she viewed the buttons, then shrugged. Everything would have to be sewed properly, or they would disappear in an instant, was her

21

opinion. Diana tried to look as though she thought that this was perfectly reasonable of her, as though she would, of course, be resewing them herself if it weren't for the fact that she had to go apartment hunting.

And was it by way of further excuse that she said, shyly, *"Aujourd'hui, c'est mon anniversaire. J'ai trente-six ans."* How funny it sounded in French, I have thirty-six years. Or they had her. *"Nel mezzo del cammin,"* now indeed. To her surprise *Mme. Rennet* nodded and announced that was her age as well.

Then Diana rushed to Kitty's room. She was settled back in the narrow little studio bed, near her the old-fashioned turning bookshelves were filled with the books of Sylvia's two daughters, Brenda and Lyn, now grown. On the little cheminée two bright purple iridescent butterflies shone, mounted on snowy cotton in a box. Kit was in love with them.

"Darling, we won't be long. *Mme. Rennet* is here until we get back. I told her to ask you about tea, the word in French is *"thé"* and for "please" say, *"s'il vous plait,"* okay?"

Kitty smiled. Diana saw it was like a reprieve, not having to go out, to wall herself in with words, with stories more satisfying than life, which until six months ago had no conclusions. She bent and kissed her fragrant brow and left.

"Goodbye, Kit," Nick called. Little survivors of the wreck.

They locked the door carefully behind them, ran down the wide bare wooden steps, peered into the grill work of the elevator, then passed *Mme. Julien* in her kitchen, stepped over the high iron lintel and pushed their way through the grand wide doors onto the sunny sidewalk.

Diana reached for Nick's hand and took Tom's arm. A momentary Joy. She had always loved her birthdays.

* * * * * * *

Ronald had proved to be a true prophet. "It always takes ten days to find an apartment in Paris," he had said. "We call it our rule of desperation."

That night they hadn't gone out to dinner, by evening all of them except Nick, who ate quantities of sandwich de jambon, felt sick. "Enterovirus," pronounced Ronald, "Time is the only cure, and it knocks everything out."

They were sitting in the kitchen drinking cup after cup of tilleul, its leaves fanned open and made the water a pale yellowy green. At *Aix-en-Provence* it was the tea *Madame Bourdet* had given Jessica and Diana when they had their periods.

Ronald told them about the summer the Cohens had spent on a small Danish island. Diana wondered why she and Nora had never been closer. Was it that between different cultures there was always an imperfect understanding? Like the blind feeling the raised form of the letter, one perceived the outlines but never the finer truths and shades?

Nora's parents, seen once, had been a dramatic sight. Her mother was almost six feet tall with pure white hair, exquisite blue eyes, and she walked with the bearing of a Norse goddess of house and home. When she sat, large broad hands folded in her huge lap one could imagine her midwifing the birth of children and animals, making the sick well, blessing the harvest. Nora's father was no more than five feet, his face was lined with tensions and nerves, it was a desperate face, and he stood by the side of his Freya, a small anxious child, a brilliant scientist, a Jew. Diana had hummed afterwards, *"Mon pere m'a donne un petit mari quel homme, quel petit homme..."* And he had fathered six children on his giant wife.

"There wasn't a single day of rain the whole time we were on Danebro," boasted Ronald in his familiar way that gave himself full credit for having pulled off a meteorological coup. As usual Diana fell into a trap of admiration, How well things worked out for them, how smoothly.

"Was it lovely and sunny, then?" she mused.

"The temperature is usually about fifty degrees," he smiled, "and it is rather cloudy, but we didn't have rain."

Then he had admired for the third time the Fields' apartment.

Nick had come to say goodnight. He kissed Diana and flashed at Ronald his irresistible smile of Pan, still miraculously carrying the stamp of pure infant joy. The dimple in his cheek flashed; Ron grinned back. No one got that smile unmoved.

Ron yawned, they all yawned. He told them about the bargain they had got when they lived in France the last year. It was in Bure. "And we got in twice a week to eat out," he said triumphantly. Diana shuddered at the thought of twice a week. She wanted to be right in the center. They walked back through the grand salon and stopped to admire the Buddha head on the white marble mantelpiece, the huge mirror behind it reflecting the room, the lovely inlaid screen behind one small brocaded sofa. Before the large windows two old garden urns held pots of cyclamen and fern, beyond the windows the small fountain of the Place was illuminated, the focus of the pentagon of streets and the grand hotels which looked onto it.

Ronald had to catch a plane. Diana kissed him goodbye sending love to Nora and the four children. No word about her, but what could he have said? Wearily Diana had turned off the lights. Where would they ever find a dwelling, a refuge she had wondered?

* * * * * * *

They were jubilant a few days later telling the children. And just a trifle hesitant, because the one flaw was that the children would have to share a bedroom.

"It's perfect except," Diana heard herself saying, and quickly changed to: "And you children will have your own balcony from your room. And Kit, it has a piano that's nicer than the one in the place on *Rue Cambronne*." She shuddered as she remembered that one and relived her gratitude to Tom for not making them take it. It had been only ten minutes' walk from the lab, and one metro stop from the children's school, and he had been so weary of looking. But it was a horror of a place. True, it had the three bedrooms they were asking for, but a violently ugly fireplace covered with imitation brick paper in a narrow living room-dining room. The dining room table was just large enough to hold four plates and was surrounded by white metal patio furniture. Only two of the apartment's windows faced onto the outside, a tiny dingy street. It was right after they had refused that one that the agent, an energetic blonde who drove a Quatre Chevaux with brio through the impossible traffic, had taken them, shrugging, "because you said you want three bedrooms, but this only has two, but it is near the school for your children," to the apartment.

No concierge had been visible as they had entered the neat marble lobby and taken the tiny ancient *"ascenseur"* to the seventh floor. The tiny red carpeted stairs were clean and neat as they slowly ascended. On the seventh floor they had knocked at the door on the left. They heard steps, The door was opened by a boy with a high-cheek-boned thin face, a typical French face, wide at the top tapering to a pointed chin. His complexion was sallow, there were a few blotches on his forehead, and his eyes appeared blue or gray behind colorless rimmed plastic glasses. He was dressed in turtleneck, tweed jacket, khaki pants, and he smiled hesitantly when he saw them.

But Diana noticed the windows behind him. They were windows without curtains, open to the sky and the neighboring apartment house, where pigeons contently were roosting on the old copper ledges. In front of the French windows was a lovely long simple French desk with a worn green leather inset. To the right a chair and a small fireplace with white marble mantelpiece over which hung a huge mirror. No rugs. Through glass doors on the left one saw the dining room, bare wooden floor, French windows which opened onto a balcony one plain wooden Provençal table, four rush chairs, a thick heavy wooden chest, a *bahut*, used for storing plates, crockery and glasses and against the far wall, a dirty cot.

The agent who had apparently never seen the apartment before, lit a cigarette and let the boy take them around. Two bedrooms opened off the tiny entrance hall. One had two beds in it, a wardrobe, a chest of drawers. It had doors which opened onto a balcony that faced onto the avenue, the broad sidewalks lined with plane trees. Over the trees one saw the gardens of the UNESCO, to the left the Eiffel Tower and the honey-colored elegant barracks of the *École Militaire*.

The second bedroom, the master bedroom, had a double bed, one chest of drawers, one bookcase flanking a small fireplace with mirror above it, and, in one corner, a little bathroom with a sink and shelves. From the bed the whole of the *École Militaire* was visible and through one set of French windows one could enter the balcony shared with the other bedroom.

The three of them opened the doors and walked out. The noise of the traffic was far away and slow on that quiet September day. They could look down the block almost to the children's school. Wide quiet streets. Buses plied the avenue in front of the *École Militaire*. Diana's heart had been pounding as they followed the boy back through the hall through the door, which led to a minuscule hall, closet, locked, then a WC and to one side a narrow room with a bathtub and finally to a kitchen just large enough to hold a small table, pint-sized stove, an old American refrigerator, and a sink whose narrow low rimmed basin was supported by a faded blue wooden base. A high window next to it opened out onto a quiet back street with a public building of some sort on it. And there was a door with a big old brass key stuck in it, which opened onto a landing in stone and led to a flight of stairs, which went down to a back courtyard and up one flight to the chambres des bonnes.

The agent had tapped out her cigarette as they started to make a second round of the place. Diana had been tormented by one thing alone, the children would have to share a rooms. It seemed unthinkable by American standards. So much that was strange and new was going to happen to them, they would have to make so many adjustments, was it fair to ask them to be crowded together for so long a time? And to ask them because their mother had fallen in love with the windows and the light?

The agent departed, explaining that she had previous appointments and that the boy was the *"fils du proprietaire"* so they could make arrangements with him.

They went over the price with him, the heating arrangements. The rent was reasonable, but they'd have to supply a great deal in the way of kitchenware, chairs, sheets. All this in French with the boy. And Diana had turned to Tommy to say in English that they just couldn't take it, they have to think about it because of the children.

"You'd be in the place the most," Tom had said going to the heart of the problem, as usual. But Diana had thought he was put off by the lack of a chair to sit in and read.

They had decided to think it over. In French, Diana said to the waiting boy, *"Bon, nous allons réflechir un peu plus."* He bowed slightly, rubbing his hands together in a queer way he had, and let them out.

How dark the hall had been, how slow the creaking trip down in the ascenseur! They had clanged to the bottom. Out on the street an old man in a neat, faded gray suit was sitting on a bench in front of the house, by his side a hairless white dog with a stiff and stupid expression on its face. With every step away from the building Diana felt worse. The street under those trees was dark, dark, dark.

"Let's go back, let's take it. The children will be able to walk to school, and that will make up for the bedroom." Quickly they turned and reentered the building, got into the elevator almost guiltily… the unfamiliar doors eyed them hostilely. They had rung the bell again; the boy reappeared. He smiled distantly, curiously, his brows raised in question.

"We'll take it," Diana had said. And he had smiled broadly. And she saw that his eyes were very blue behind the thick lenses. He murmured that he was sure that they would love the place, he would call the agent and tell her.

A family of six Columbiana had previously occupied the apartment, and they had been quite happy. He gave them his name again, Patrice Montcheval, (My horse or horse mountain? Diana had laughed to herself.) and he lived at *Cité Universitaire*.

They went down in the elevator together. He told them his father was a business man, who had been to the States. Did they have children? he had asked, that was nice. He was sure they would love the place. They shook hands. Diana was deliriously happy.

Now telling the children, she could hardly wait for the light, the sky; Sylvia's was dark and confined. The children were so thrilled about getting settled, about a balcony, they had never said a word about sharing. Hadn't she thought, she wondered, that they might even prefer it? Hadn't they come away so they could knit together, form fresh familial tissue over the lesion?

"We found our apartment on Friday the Thirteenth," said Nick, with a grin.

They laughed.

¤

Chapter II

Wearily, Diana turned off the vacuum cleaner and decided it was time for a bit of lunch. It was the second day since school had begun, and she hadn't gotten used to the absence of the children. And there was still so much to do. It seemed to her that they had been settling in forever. First they had decided to paint the bedrooms and the kitchen. A week ago they had given up on the kitchen and had hired a man to do the salon and dining rooms. He was a hardworking wiry man who came in the evening after he finished his own work, and, being conscientious, it soon became clear that both rooms would need two more coats than they had bargained for.

She brought a sandwich out to the terrace and sat at a small round table they had bought with its complement of four yellow chairs. She gazed off into the late September sky. So much buying. Trips and trips and trips to get knives, wire, paint, brushes, lamps, pots, pans….still no comfortable reading chair. They had not moved in until they had painted the bedrooms. It looked, at the rate things were proceeding that it would be the middle of October before they were really settled, and she would have time to crawl into some tiny shelter of time and quiet and try to work. Tommy had thrown himself into the fixing up in a way which surprised her. His French was becoming a bit more confident, it was nothing like hers for speed and fluency, but it some-times had a way of being more accurate. For so many years now she had been the ruler of the home, so that she had forgotten he had his own homemaking abilities. He could fix anything and was a meticulous painter. And he liked comfort. It was he who buoyed her up on their thousands of errands and continued to paint when they got home, while she would collapse on the bed. His lab wasn't ready to open until the rentrée, and he had energy to burn. Besides it was a challenge of sorts. At the moment he was out trying to buy a piece of wire to pick the lock of the cupboard closet in the little hall outside the kitchen. When he had asked M. Montcheval what was in it, the latter had shrugged.

"Ah, just things my family wished to keep," he answered smiling, "I'm not sure what things." A vaguer smile.

"But where's the key?"

"Ah, well, I couldn't say, they probably have it."

"That's space that would be useful for you," said Tom to Diana wasting no further time on him.

It was Diana's turn to shrug. "I'm sure I can manage" she had answered. They had the office pantry shelves where the maimed crockery, random chipped plates and glasses from the kitchen middens of previous years were stacked.

Tom turned the handle of the door under the eyes of the other two. "We have to get it open."

Nick's first words on seeing the apartment had been, "It's really dirty, but it's nice, the windows. What are we going to do to fix it up?" Kitty said, "We need some birds." But both of them could scarcely conceal their terror when they were presented to the concierge by M. Montcheval.

On that day he had been waiting for the *"brocanteur"* – the junkman – to come and take the *bahut* and the iron cot away. They had all met in the lobby. The concierge could have been sixty or eighty. She was a stout personage, composed seemingly out of two pillows, tied around the middle with a string. Her hair was the white of someone who has once been blonde. Her eyes were hard and blue, and she smiled with all the formality and suspicion of a French woman of her age and class.

When the children were presented to her she warmed one tiny degree and informed Diana that the four Columbian girls of the previous year knew not one word of French when they arrived but by mid-year they spoke French *"comme des petites francaises."* Next they had been taken on a tour of the tiny back courtyard, where there was an ancient faucet for water, some buckets, a rug on a line, and some spindly houseplants being aired like convalescents. Here was the place for the *"poubelle"* (a word the children found enchanting). Here was the beginning of that stone staircase which would wind round past everyone's back door and a splendid view as well of all the tiny kitchen windows with their ancient meat safes below them, theirs notable for being the shabbiest.

Madame Guillemin, for that was her formidable name, had assured them that she would be happy to bring them the courier in the morning and do their menage as she had done for *Mme. La Colombiane*. And one thing more; the children were never to come down in the elevator. Diana assured her they would not. Throughout all of this *M. Montcheval* had stood hands folded gravely, head to one side, listening attentively to *Mme. Guillemin*.

It was later that same day that Diana had realized for the first time that he spoke English, perfect English in fact. Diana had found them all on the balcony; his hand was protectively on Kit's shoulder, and he was pointing out points of interest on the horizon. Nick was watching him warily but learning what he could.

"So you speak English," Diana had said, almost blushing because she remembered speaking English to Tom in front of him. He smiled shyly and answering in French had said,

33

"Yes, but I am very timid. My English isn't as good as your French." That was nonsense of course. Diana vowed she would only speak to him in French, it was marvelous practice. He could speak what he liked to the children.

Since then he had been extraordinarily helpful. A week ago he had insisted on taking them all to dinner at a restaurant at the end of the small street off the *Rue de Commerce* in the Fifteenth which lay at their back door. Somewhat deprecatingly Patrice, as they now called him, referred to it as *"un peu Populaire."* It reminded Diana of the old restaurant Julien on the *Rue Soufflot* where she always had lunch after her lesson with M. Durand, her tutor in Greek during her Junior year. How she had loved him in his little cheap pantoufles and threadbare turtleneck as they went over Antigone in the chalk filled rooms of the *École Normale*.

Now, in this place with its dark bentwood chairs with cane bottoms, long tables covered with white paper, it seemed to her that the same elderly, fatherly harassed waiters running up and down the aisles. The restaurant Julien no longer existed, perhaps though in a Buddhist heaven of waiters their souls had transmigrated to this one.

That night Patrice had sat with his arm around Kit, whom he called, "a little princess." She had been frightened by the noise and the crowds and eating with strangers; at their table had been two tired looking older men, one in a trench coat, the other with a newspaper. Nick had ordered a dozen *escargot*, followed it with *steak au poivre*, then gone to the bathroom, thrown it all up, and ordered a giant gooey dessert. Patrice had told them about his family and his studies. He had one sister, Isabelle. His father was a business man who had traveled all over the world for his company. His mother was the daughter of a very distinguished lawyer. It was that grandfather who had originally owned the building they were living in, and the family still owned three apartments in it. *Mme. Guillemin* had come as a young girl to be the family's own bonne. On Patrice's paternal side were French Protestants and English. The Montcheval clan was all over the world, it appeared.

The night after that had been the eve of Kit's birthday, and Patrice had turned up unexpectedly, bearing two boxes. "I brought these for you," he said to Kitty, "for your room while you are here, they belong to my sister Isabelle and I know she would want you to share them."

He presented Kit with the boxes. One contained a moth with slender furry antennae and huge eyes at each corner of the wings, the other a Monarch, regal in its purple reds.

They had all admired the specimens, Kitty glowed with pleasure. Then Tom had gone back to reading on the bed, and Diana had returned to the kitchen where she had been doing the dinner dishes. Patrice followed her after a minute or two. It was agreed that they would speak in French. "But let me help you," he exclaimed, "I love to do dishes." He had looked with disfavor on the pegboard where American style they had hung pots and spoons and cups.

"It is not so good without a system," he murmured. Diana had laughed. She was without systems, without organization, no formulations. Wasn't that her problem? Drying a dish Patrice had walked to the dining room and peered in. "The *bahut* was useful, I think," he said regretfully. And suddenly Diana remembered that it once was his home, and he and Isabelle once shared the room Kit and Nick now shared. Politely Patrice complimented Diana, as if to make up for the remark about the *bahut*. "You have done so much work to improve the apartment. When my fiancée is done studying for her exams she will come and help you paint." He beamed.

"She is very good with her hands, not like me. She is only sixteen, and she is, I'm afraid, a *'jeune fille du seizieme,'* you know, very proper mamas and papas, and her father is the brother of a *'haut-fonctionnaire',* but the father is very simple and sweet. He and my family are good friends. Michelle and I plan to be married as soon as we can. Just now she is very busy studying for the *bachot*, and I, too, will try for entrance into *ENA*, ah, perhaps you do not know that? The *École Nationale d'Administration*.... If I succeed I will then try to apply for the foreign service part. Michelle and I want to go to China. She is very beautiful, and if I don't save her, she will be nothing but a boring young woman thinking only of receptions and all that sort of thing."

It was nice to have him rattling away in French. It would be fun to meet his fiancée. Dormant memories from her Junior year arose. The two Bourdet girls, Madeleine with some mysterious disease that had the whole family worried about her, and Genievieve the hearty, dumpy, girl-guide leader with her pronounced moustache, slated by the family for energetic spinsterhood. In the end, some pale and bespectacled youth had, by a *bourgeois* miracle, been found for her, and an endless round of formal dinner parties ensued to celebrate the unimaginable.

"And you, Diana, you are very modest but what do you do, something, I'm sure, you are a writer?" Patrice's voice entered her thoughts that were wandering, darkening with the oncoming dusk.

Diana had answered, hesitantly, "I write poetry."

"Ah, of course, but perhaps you will show me your poems sometimes."

Diana had smiled vaguely. It was so unreal. What were a few poems in the scale of human life? What were a few poems, all that she had. Her voice, desperate and tense saying to her mother, "I must write, I must get a chance to write," already worn from Nora's month of unexplained illness, the night cries, the trips to the doctors, all insinuating it must be psychosomatic, and finally she seemed weak but on the mend and they brought her to Diana's family's summer house where Nick and Kit had been sent. The next day Nora had announced she could no longer see from her left eye. Diana had rushed her back to Boston by plane. She was x-rayed on that hot sticky July day, the x-rays showed what hadn't been there a month ago. The doctor had smiled when he told them, "A brain tumor." Why had he smiled? "Leave her with us, we think we have the only treatment that may knock the thing out."

Patrice continued, "You must meet Robbe-Grillet, have you read his books? and Natalie Sarraute? She is very very busy but I know she would love to meet you. They are both friends of my parents. I will telephone her and tell her about you."

Putting down her coffee cup now, staring out at the sky Diana tried to imagine being Natalie Sarraute, writing every day, never being disturbed, never circling around it, simply doing it. In a little while they would be settled in, and then it would be easier. The sky absorbed her. She was queen of the air. In the apartment house across the tiny side street she looked into an elegant bedroom on the floor below, in faded housedress a maid was smoothing a green silk bedspread on one of two twin beds. Behind Diana, behind the open French windows, their bed was, of course, unmade. The sun poured down, making her sleepy. Through the open windows in the dining room she heard the parrakeets chirping companionably to each other. At one of the windows of the *chambre de bonne* across the way someone had hung a small cage out of the window. She decided to move the birds onto the narrow balcony outside the dining room. The birds fluttered about and burst into louder trills when they felt the sky above them. The bird sand sparkled on the floor of their cage.

Leaning from the railing on this balcony she stared out towards a little park at Place Cambronne, beyond it the raised lines of the Metro could be seen. In the park children were playing, some old people sitting hands idle in their laps. Blue smocked, dark-skinned Algerians were sweeping the water in the gutters with old-fashioned brooms, sharp and jagged.

The view from the air, things receding, diminishing, falling into a new order. She compared this view with the one from Notre Dame where they had gone for Kit's birthday on their way to the Quai where the birds were sold.

That morning Nick had brought Kit breakfast in bed. "Just to keep her from messing up the kitchen," he had muttered to ward off Diana's expression of pleasure. He was too close in age to Kit to play the older father-brother, and it had been Nora who was his kindred spirit and favorite. She could hear Nora's voice calling Nick's name in some intense family game they all played, hear Nora, direct and proud at the age of four telling her, "Nick loves me, better than he does Kit."

The sun was shining and they were all very excited. Tom wished them luck as he went off to the lab. Patrice's warning rang in their ears, "Don't let them sell you a sick bird, you know." Crossing the Ile de la Cité they found themselves at the far end of the Place de Notre Dame. Once again Diana was shocked by the sight of Paris, white and sparkling, instead of the sooty grey-black she remembered. Scaffolding like a straw cage boxed in Notre Dame, and on the corners high up men were still washing and scrubbing at the stone with powerful jets, peeling off layers of time from the core of stone. Slowly they walked towards the Cathedral drawn in by the power radiating from its presence. Crossing the Place, Diana felt herself diminished, crosshatched until she became, with the children on either side, a small figure in an eighteenth century etching. All the while, as they moved closer, buses pulled up and dispensed tourists. Closer still, they saw the guides leading their little flocks from portico to portico intoning dates, naming saints. Closer still, they strained upwards, the children and she, to view the gargoyles, leering wide-mouthed and slant-eyed over the populace of their city.

They went in with a shiver, and stood, hearts wrenched, gazing up at the joyous acrobatics of the stone, whose movement of voûtes and columns appeared merged, disappeared, re-emerged. Backs to the altar they faced the great rose and blue window of the central nave. The children were visibly moved. It was the first time they had ever been in a church. The black robed priests and nuns sailed up and down the aisles and the stones rang with footsteps. To the right of them a steady line of people disappeared up a flight of steps. Diana reluctantly agreed to their walking up to the top along with the crowd eager for the view. It was so narrow on the steps that she warned the children they could not turn around once they started up. The ancient worn-to-satin steps turned and turned and turned, a line of people snaked their way up, another line snaked their way down, brushing each other good-naturedly. Diana's legs ached; people rushed past them. Nick disappeared from view. She and Kit plodded on. Finally they burst into the air. Shoulder to shoulder they found themselves along a platform nestled in with the gargoyles, open to the blue sky. From there they could see Sacré Coeur, its white dome floating like an eastern mirage at the other end of Paris. The Seine sparkled in the light moving sinuously under the bridges which arched over it like ribbons gracefully tying the city together. Nick was clearly excited at the prospect of the city, but Kit was awed at finding herself cheek by jowl with the gargoyles. Diana stared at one leaning its face in its hands gazing out sardonically, a demon no doubt, for it mocked faith and trust and all that animated the men who dared to put it up alongside those spires which soared up away from despair. She remembered the postcard Tom had sent her, from Paris, of that very gargoyle. She had just learned that she was pregnant. On the reverse side he had written, *"Bonheur a la jeune femme enceinte."*

She had been filled with a sense of foreboding with that pregnancy of Nora. She had been convinced that she would miscarry. Then she put it down to nerves because she had had a miscarriage between the birth of Nick and Kit. You can be haunted, she told herself by failures, by ghosts of the unfulfilled. Surely that is what death is, failure. Hadn't Rosalind Farber, Roz, the well-analyzed child psychologist, written to her when Nora died. "Things like this just don't happen to people we know…" as though death were a lack of talent, money, or will. The Farbers had been friends for years. Diana had crumpled up the letter and thrown it away. It was bitter in her mouth. All the dinners, all the shared jokes, the pride of caste. We are the wives of men of accomplishment, men of highest intelligence. We raise perfect children, and develop ourselves as well. And money, money, money always the overriding topic. What things cost. What chic imported furniture costs, what wines cost, what camp costs, what private school costs, what help costs, what building on a new patio costs. They entertained each other well and often; the women in a friendly rivalry, who could prepare the most difficult recipes, who served the most elegant dinners.

A breeze sprang up, across from them flags waved before the sprawled buildings of the Prefecture of Police. Drawn along the curb, the Black Marias, like shiny dark beetles, waited. What wouldn't they have seen, she and the children from this vantage point, had they been there in May? The wail of sirens, screams, the clash of paving stones. For fear of future clashes, the city fathers, in their wisdom, were removing the ancient cobblestones and covering the streets with macadam.

They made their way down to the bottom, legs like jelly, dizzy with the turns, throats dry and headed for the nearest café, where the children could indulge their new learned love of citron pressés and sandwiches jambon.

At a nearby table sat an old wizened woman, very neatly

dressed in black. On her head was a broad-brimmed black hat with red velvet trim, a large yellow ring glittered on one withered finger. Haughtily and with great care she sipped a tiny cup of coffee. To her, a family of large roughly dressed people, mother, father and two teenage children, made respectful salutations as they left the interior of the shabby cafe. In these old quarters thought Diana what roots send up their networks of leaves, what stability of relationships. Perhaps that woman had lived here for decades, she has her place in the sun, her due is paid her.

As Diana signaled for the *garçon* she thought of her old friend, Caroline Richardson. How she had lived out her widowhood faithfully buttressed by Gino, former Italian quarrier helper, handyman, and chauffeur to her and her dead husband, the sculptor, and Gina his wife, who was cook and *femme de menages*. Diana was twenty when she knew Caroline, a woman in her sixties, without family, deserted by almost all of their old friends. The celebrity filled weekends, the dinner parties, the receptions had passed away.

The *garçon* appeared, smiled at them with a warmth which the sight of the two children seemed to bring out in everyone, pocketed his tip, and bowed. The old woman reluctantly put down her cup, got up stiffly, taking in one hand her dark green marketing bag, heavy with wine bottles. In the other hand she held a cane and started to move off, like a bug, dragging a stiff leg, when suddenly she stopped a few feet beyond the cafe, turning her face to one side with a peculiar grimace of shame. Between her legs a puddle of steaming yellow urine sparkled in the sun.

When they came to the *Quai de la Corse* all the bird shops were deserted except one, so they wedged their way into that. The dim interior coruscated with color, and they were distracted by the trills of the birds and the passionate conversations of the buyers and attendants who, dressed in dun colored smocks, darted about making explanations.

They studied the birds that lined the plain wooden shelves in their crowded cages. How to make a choice among so many? Adding to their indecision were Patrice's horror stories of people who had bought birds that seemed in perfect health but succumbed instantly on arrival at the domicile.

Finally, exhausted, they bought a male and female parrakeet, a huge cage, thousands of francs worth of bird equipment; beak scratcher, sand and gravel, biscuits, paraphernalia for cleaning the cage, etc. and staggered outside, too burdened to do anything but hail a taxi and return to the apartment. It was only when they had installed the birds that Diana noticed that the female had a sore on her foot! "Well, it's not dead yet," Patrice had said consolingly when he dropped by.

That evening they feted Kit at a Chinese restaurant near the Boul' Miche. Tom had invited the Glicksteins to join them. George and his wife, Jeanie, were leaving Paris in a few weeks, after a stay in Paris of two years. They were waiting at a table when the Glicksteins arrived. George had a round smug face adorned with a fair yellow beard that gave him the look of a dandy of the late nineteen hundreds, and drawled a bit when he spoke. Jeanie was warm, outgoing, energetic, with deep set blue eyes, short brown hair, and a Chicago accent. She had brought a present for Kit and kissed them all. She was an accomplished musician and, a few weeks before, had played the Bechstein for them at cousin Sylvia's, much to their delight. Now, she had promised to arrange for Nick and Kit to have her piano teacher, *Mme. Le Gros,* when she and George went away.

They began the ritual of ordering, something which Diana never cared about in a Chinese place, so she was grateful that Tommy did it so well. He read every item with care, made notes on the napkin, listened to everyone's request, harmonized the affair. Years ago when he came to travel with her in the summer of Junior year he had been so shy and inaudible, it had been a torture for them both to have him order. Shifting her weight on the banquette, flanked by the children, Diana remembered the letter a poet who had loved her had written hearing she had married Tom: "You're making a mistake, you're not a domestic animal."

She hadn't even known in what context to think about that remark. What was domestic about wanting to marry Tom? It was not a decision she had thought about. Or had she, that day her father had lost his temper and said, "If you think I'm going to support you, while you go to England, you're mistaken." How did you set out on one road rather than another; what answers lay in that question? She woke to hear George saying, "The speeches went on for days at the Sorbonne, in the courtyard, in the classrooms."

"You would have loved it, Diana," Jeanie added.

"People were writing poetry on the walls everywhere, and slogans, and there were marvelous posters that appeared on all the buildings."

"When they started to throw a cordon up around the streets near the Jardin de Luxembourg," George continued, his face glowing in a way that Diana found annoying, but could not say why, "these old *bourgeois* couples, as proper as you can imagine, pulled kids into their homes, hid them from the police, *'la flickaille'* who were gassing and rampaging and picking up everyone that remained on the streets. It was great. The workers were with us..."

Jeanie broke in, "You see people loved each other. People stopped each other and spoke to each other on the street everywhere, and you know what Paris is like, it seemed as though we were really going to win, as though the world were us."

Like a swarm, like a crucifixion, the adrenalin pumping of the body, war, all out mobilization, the bonding of isolated social elements, a return to the One. Diana regretted that they had missed it. What would it have been like to live even momentarily as though all things were possible, to believe that you could actually shape your own destiny?

Tommy waved his arm helplessly. He still had difficulty attracting waiters. George leaned back in his chair, "Garçon," he called. He had a good French accent. An Oriental waiter materialized instantly. George with his smile, "bon gars," delivered the order, so carefully planned by Tom. Then he and Tom pushed off into a long conversation about the lab, the people who worked there, and all its inconveniences.

Jeanie turned towards the children and Diana. "The piano in your new apartment, the Gaveau, is really a lovely one," she said.

"But not as good as the Bechstein," said Nick quickly, and Diana sensed his fear of inaccuracy and exaggeration. Did he see her as untrustworthy, unreliable?

"Oh, certainly not," Jeanie answered approvingly. She went on to tell the children about her teacher, who was wonderful and young and would love to teach them, if they'd like it. They both seemed pleased. "Her name is *Mme. le Gros*"...

"That means 'fat'" said Kit quickly. Everyone beamed at her. Her hair fell in two wobbly braids.

"What a beautiful accent you have," said Jeanie admiringly. Kit looked confused and pleased.

"This is a more beautiful Chinese restaurant than the ones at home," she said, shyly. At the Jardin Imperial the tables were covered with heavy white napery and set with lovely porcelain bowls and glasses for wine, an innovation which the children found extremely funny. The walls were hung with silk scrolls and decorated with red and gold lacquered characters.

"Well," George drawled, turning back to the women and children, "I'm not sure what Jeanie and I will do next year. We're going to look for a boat in Scotland, a big one, and maybe sail around the world, right, cheri?" He leaned over and kissed Jeanie at the nape of her neck. "After all, with her father's money, why should I work?"

Jeanie looked down in embarrassment, but he persisted, "My father is rich, but Jeanie's father is wealthy."

The waiter appeared to everyone's joy, with spring rolls, spare ribs, and hot and sour soup. The children glowed; it was a bit of home. Looking at the Glicksteins Diana saw herself and Tom, years before, their first two years of marriage spent abroad in England, with marvelous long vacations in which to visit France, Switzerland, and Italy. Then, anyone who had two children the ages of Kit and Nick would have seemed as old as their parents. Did they look that old to Jeanie and George?

As if he had overheard her thoughts, George glanced at Jeanie. "Jeanie's getting older," he said. "She's twenty-six. I think it's time to trade her in. I'm two years younger than she is," he boasted as though it were some sort of cleverness on his part. "And older women after all *elles ne sont pas pour toujours.*"

As if he had struck her, Jeanie flushed crimson. Diana wanted to hit him. The first time they had met the Glicksteins, George had put Jeanie down all evening for the way she spoke French, her music, and her understanding of the French political situation. Looking at that callow face, Diana wondered for the first time what it would be like to be married to, to love, someone who was cruel, or someone you despised.

"Oissive jeunesse par tout asservie par delicatesse j'ai perdu ma vie." Why did that line from Rimbaud sing in her

45

head? Indolent boy, shouting with workers, masturbating his guilt at being rich so deliciously, and humiliating his wife. She had heard so much political talk growing up. Her father fought for the rights of Blacks, Jews, Indians, all oppressed people, but whenever her mother spoke up at the dinner table, "Sara," he would roar, "will you keep quiet, that's stupid; you don't know what you're talking about."

"It's always for themselves, all this talk," her mother would explain, with a smile and a shrug, to Diana. "For their own egos. The workers, the workers, they argue, argue."

The dishes piled up around them. The children were tipping like drunken roses, their cheeks aflame with the food and the heat. The Glicksteins were off to a movie. They all stood outside together on the *Rue de la Harpe* in the warm clear night. Sniffing the air Diana's heart raced. Somewhere her other self still walked those streets, head *"dans la lune"* as *Mme. Freilander* would remark about her dreamy absentmindedness. Self-absorbed, aware of others but only at their boundaries, virginal, imagining herself as a poet, and frightened that she wasn't a woman. Little girl, so naive, she was still out in those streets. But Diana couldn't laugh at her any more than she could feel sorry for the ghost of that young wife, who told herself she would write but who, like the little mermaid, had acquired a set of limbs for love at the price of becoming mute.

There was nothing that she had to look ahead to, except perhaps, once more, a chance to work. She put her arm gratefully through Tommy's. Behind them the children, excited to be out at night in a big city; whispered and giggled. They all strolled slowly down to the river, and, once more that day, she and Kit and Nick faced the rippling calm of Notre Dame, now just beginning to shimmer in the moonlight like the ghost of an idea.

Chapter III

Now the days began to have a rhythm. First thing in the morning Nick got up and went for the papers and a fresh *baguette* at the bakery near the *Rue Cambronne*. Then Diana wrapped Tom's bathrobe around her and made them cocoa and tea and braided Kit's hair and kissed them goodbye watching them begin their descent down seven flights of stairs. They were dressed in their school uniforms, gray with blue blazers. Each carried a *"serviette"* filled with pencils, papers, books. Watching their procession down the street from their corner or the balcony she saw how they tipped on their *serviette* side, how companionably they bumped together. Then she would get back into bed with Tom, falling into sleep again, always briefly aroused by the concierge's sharp ring to announce the mail, then drifting off until Tom stretched and began his slow waking up. They made love every night; sometimes they made love in the morning, afterwards Diana would make Tom his breakfast, and they would read the papers together. Reluctantly Tommy would depart around eleven and often Diana would get back into bed and stare out at the view. Or she would do her marketing before the stores closed for lunch, eat something, and then get back into bed and fall asleep until a half hour or so before the children returned. Then waking with a start, she would hurriedly get dressed, splash water on her face and lay out a *"gouter"* for the children. Her tiredness and her need to sleep never came to an end.

Frequently, at the same time that the children arrived home, Patrice would appear. It turned out he had to move from *Cité Universitaire*, and had in fact been living above them in the *chambre de bonne* which went with their apartment. It was right above their dining room. The sound of his ring was always exciting since they had no company. The children would rush to open the door and there he would be smiling affectionately at them, wearing a dirty raincoat. He always invented an excuse for appearing.

"I have brought you *Le Monde*," he would say to Diana, bowing, and handing her his obviously read *Le Monde*. With this passport he would be welcomed in and they would all gather around the wooden table, eating pastry and drinking Vittel water for which Nick had almost as pronounced a passion as Patrice. The birds would trill madly, intoxicated by the sound of their voices. Often Diana would invite him to stay for dinner. She couldn't break herself of the habit of buying food for extras, she had fed such a large family for so many years: five of them, the au pair, and the never ending hungry bachelors who graced their table year after year, the lonely, the strays, who satisfied Diana's need for company and stimulation, and Tom's desire for a convivial table. So many years of Diana's "Darling?" as Tom thrust open the door followed by the eager guest, apart from the nights when they had many people in. The children would crowd around Tom, all pink and rosy from their baths and then rush off upstairs to play until bedtime. Tom and the guest would have a drink in the kitchen while she prepared their meal. After dinner Diana would do the dishes while Tom and guest, most often Tom's favorite unmarried colleague, would go back to the lab.

Here, Patrice would tell her of a movie or play which shouldn't be missed, and the three of them would go out together.

Patrice was an unlimited source of gossip and untiring in his love of politics. If he wasn't telling Diana the latest record to buy, and he frequently brought her records, he was analyzing the strategies of Couve de Murville, his hero because he was an honorable Protestant in a world of thieving conniving Catholic brutes like the unspeakable Pompidou. Or he repeated the latest story· of *Mme. Pompidou's* infatuation for the singer Francoise Hardy. Or he discussed the maneuvers of the British under Harold Wilson's leadership.

In the beginning Diana kept expecting that he would bring Michelle by for a visit. There was a day when, in greatest excitement, he had said that he and Michelle were going to hear *Barbara*, the singer, whom he wanted Diana and Tommy to hear as well A day or so later, crestfallen, he appeared to say that Michelle had been sick that evening, and if he got an extra ticket, would they like to go with him? Gradually, Diana assumed that Michelle was too busy and too shy, perhaps too French, to come and meet perfect strangers. After all, Patrice had lived abroad, and was a man – that made a difference in French terms. Indeed, after dinner in the kitchen helping her cleanup, he would tell stories about life in places as far flung as Scotland and Cambodia, where his parents had lived in the service of his father's company. Sometimes she was so busy laughing and talking to him, while she prepared dinner, that she didn't hear Tom let himself in until he had peered into the kitchen.

"I hope you will let me read your poems sometime," Patrice would say, grinning amiably, "I'm sure they must be very fine."

"Of course," she would say politely, but really what was there to show him? He might think she was a Natalie Sarraute or a Robbe-Grillet and be so disappointed. A group of poems she had sent months before to The Hudson Review came back with a note from the editor saying that they had "almost taken one." Now everything seemed far away. She heard her mother's voice saying "When I see all those books come into the house, those little books, and the big ones, I think to myself what that represents in children neglected, wives ignored, lives sacrificed to a handful of pages."

It was impossible for her to work in the morning unless Tom was out of the house, and he almost never left before noon. When she sat at her desk, stroking its worn green leather top, staring at the pigeons across the way, watching the clouds and the sky, she day-dreamed or wrote a bit in her journal.

One day she got a kind of flu and lay in bed almost unable to move, bundled up in Tom's bathrobe because she was cold all of the time. Now she slept in earnest all day long and all night too. For a while it halted their passionate lovemaking, lovemaking which had a new dimension to it, but Diana couldn't think why. Was it because they were in a new city, new place, free from the vibrations of the old life? Yet night after night she wept, her whole body racked with sobs alongside Tom's quiet deep breathing, crying out to Nora, wanting her, aching for her. She recalled how she had felt about their making love when they had first learned the truth about Nora's illness. It had seemed unthinkable, sacrilegious, but then, more superstitiously it had become a fertility rite of life forces that would protect Nora. If their love were strong they could ward off the danger to her.

A week went by and Diana wasn't better. Reproachfully, in the evening everyone piled into the bedroom, Patrice included, to beg her to get up and come out to dinner with them. "Come on," said Tom, "it's no fun without you." She looked at him wanting to cry. Why couldn't he leave her alone, why couldn't he ever let her be, why did she always have to be there? Weren't the children his as well as hers? He had never even taken them for a walk unless she would come. She was a prisoner of this love that was eating her up. He would never if she was sick, and she was sick often, bring her food or even feed the children. She would stagger out of bed, take care of them and herself, while Tom said, generously, "Don't worry about me, I'll eat out."

And here he was once more with his demands. "Do come," said Patrice solicitously, "it might do you good to come out." She tried to smile. "I'm afraid you're on your own." But she wanted to scream, amn't I ever to be allowed a minute, a second, to myself? She was conscious of Nick and Kit looking at her worriedly. Did they suppose she was going to die? "Bring me back something nice for dessert," she added. And turned over with relief as soon as they'd all left, and fell back to sleep.

In her dreams she dreamed a dream she had had before; the same dream with variations: the doctors had told her that Nora was seriously ill, but then she wakes up and finds it is only a dream. Or Nora has been seriously ill but now she has passed the danger point, and the doctors say she will recover. Or she is watching Nora knowing Nora is not out of danger yet but years have gone by, and Nora is healthy and growing with no sign that it has come back, and she knows that she must always live with this uncertainty, but Nora at any rate is there. And then she wakes up.

In two weeks Diana felt better, the weariness which had engulfed her retreated like a tide. One bright clear Sunday they decided to visit the Marche aux Puces. Tom had in his pocket his beloved Plan de Paris, and he and Nick poured over it together, tracing their voyage on the Metro. The flea market opened at 1:oo on Sundays and they were among the first to arrive. Up and down the little streets they went entering almost every stall. Everywhere it seemed to Diana things cost too much There was a stall of French Provencal plates, the special plates of pottery, the Breton Quimper plates which her mother loved so much. On them Breton peasants stood stolidly in baggy blue pants, curved yellow jackets, in the pottery sky the wide V-shape of a bird hovered forever.

As was the French custom the stall sellers all had a great deal of camaraderie among themselves and showed sullenness or hauteur towards the customers. Each little stall was an underworld grotto where the inhabiting fish scarcely noticed them as they swam in and out. In one grotto, the most exquisite 18th century furniture was presented; in another you would have thought the world was filled only with pots and pans and preserving jars. Nick and Tom became fascinated by a shop which sold old weights and measures, while Kit and Diana walked on and then stopped before a shop filled with antique dolls. Some had been placed on tiny rush chairs and sat in the sun like faded pensioners. Others hung from the pegs around the stall door, like dispirited angels. Their full porcelain cheeks were as white as death, each with a hectic spot of red. Most of them had lost their hair, and those without clothes fully revealed the rigor mortis of their limbs. The naked ones, some, had stockings and shoes painted on their legs in a fashion which made them shameless and provocative, but others were still clothed in their original long dresses, torn lawns and silks of the turn of the century. Their dark eyes stared unwinkingly into the sun.

The arms which held them and loved them had long ago withered to bone, disintegrated to dust. These little strumpets had outlived the living of warm rosy arms, dimpled wrists, tenderly kissing mouths, high pure voices. Perhaps that accounted for the aura of perversity which emanated from the dolls.

All Nora's possessions, the bed in which she died, had to be got rid of. Day after day Diana had to enter her room, her little pyramid, and strip it as thoroughly as any graverobber. Upstairs in the attic in a red case was the hundred dollar wig they had bought her, because the chemotherapy had made her own thick, curly blonde hair, of which at five she was already so vain, fall out. Gamely she had worn it once and never again, it hurt her head, too hot, too scratchy.

"Do you like those dolls?" Diana asked Kit.

"No, I like furry animals." She tucked her plump hot hand into Diana's as they walked on. Diana's other hand still felt the unaccustomed emptiness, like an amputation.

She wondered what Kit was feeling. "All I ever wanted when I was little was to walk down the street with my Mommy holding my hand, that was my idea of bliss," her mother had once told her. And so her mother had wanted that bliss to be repeated with her father. But what did Diana want? Was the world divided into two sorts of people, those who wanted the oneness to come from the merger of two in love, and those who didn't want or perhaps didn't feel the need for that oneness? Diana was afraid she was a very selfish person. They all loved her, but she wanted to be left alone.

At the next stall they saw an old bottle, about three feet high, with a wide irregular neck, the green of the sea caught as it eddies around smooth old rocks, a dark, mysterious and changeable green. For some reason it made Diana think of the death of *Madame Bovary.* She bought it.

* * * * * *

Every day Paris quickened more with the bustle of the *"rentrée."* Tommy had bought the guide recommended by Ronald, the Guide Julien, and at least twice a week they would pick a restaurant to go to. Diana would pitch her voice several octaves higher than normal – she had learned that there is a pitch below which one cannot speak French and be understood on the phone – and make a reservation in advance. How intriguing, the thought that if they didn't come that table would wait for them faithfully all night long. She would prepare a simple dinner in advance for the children, clean up, and then the children, quite content to be left alone, would see them off at the door and wait for them to enter the elevator. Often Patrice would come by and offer to be with the children, help them with their homework, and keep them company. Diana, her face animated with excitement, her eyes very blue, wearing a coat she loved, which loved her, would feel the sweetness of it, Tom's pleasure in their going off together, the rosy cheeks of the children, and Patrice's eyes, very blue, looking at her with admiration. It made her feel very *"grande personne,"* she told Tom, loving the seventeenth century pomp of the expression in French, so much loftier than the flat finality of "grown-up" in English.

They would clank down, slam the heavy elevator door then press the buzzer to open the big doors and head out into the night. Out would come the Plan de Paris and Tom would chart their course. Sometimes they went into quartiers filled with mean and sordid streets, sometimes into the old grand quartiers, but always the ambience in the restaurant was the same. A warm interior, the friendliness of the host, people already at tables, they were about to partake of a ritual, a national ritual, the emphasis on pleasing, the meal to unfold with the decorum of high mass. It was the event, it was the evening, one didn't rush off to a play or a movie. She and Tom would settle down to the menus; Diana always thankful that Tom was going to take charge of the wine, such a serious affair. Then after that one could lose oneself in tastes. The wine drinking slowed Tom's usual speed, and he was almost as leisurely as she was. Diana remembered those first days in Paris when he was courting her, and their first year of marriage. She didn't find him dull now. Once again she found herself looking back at the foolish person she had been. "I gotta use words when I talk to you?" Tom had always teased her with Sweeney's line. "Don't you know words don't count," he would grin kissing her. But words had counted for her. And after they had made love in the beginning, hadn't she always wanted him to talk to her about anything really but somehow to put the closeness into words. "That's the trouble with American women," a Cambridge don had once remarked, "after you've made love to 'em, they want to talk about Proust." Tom always teased her with that crack, as well. Things the body knew, but the head didn't, and the other way round. Each cutting the other off from vital information, and years passing before one had begun to understand. The question of exchange, of need. Sex, of course, was something which was there. It had gotten better and better, there were moments when it was superb, others when it was mechanical. With the birth of each child she had grown more voluptuous, and with time. Even so, Tom's ever present desires left her weary, conscious-stricken at times when she wanted to say "no." To say "no" was apparently unthinkable but they had compromised finally after years and years on a phrase, "I'd love to, but I'm too tired." She was the one to use it. Did that mean she didn't love him as much as he did her?

"You are a whore if you go to bed with your husband when you don't feel like it," said a voice in her head. "Not at all" answered the voice of her mother, "you are merely being loving." "But if you don't feel loving?" The dialogue stopped.

"L'appetit vient en mangeant," said Diana to Tom as he studied the menu, for that phrase was his final one about sex.

"I'll have the *potage parmentier,* the *pâté maison,* and the *specialité de rognons,* and for dessert, the *tarte de mademoiselle tartin* because it's in my cookbook and I've never made it." She always made up her mind before Tom. She was very quick at knowing what she wanted. He depended on that.

After some minutes of agony, Tom made his choices. Magically the waiter appeared. He and Tom sorted out the question of wine. They gazed at each other after he went off, a fatherly waiter, with a bit of a pot belly and the land look of a *député.* The room they were in was small, not more than ten tables in all, very simple, flowers on each table and on the old walls a creamy wallpaper down to the old brown wood. From the ceiling hung some old light fixtures which shed a soft yellowy glow on things. Diana took a deep breath. Around them the animated voices of the French rose and fell. A very young looking strikingly beautiful girl was gazing intently, her head charmingly to one side so that her blond hair fell like a cloth to her shoulders, at a much older man whose heavy lidded eyes bulged as he spoke, his hands gesturing expansively, his hairy wrists revealed when his shirt cuffs pulled back. On one wrist was a heavy gold watch, and on one finger a gold ring with a ruby in it.

"You're looking beautiful," said Tom to Diana.

The waiter appeared, solemnly presented the bottle with label to be read by Tom. Then he took it aside, uncorked it and brought it back, putting a bit into Tom's glass. That was the part that made Diana nervous. What if Tom found. it bad. Would he return it? Tom took the obligatory sip and motioned that it was good. The waiter seriously filled his glass and then Diana's. "How are things going at the lab?"

"I still haven't got things in working order. Now that everyone's back it's noisier, and, with three of us in the space we share. it's hard to move. I discovered today that there's one little man in charge of drilling holes in corks for pipettes, and if you want a hole drilled, you have to find him, then have a conversation with him, first about the weather, then any other topic you can think of, and then place your request for holes and then hope that he'll have time to do it for you in less than a week. Since he is a functionary just as much as Roger or Philippe, everyone at the Institute is hired for life, he's in no hurry."

"And Roger and Philippe, do you see much of them?"

"Well, I'm not working on the same things that they are so

they're not terribly interested in me. We all get together at seminars though and big lab lunches. It's wild for the students, though. For instance, there's no real library at the Institute, and the current journals that arrive are all taken off by Roger or Philippe and kept locked in their desks, and the only way a student gets to see it is if they think there is something the student could use for a piece of an experiment, in which case the student is allowed to read that portion. And the students, when they are told that a piece of work has been done by Philippe or Roger, believe automatically in its correctness. They never question things the way we would at home, even the guys higher up don't question."

The smooth dark satiny *pâté* with its aureole of aspic shining up from its bed of lettuce was placed before each of them. A bit of *pâté*, a bite of crusty French bread, a sip of the wine. The *pâté* is rich, but not too rich, the wine played under that richness, enhanced it, began to spread out through their bodies gently, gently a warmth they weren't even quite aware of, just a feeling of "good."

"A guy, Daniel Martin, very bright, one of the junior people, gave a seminar the other day. All very fancy theoretical work, but it had obvious experimental weaknesses, which I think he knew were there, but he ignored them. And nobody even questioned him, until I did. It was patent that the thing wasn't going to work, but he got huffy, when pressed, and started making really ridiculous assertions to defend himself. If he hadn't been so sure that no one would question him to begin with, he wouldn't have tried to bring in an idea like that. But around here when a man's built himself a pretty little structure that's often as far as he'll go. They just don't like to check these things out with any kind of hard work."

Tom was smiling his characteristically pleasant smile. He never, like Diana, became angry and bitter at people's shortcomings, perhaps he had lower expectations of them. Perhaps he saw more clearly. For so many years she thought he didn't see at all, because he never made comments about personalities. It was the work he cared about. But he noticed people, just the same.

Still Diana was resentful that neither Roger nor Philippe had made any effort to see them socially. There had been one occasion at Roger's house, clearly their night to have the foreigners in, since the visiting professors, those about to depart, the Gerolds, and themselves, and one or two others who spoke English, had been invited. Diana remembered so clearly the time they had had Roger and his wife to dinner when they were visiting the States, how hard she had worked on that dinner, and how their beautiful Swedish *au-pair* girl had made such an impression serving the table. The children, delectable, had appeared briefly and Diana had made even the hot *hors d'oeuvres*. It was thousands and thousands of years ago.

The *rognons* arrived in a dish of glazed terra cotta, small onions bubbled to the surface of a ruddy sauce gleaming like pearls. Tom's *steak au poivre* was ignited at a small table alongside them then basted in the dying flames of cognac and drippings of butter and cream. Everyone else looked over enjoying the romantic wisps of blue fires. The waiter wheeled away the spirit lamp and utensils on his little table, a high priest who waits in the wings.

"Jim Gerold told me he didn't get a damn thing done the whole year he spent here, but he loves Paris so he doesn't care."

Diana sighed, then cheered up seeing how Tom was eating. He loved Paris. They could have gone to England; it hadn't been her choice. Even to come abroad. She saw herself leaning over him in bed. "I don't care about going away," she had said, "I can go to New York once a week and have a poetry workshop there." Had that been a threat? She had never spoken or thought of leaving the house before, alone.

They decided on another bottle of wine. The waiter beamed his approval. Between her legs Diana felt desire quiver. She stared at Tom lovingly. So many years, so many years, the words over and over in her head like a train on a track. He felt her gaze and beamed back.

They were the last to leave the restaurant, the chairs pushed back, the crumpled napkins on the uncleared plates. The waiter bowed, the tip had been generous, but he looked weary, *"Bonsoir, M'sieur, Dame."* Giddy, they hailed a taxi and magically entered the dark of the apartment. The children's door was closed. On the table, the dining room table, an empty bottle of Vittel shone in the moonlight. "Patrice must have drunk himself into oblivion on mineral water," giggled Diana. And they fell onto the bed and made love, under the blind eye of the moon.

* * * * * * *

Cousin Sylvia was visiting. She had called that morning, her voice, not heard for years, unexpectedly high pitched mincingly precise. "Diana, dear, I'm back in my beloved Paris. How is Tommy and how are the children? Are you settled in? Are you free this afternoon? I can give you some time."

An hour or so later, having walked, she arrived, dressed impeccably, but casually: a red suede jacket over a natural silk blouse, a navy blue pleated skirt, comfortable low walking shoes, in blue, and a red leather handbag. Her once jet black shiny hair was a stunning white and cut short. Her delicate haughty lustful upper lip fitted neatly over the top of the slightly protruding lower one. Her nose was arched, small, with flared nostrils. Dark brown eyes that at times looked almost black stared out from under slim arched eyebrows. Eyes and eyebrows set off by a skin with the warm ivory tones of Spanish women. Tall. a perfect model size she shopped untiringly at all the boutiques during their twice a year soldes. Her family had been desperately poor; her father was a painter. her mother had killed herself with a fatal cancer. Her brilliant, beloved younger brother had died at the age of twenty-one from a tumor, and she had been under the sentence of death all her life.

The children, pounding up the stairs, bursting in the door after school, were awed and thrilled to find her, a splendid bird, in their humble surroundings. They all sat down to "*gouter,*" and Sylvia told them the story of the *perruches* which she had had for her children.

"We had put a little marble egg in the cage to encourage her to lay and forgot to take it out. Well, she laid twenty eggs! And we were frantic. I had to make a special mash and feed them myself with droppers, and one morning, can you imagine – a little canary flew into the cage when it was open for cleaning in the kitchen. Oh, how we laughed." She laughed, a high trill. Suddenly Diana realized that she is the same age that Sylvia was when Diana was at school in Paris. So that was how it looked to be thirty-six, to a twenty-year old!

"Come," said Sylvia to Kit, "your braids are all coming out." Fascinated, everyone followed her to the children's room. She took a comb out of her bag, and, standing over Kit. pursed her lips as she drew a part through her hair. It was an exact part, white, even. Then, with short, stubby, yellowed fingers she started to weave the braid. Kit's little face bloomed into the dreamy voluptuousness of nerves gently caressed. First one braid, then the other. Sylvia stepped back. Each hair lay flatly sleeked, one against the other. The two braids were of equal rotundity and length, the rubber bands were at the same place on each braid. Such concern and effort, yet Kit's head had become under those hands, an object, a thing disassociated from the living child. "It's not perfect," murmured Sylvia to herself.

At that moment the bell rang. "It's probably Patrice," explained Nick, to Sylvia, adding gravely, "He's the son of our landlord."

Patrice was as overwhelmed as the children by the sight of Sylvia. He bowed with a special unctuousness, his blue eyes sparkled with excitement. Diana had told him about the Fields, and he was gratified in his heart of petit snob. Ed was a very important man, in a minor way, Sylvia stood straight and proud, allowing his homage.

Patrice turned to Diana. "I just came to bring you a book I thought would interest you," he said, handing her a book of poems by Raymond Queneau, "but I must go now." He turned and bowed again to Sylvia. And departed. To be present at a family visit uninvited – there could be no greater social crime in France.

"He's an absolute darling," Diana explained to Sylvia when the door had closed behind him "You can't imagine how good he's been to us and the children, he's always popping in with something fun.... those are the flowers he brought yesterday," and she turned to a glowing bunch of anemones in a simple glass vase.

"You mean," said Nick sharply, to Diana's surprise, "he comes here to dinner all the time. He's just plain hungry."

"He thinks we're lost, and he's adopted us," Kit said softly, and they all burst out laughing.

Sylvia looked faintly disapproving. She too was a snob and Patrice did not pass her test o£ people who one should waste time, or food, upon.

"You really must have some curtains," she said, dismissing Patrice. "I think I may have two pairs that would just do for the bedrooms." With that she took from her bag a tiny tape measure and, to Nick's delight, asked him to help her measure, in centimeters.

"You know about that already, do you?" she remarked approvingly, seeing he could do it.

Sylvia wanted the most that she could get from people, their money, their brains, their looks, their talent, and she wanted it the way she desired to sink her small even teeth into a piece of ripe fruit and devour it. But if I had grown up with poverty and death, thought Diana suddenly, mightn't I be the same?

¤

Chapter IV

The autumn was coming on in earnest. The leaves were going down, not crisp and blazing as at home, just sallow, sere, and subsiding. People were beginning to cough everywhere, the universal cough of Paris in the dark months. In their weekly guide to Paris they read about an exhibition of mushrooms at the *Jardin de Plantes* and through a light fine rain they made their way across a town changing on the Metro three times to enter, finally, the dreary grounds of the *Jardin*. It was a Sunday, and it seemed that every proper thinking Parisien was there with his family. Most of the people had the look of working class; something especially neat, especially washed about their rough chapped flesh. And there were the middle-class *"petits"* the *petits fonctionnaires, petits bourgeois,* careful faces, thinning hair, anxious, watchful faces, angular and distrustful, the true French look of *"mefiances."* Here and there they could see some jolly folk who simply liked to eat mushrooms. They were caught in a line which slowly wormed its way from case to case.

On the walls there were charts, and the Latin names of species in big block letters were placed around the room. Under glass cases the mushrooms, so real as to look unreal, displayed their amazing range of shape and color. But the deadly Amanita, reddish, with white spots, was the star of the show. It received the homage paid only to death. It was the focus of the crowd's unspoken terror. It was the death that lay in wait for all of them, the beautiful death, the insignificant death, the seemingly harmless, the hidden seed they carried in them from birth, the spore that would multiply to their destruction.

"Ah, ça vous donne des frissons, non?" said a coarse-faced man wearing a beret, standing in front of Nick. He pronounced the words with enormous satisfaction.

In the damp cold, the heat and press of the bodies gave off its own odor, pungent and dreadful: sweat, garlic, and flesh, rank and enduring. Tom was absorbed in the catalogue, as usual, reading quickly and pointing out the most interesting and unusual features of the exhibit. It maddened Diana how he read faster than she did and remembered everything he read. These days, more than ever, she was conscious of how dependent she was on him.

Kit tugged at her hand. She had turned so pale that Diana thought she might faint. In turn, Diana pulled at Tom's sleeve. "Kit and I will meet you outside." She wondered grimly what she would do if Kit started to throw up, but outside Kit's color began to return. They looked out at the umbrella trees lining the gravel walks of the park, branches like spokes. A few days ago Kit had received a letter from a small friend of hers at home, and she had dictated a poem to Diana to send to him. It was called "Sunshine."

The Sunshine brings tears to the eyes
And sad memories to the mind
Keep your voice from weeping and your eyes
from tears, for all comes right some day or night
when I come back from over the sea.

How frightened Diana had been all those months of Nora's dying that the children would ask the unanswerable question. But they never did. Nor did Nora. When the children came home from school that April afternoon, Diana told them. "Nora is dead." They wept. She wept. Kitty saw their neighbors and Betsy, her little playmate, and rushed out to tell them, but Nick sat in Tom's armchair, tears rolling down his cheeks. That night Kit had said, "Now Nick will love me the way he did before Nora came." Poor little woman, Diana had thought, what love pangs you have already endured. "She was like a judge. She was always fair, and she never got angry; she was the best person I ever knew." And then with a directness that was that of an adult, Diana's peer, she suddenly said, "It must have been awful for you to have to keep that secret so long."

And Nick, as she tucked him in, "Can we catch what she had? Will they find a cure for it?"

"Perhaps what Daddy is doing now will help to do that. Perhaps you will find a cure when you grow up."

"But it is too late for her," he said, and paused in the dark. Staring straight ahead he said, "We should never think about this, never again."

When they had first learned what was wrong, Diana had begged Tom for a baby, that too would have been a good magic, like their lovemaking. At last he said, "Won't you need your strength for Nora?" Now from time to time in Paris, she asked, "Should we have another baby? Look how the children adore André?" André being the fat gargantuan baby of the Rosens, a couple in the lab. Now she knew she could ask, because she no longer wanted a child. How could she have thought that life could equal a life?

"We should never think about this, never again."

But Death is a rape. How to stop it playing over and over in your head! Recently Kit cried, and said she wouldn't go to school, because there was a girl in her class who had a little sister, who reminded her of Nora, and she was too jealous and sad, when she saw her. "Nora's little hands were so soft," she wept, "I used to think she rubbed talcum powder on them." Diana burst into tears, and Nick found them both weeping. His face turned stony and stern "Look here," he said to Diana as if he were a grown man,

"You've got to stop that. You.... you might go crazy." He frightened her then. If you had suffered your sister's death, did your mother have a right to add her suffering to that already intolerable burden? He had made his choice, his way of protecting himself, now she understood. The world was mad, and if one thought about that, one could go mad also. She needed to weep night after night, but he needed to protect himself.

He was so like Tom. Was it a strength or a weakness to be able to banish unpleasantness from one's mind and to live in the present, neither imprisoned by memories of the past nor fearful about the future? How many hours before Nora's illness she had wasted in futile self-recrimination and paralyzing worry, until now the lesson imposed upon her had read: there is only the present, and that is to be lived through until its bitterest end?

Tom had tapped her gently on the shoulder, and she had come awake from her exhausted sleep. "It's all over." It went through her like a knife ripping at her, why hadn't she been there at the end? She had heard the hoarse morphine rasp of breath night after night as it had labored in Nora's throat. She had been up with her night after night for weeks. Tom had gone to England for a conference, and when he had returned she could go on no longer. They had put in a call for help, but lying in the bed she had said to Tom, "You have to be with her for the next nights, until we get a nurse." He had looked grim and displeased. There was his work in the lab, his famous important experiments, and the teaching. There was a pause. And in her head her voice said. "If you don't help with your child now, I will get a divorce later.'

Tom wept strange tears, high gasping sobs from some part of him where the hidden infant lay concealed. They wept clasped together.

* * * * * * *

"Where are you going for the *Toussaint*?" Patrice asked Diana as they stood in the kitchen. finishing up the dishes together. In the dining room, Tom was listening to Nick memorize his irregular verbs. Kit was playing with a set of *Cuisenaire* rods. They were supposed to be helping her understand mathematical concepts, but she was building little villages with them and putting small beads inside for people.

"You know," Patrice continued, "It's a big holiday. Everyone goes out of Paris. You and Tommy never go anywhere, I think." He paused. "You must meet my friend, Henri Drouot, and his wife, Marianne. They would love you and Tommy. And you are a writer and so is he. He wrote a very good book against the war in Algeria, a novel about his experiences there; and one about a peasant in Brittany. He's really a philosopher, and he is very fond of me. We were very close when I was at school. Now he writes me all the time and asks me to come and visit them. Wouldn't you like to go there? The children would love it, he lives in the country in a lovely little chateau. Kit would adore the animals, cows, pigs.... everything."

Diana laughed. Was it because they always spoke in French that everything Patrice said sounded slightly unreal, amusing, exhilarating?

"But really, they may want to see you, but we are a family of four," she protested.

"No, no, really, he and Marianne are very lonesome out there, and there is no one like you, you are at their hauteur. And you will see something of France besides Paris."

"But Patrice, Tom is just getting the lab set up."

"And I think it will do him good to get away. I think he is looking a bit depressed."

Diana looked at Patrice fondly. He really was so good to all of them. She was very touched that he would notice Tommy's mood. She thought of all the people she had fed, not one had ever thought of her, given her a token to show what she did was appreciated. When Patrice brought her flowers she really was moved. That someone should say thank you, to her! And, of course, flowers were what she always longed for. By now she knew that Tom would never buy them for her. On her birthday, or on any special occasion, she bought them for herself. Once Tom had said, years ago, when she mentioned how sweet it was to be given flowers, "A man only gives flowers to a woman, when he isn't making love to her." "Or if he feels guilty," he added. Since neither of those two things were ever the case with them, thought Diana, ruefully afterward, she guessed she would never get flowers from Tom.

"Just the other day," Patrice continued, "he wrote to me asking me if I could come there. Why don't we all go together? They are even thinking of emigrating to America, if things don't go better for him in his career. You know he is almost in exile out there in Cluny, nothing but peasants and the internats at the boarding school …. *les adolescents* the way I was." He winked gaily.

"Oh, that's crazy, " protested Diana, who was now really tempted. "But we might all go and stay in a hotel."

"No, no, no," insisted Patrice. "He has a huge house, they are always entertaining. They love people, he and Marianne. They would be thrilled to death. I'm sure he has heard of your father…."

Diana's father was a well-known lawyer with many admirers abroad, That had impressed Patrice.

Suddenly Diana began to feel how desirable they were to this fellow, Henri. She was seized with a passion to leave Paris, leave the apartment, to see new people. any people. They had seen no French people at all since the one stiff dinner given by Roger.

"Impossible," She repeated.

"Henri owes me a big favor, you know. I got Michelle's uncle, the cabinet minister, to come and visit him. Let me telephone Henri and tell him about you. I wrote him only the other day and said I might be able to come."

"But you can't just invite a whole family down on top of him."

"*Non, non,* what do you take me for? But will you come if he can have you?"

"I don't know," said Diana weakly, "it depends on Tom."

"Let me use the phone," he said and took the phone from its little stand in the hall and went into the children's bedroom. Diana went to tell Tommy and to her delight he looked interested. They all needed to get away. She was sitting holding her dishtowel dreamily when Patrice emerged beaming from the bedroom.

"There, just as I thought, he is absolutely delighted to have you come. Will you go?"

"Yes," said Diana, "Tommy wants to."

Patrice grinned even more broadly. "Now I have to find out about trains." He went back into the bedroom and made some more calls. Diana felt very lighthearted. She longed to be distracted.

****

They had taken a train to Chalon, where they had rented a car and started to drive to Cluny. Weary, as the pitch black Burgundian night fell, they had luckily found an inn with one room vacant. They were giddy with the excitement of being without the children and at dinner drank two bottles of white wine without noticing.

"Don't you think you'd better call Patrice and let him know we're alright?" said Tom responsibly.

Diana staggered obediently up from the table. Everything seemed hilarious, the woman's high-pitched voice on the other end (Marianne?) and Patrice's exasperated worried, "But good heavens, where are you, I thought you must be killed on the road."

"No, no. We're fine," Diana giggled, "how are things there?"

"Good, but you sound so strange."

"It's nothing, just the wine."

"So," he said thoughtfully, "you're drunk, a bit."

"A bit," admitted Diana. All she could think of was getting into bed and making love. Could he read her mind?

"Ah, I am the only responsible one," he said some-what chidingly.

"Well, we'll call in the morning and get directions. Do the children want to talk to me?"

"Oh no," he replied quickly, "they're having a wonderful time with the Drouot children."

Upstairs their bedroom was drab, with a bidet on wire legs to be filled with a pitcher from the sink. The twin beds had two plump green comforters on them and the hard round old-fashioned French pillow. Outside the wind began to howl and the rain to slam against the roof. They made love with a small light on. Diana shuddered and screamed in pleasure, freed from the restraints imposed by the children sleeping nearby. Her mouth was parched with passion, and she opened her eyes for a second, and saw Tom above her, his face assuming as it always did the delicate sensual tenderness of an Indian god, with a god's full cheek bones and curved full lips. These days they made love differently, with a passion that never diminished.

Diana was seized, shaken, drained, exhausted but day by day grew into a new sensuality. And Tommy reached for her like a drunk for a bottle. Diana thought of Cleaver and Mailer, the male *desouevré* has only sex to occupy him. Tommy was out of joint with the lab, his work was going terribly, there was no stimulation or excitement in Paris. All the things he had felt would happen if he came abroad seemed to be happening, but, Diana reminded herself, one good experiment and all that could change.

She hugged his round, furry body with its broad shoulders, his lovely buttocks and nice legs. He was getting a pot belly, and his forehead rivaled Shakespeare's. She had never thought him handsome, and now she found him beautiful. Even his brown eyes, which she had always wished were blue, could pierce her with the intensity of their expression of love, or of burning intelligence.

Before she fell asleep she reviewed the morning. She had gotten up at six with the children to feed them breakfast. Excitedly they had packed their little gym bags, Patrice had looked at her tenderly, she thought, in Tommy's old bathrobe. "Don't worry"" he had said at the door like a dear brother, "I'll take good care of them." But he had added anxiously, "Call as soon as you get to Cluny, and I'll give you directions." And, as he turned to lead the troops, "Don't change your mind!" As the door shut behind them he was saying in a soft voice to Kit, "Goats...." It made Diana laugh just to recall it, "Goats" said so silkily, so hypnotically, a magic spell. She fell sound asleep.

In the morning she poked Tom to wake him. He wanted to sleep later, of course, but responsibilities rolled over her duties, les *"devoirs"* the "oughts," what was eternally owing to others, to the children, to Patrice, the Drouots. Last night's intoxication had vanished. Outside the day was surly as though the rain had not rained itself out. Over the big cups of café-au-lait and rolls, the landlord gave them directions for reaching Merzé par Cluny. The little country roads were sodden from the night before. The white and brown cows, les charolles stood forlornly in the mud of the wide fertile plains with little meandering rivers and gentle rolling hills. Up and down the lanes they wound, worried about getting stuck in the muddy ruts. The farmhouses were very distant from each other, miles apart it seemed in the muddy fields. The landscape was not a friendly one, and Diana was wondering how they would manage if they got lost when they turned at the top of a narrow path, and began to come down a rutted lane. Ahead of them they could see a little Simca, a wooden shed, and there, surrounded by two peasants, three turkeys, and a small runny-nosed child, was a man who looked as though he had dropped from the nineteenth century. He was a small man, straight as a ramrod, wearing an impossibly romantic black cape, fastened at the high collar with two military chains. He wore steel rimmed round glasses on his angular beaked nose and was staring steadily at them but making no sign of welcome. The car slid to a halt.

"I think it's the French version of Mr. Rochester," Diana giggled nervously, "I wonder if he has a gun." The figure moved majestically forward now that the car had stopped.

"Monsieur Drouot?" asked Diana tentatively.

With a moat serious expression, his lips pressed tightly together, he bowed. *"Mme. Field, M. Field, soyez les bienvenus."* Motioning them to follow him he strode in his riding habit along a path, bordered by a high old country wall on one side, by an open field on the other, and led them under a small archway.

Inside the courtyard to one side was high straggly chicken wiring that penned up some bedraggled fowl, a pheasant, a guinea hen, who all seemed to bear a striking resemblance to their owner. *"Mes oiseaux,"* he murmured with rotund offhandedness. To their left and straight ahead was a charming old stone house, long and low, with a big front door at the top of four worn soft stone steps. Beyond the house, off to the right, were some shabby worn structures of a faded blue that looked like barns of some sort. As they stared off, the big door was flung open, and a cluster of children appeared in the doorway, behind them a dark curly-haired round faced woman, her cheeks rosily flushed, the same diminutive size as Henri. She smiled shyly, *"Ma femme,"* said Henri. in rather the same manner as speaking of his birds, then *"mes enfants."* A series of round and hot little hands were offered Diana and Tom. To Diana's eye, les enfants, Jean-Paul, Elizabeth, Claude, and Marie-Therese, all looked to be under nine years of age. Behind them stood Kit and Nick, in what seemed to be a state of shock.

"Where is Patrice?" Diana whispered to Tom as they were being led into a hall with flat red tiles on the floor. Their coats were taken by Marianne, and Henri led them into a large room with low dark woodwork and plaster walls. Above a gigantic fireplace there were two family portraits, one of a man and one of a woman in eighteenth century dress. Many chairs were scattered about, all different, all ramshackle. Diana was escorted to the least fragile looking one pulled close to the fireside. On the far side of the mantelpiece was a massive old writing desk of a rough, countrified aspect and some smaller shakier-looking tables

They all sat down, and Marianne was sent to make tea. "We will have some tea," Henri announced. "You may be cold from your drive.

They all smiled. Diana was suddenly conscious that she was wearing black suede boots, a mini-suede skirt and vest, and a bright red cashmere sweater that emphasized her breasts. She was an American woman, and at that particular moment that meant someone in defiance of the natural order of things. Marianne's dowdy figure and shapeless dress were reproaches. Marianne was only a year older than Diana, Patrice had said, but she looked the way mothers are supposed to: middle-aged, worn, cheerful, preoccupied. Looking at herself through Henri's eyes, Diana fell short of the traits of the good dependable middle-class wife.

Marianne appeared with the tea and disappeared again. "You must excuse my wife," said Henri, holding his cup in an aristocratic manner, "she must attend to the children." Focusing on Diana, he added, "Your husband must excuse me for not speaking English – an unpardonable fault these days."

The woman in the powdered wig seemed to be winking at Diana. The situation was so awkward that it was terribly exciting.

"Oh," said Diana quickly, "but he understands and speaks French." She felt the burden of being the only one to make things go well. And where was Patrice?

"We are delighted to have you with us," Henri went on; inclining his head graciously. "You are close friends of our *cher* Philippe and Flora Montcheval?"

There was a silence like thunder. Diana hadn't even known the first names of Patrice's parents. What had Henri been told? And how was she supposed to respond?

"I, well, we feel as though we know them, Patrice has been so welcoming and has told us so much about his family." She breathed heavily hoping that would cover the surprise. Henri looked thoughtful. "So you did not know them in America?"

"Ah, no," Diana felt herself flushing, and becoming furious with Patrice for putting her into such a situation.

Passing it over, Henri went on, "I understand your father is a famous lawyer, I am sure I have heard the name. He defends those who are against the war in Vietnam, so like our former situation in Algeria. You will see, you will have to get out eventually as we did ourselves." He stopped.

"But I must not talk to you about your *politique* on which I am, alas, very little informed. You, how do you find our beloved France after the turbulence of our recent upheaval?"

Diana gulped, and looked hopefully at Tom. No help was coming from that quarter. He could remain comfortably silent without speaking a word longer, with the exception of his mother, than any living human being. Diana searched desperately for the right piece of rhetoric. Listening to Henri's elevated French made her feel that she should be speaking in the *passé simple*. She tried to compose a sentence beginning with "Unhappy France," but gave it up.

"If Edgar Faure's educational reforms are pushed through, do you feel that would have a 'beneficial' effect on the students?" "There" she thought proudly, "beneficial, has just the right note, dry and pedantic."

Henri rose happily to the topic. "The youth, our unhappy youth, is filled with vague desires to improve the lot of man, but, alas, they have not taken the time to understand exactly what that lot is. Nor have their mentors, those older and more instructed, who should, bien entendu, enlighten them, been, shall I say, unreproachable in that respect, being unhappily more concerned with their own notions, notions occupied with making their names known in the world, the little sphere they seem so absolutely to be the monarchs of.... "

It was clear that Henri could go on forever, but at that moment footsteps were heard, the door to the salon was gently opened, and a young man, followed by Patrice, appeared in the doorway. They both were grinning madly. With great alacrity Patrice came forward and bent over Diana's hand. The young man followed suit. *"Madame,"* he murmured.

"May I present my pupil, *Jean-Francois de Longvilliers*," said Henri with relish, as he sounded the *"de."*

Cautiously, Patrice and Jean-Francois settled themselves into two spindly black chairs. Henri turned to Jean-Francois. "And what do you hear from your dear sister, *Mme. de Sablonnet?*" he asked. The boy blushed and muttered something about her return from the country, and her sending her regards. Diana was sure it was a lie. No one would ever tell the truth to Henri.

"Be sure to send her our regards when next you write," said Henri. Diana tried to imagine what it had been like for Patrice to be a familiar in this household. Patrice's words came back, "I was Henri's great confidante, he told me everything, all his hopes and plans, all the plots against his career."

Henri was determined to tackle Tom. He began to ask him about teaching in the States. Diana relaxed and drifted. A man bending over a woman's hand. A quaint gesture fallen into desuetude, but it resonated, set up a reverberation in the blood, the imagination. The man bends over the woman. The first salute-like the opening of a duel. Something in her responded as to the opening bars of familiar and stirring music. She crossed and uncrossed her legs.

"We have taken a room for you in Cluny at the nicest hotel, the patron is a good friend of mine, and we will go there tonight for dinner. But let me show you something of our little *propriété* now before it grows dark."

Diana looked closely at Patrice. He seemed very pale and strained, but he smiled in a guarded way, feeling her glance. Like a gaggle of geese everyone put down their cups and followed Henri's lead.

On the way to the cour they were followed by Claude, a curly haired five year old. He waited patiently while his father pointed out trees, landmarks, told of plans for future planting, the state of local government in Burgundy.... Finally Henri drew breath. Then Claude began quickly to tell Henri how Jean-Paul had cheated him. It was a long involved five year old's account of treachery, but told with more haste than art, as though any minute Jean-Paul would appear to cut him off. He ended abruptly and waited, like a patient courtier for the King's response. It came instantly in a lofty volley of subjunctives.

"I would have wished," began Henri, "that you had not seen fit to come to me with this petty trivial affair between two obviously ill-behaved little children without the most rudimentary ideas of what constitutes conduct and harmony among civilized individuals...." He went on in this vein for several more minutes. At the end, Claude ran off happily, having understood not one word, but quite content to have gotten one up on his older brother.

When they got to the barn, there were Nick and Kitty. "I'll

show you the cows," said Kit, rushing for Diana's hand. They entered a dark low unkempt set of stalls, heavy and sweet with the fragrance of dung. Kit pointed to a lone horse. "His name is *Ronceval*," she said her mouth tasting each syllable, "and the cows are called *Bonne* and *Belle*, and *Belle* is really beautiful because she has a white mark like a star on her face."

The cows leaned over their stalls, their large rough tongues drooping, their breath mingling with the scent of dung and straw. In the last rays of the setting sun the straw gleamed gold enough to thrill Rumpelstiltskin. A hen pecked and scratched in the dust. Henri was patting *Ronceval,* proudly, talking to him. "Do you ride?" he asked Diana and Tom. They shook their heads. "My family has been in the Army for generations. The Cavalry was their life. I have deserted the tradition by becoming a teacher." Neither of them knew how to respond. But he went on, "We have our own milk, eggs, we even make our cheeses. It is a very simple life I lead here, a bit as though I were in exile, I often feel. The peasants and the *bourgeois* around here are a primitive lot. Indeed this is a country of witchcraft."

"I felt that when we drove up here," Diana said, liking him for the first time.

"Ah, you felt that too," he answered looking at her, happily.

They left the barn and walked gingerly through the muddy path towards a clump of trees. Some boards, arranged on a low branch, bore small circular white mounds under a cover of netting. They appeared like offerings of some sort.

"Our fromage de compagne," said Henri.

"Yesterday, it was so muddy that Patrice had to carry me in his arms to see the cows," whispered Kit, "because he wanted me to see them before the dark."

A goat was tethered to the tree, a he goat with a cynical and lecherous look in its almond-shaped eyes, its dapper French politician's beard moved up and down, soundlessly, like a silent film. From where they stood the house was no longer visible, but the sun was beginning to shine.

"There will be some nice weather ahead for several hours," remarked Henri. "There are some lovely examples of early eleventh-century churches nearby. I, alas, must work before our dinner, but Patrice knows how to direct you."

They nodded, like children being let out of school, and all piled into the rented car. Jean-Francois who had been part of the entourage until this moment disappeared into a white plastered one-story house next to the main house.

"That's where Patrice stays," said Nick.

Patrice broke into a real smile for the first time, but chided them for not calling sooner. "I was so worried, I had all sorts of anxieties," he said, "you might have gotten killed." Diana was shocked that he would say such a thing in front of the children.

"Well, children," she said hurriedly, "Is it an adventure, to live with a French family?"

"Last night we had the most terrible dinner," reported Kit in lugubrious tones. "I couldn't even tell what it was until Patrice told me it was turkey gizzards fried in fat. Ugh." Pause. "Mom, Henri slapped Jean-Pierre because he didn't finish his noodles!"

French family life, thought Diana to herself, "What do you think, Nick?"

"Henri's strange," he said concisely, and relapsed into silence.

"Henri is a bit strange," said Patrice hurriedly, "but I see that already he adores you as I knew he would.... He loved your agreeing with him about the witchcraft. You'll see; tonight he'll tell you about his fight at the Sorbonne. You know, they treated him very badly, and he even insists that André Marcel stole part of his thesis material on Schopenhauer and then turned his thesis down. That ruined his chances for him. And the worst is that André Marcel is a cousin of Marianne's, she comes from a very distinguished Jewish family of scholars, those are her ancestors in the salon, and she herself is a mathematician."

Diana was taken aback. She had gotten everything wrong. Henri who looked Jewish and scholarly was Catholic and army. Marianne who seemed so *bourgeoise* and French was Jewish and distinguished. No ordinary housewife, she must be going mad here in the country with nothing to do but tend to an exigent husband and her large brood

As if he read her mind, continued, "That is the worst of it for her, because if only Henri could find another position closer to Paris, or in Paris, she could find work again for herself. As it is, they are helpless here."

They were going up a hill, and a golden sun going down in the west began to spread pools of gold and red across the sky. They passed through a small village with no one in sight and came upon a white plastered Romanesque church, its rounded arches lovingly encompassing small windows. Alongside it stood a tree that still had all its leaves, leaves which were miraculously golden. They stopped the car, got out, pushed the ancient wooden door quietly open.

A cold damp silence lay over everything, over the simple wooden pews, over the altar, over the fount, an open empty shell of stone. But the silence was the silence of places that for centuries have held life within them, a silence woven into time past, an inhabited human silence, a silence defined by sound as the space of a Japanese scroll is defined by a solitary branch bearing a single bud. The sun stained the windows and cast warm colors on the cold gray dials.

If Nora were buried here in the old graveyard, she would be comforted. To have a place to kneel, to feel the earth hallowed by her actual presence. To bring flowers on the *Toussant* – All Souls Day, which was on Sunday. She would stand clothed from head to foot in black and kneel and let her knees, through which Nora had come into this world, touch the lower world where she now lived, feeling the warm sponginess – the living tissue of the earth palpitating with Nora's energy. Then grief could come all in black, black, black and she would no longer have to contain it in herself like some monstrous birth, which would have no term, for there were no ceremonies any longer that could help or heal. All she could have or hope for was Nora restored to her in dreams at night. By day, there was only moving quickly past a vast abyss, pretending it wasn't there.

"This is nicer than Notre Dame," whispered Nick, and they tiptoed out.

In the car they planned the next day's sightseeing: see the Monastery at Cluny, eat at a one-star restaurant, see a recommended church of the twelfth century (one star in the Michelin). On Sunday they would have lunch with the Drouot and catch the train that afternoon back to Paris. The children sighed with relief.

Back at the house Diana asked if she could help Marianne prepare the dinner for the children. But first the two women followed Nick and Kit upstairs. The floors tilted, the window frames sagged, everything was slightly askew in a charming way. The children's rooms were a mess of books, crayons, papers. They found Jean-Pierre bent over his copybook. He had been doing lessons all afternoon with his mother: an essay on nature in the country. Marianne pouted with dissatisfaction, as a good French mother must, but seemed covertly proud of him. Jean-Pierre had a slight tic and looked like he wanted to kill. Then together they all went down to the kitchen, a small room with a pantry to one side and a larder to the other. Patiently Marianne began to warm up a variety of leftover food, a green mass of vegetable, some encrusted greying noodles, squares of farina refried. Diana felt ashamed that she had let Patrice persuade them to come. Marianne had four children to feed, dirty greasy plates were stacked high in the scullery. The bonne, Marianne explained would come to do them in the morning. The children were fussing and fighting, and she would exhort them to behave, but absentmindedly. She explained to Diana that she would like to emigrate to America, she knew English a bit and languages came easily to her, but she feared that Henri could never adjust to life anywhere but France. "You, who are a writer, like my husband," she said, "you understand how dangerous it would be to cut yourself off from your native tongue."

Diana looked down, feeling like an imposter. What had Patrice been likely to have said on that score? Could she, in all honesty call herself a poet? She hadn't written anything in months. She had sat at the long desk facing out onto the windows across the way, watched the busy life of the pigeons, observed the movements of the couples in the bedroom on the floor below, the green carpet, the matching green silk bedspreads on the bed But nothing had come, no poem, no lines, everything was frozen. She had never yet dared to say, "I am a poet," only, "I write poetry."

Marie-Therese, the youngest, was banging her fork and yelling *"Coupe, coupe."* Jean-Pierre looked at her coolly as she bent over and said, with a touch of his father's hauteur, *"Madame, votre fils, quel-age a-t-il? Quand parlera-t-il francais?"* Diana finished cutting Marie-Therese's food, assured Jean-Pierre that they had only been in France a short while, and that Nick would know more soon. She intercepted the fried farina which seemed destined for Kit and explained that she'd prefer the noodles. Kit muttered, "I hate noodles." There was nothing else to eat. Dessert was stewed compote. Wearily politely the children tried it. Afterwards they were sent upstairs to get ready for bed, and Diana helped Marianne stack more plates, put the food back. As far as she could see the noodles, farina, and vegetable mush were going to last for several months more. But it was companionable to be together. They were women. This is what women do. They cook, clean up, put away, worry about children, worry about husbands. Now it was Diana's turn, and she related Tom's problems. She didn't ask Marianne about her life as a mathematician.

When she went back upstairs to say goodnight, Jean-Pierre was beating his brother Claude. Kit had gotten into her little foldaway cot and was retelling herself a story from a French comic book, which Patrice had bought for them on the way down to Cluny. Nick was on the other side reading his Lucky Luce. Diana kissed them both and promised to send up Tom. "Get here early," whispered Kit hotly in her ear.

Later that night, in their hotel room after dinner, they threw open the window of their room, the best in the house, Lamartine's bedroom, and gazed out onto the ancient rounded cobblestones and the silhouette of the cathedral on the other side of the little place. A little lantern cast its perforations of light on the steps to the inn, and in the dark sky a few stars let out their pinholes of fires. Out there was Europe. To be somewhere else, was that an earnest of being someone else? But they were not looking for new selves as much as trying to cleanse themselves of the stains of death and failure. Like a body that has suffered brain damage, it was time to repattern brain cells; to climb other stairs, to look from other windows, to enter other doors. Behind them the bedroom had grown chilly, and from somewhere among the dark roofs of the town the smell of a wood fire drifted in; sweet and salty. They shut the casement.

Dinner had been a huge success. Diana, watching Tom expand under the influence of wine and food, had once again blessed Patrice for urging this excursion. He, on the other hand, had sat there whenever Henri was speaking with a strange little expression, boredom or contempt? on his lips, and Henri had often looked towards him with defiance as though saying, "I dare you to contradict me."

"What a little Jesuit, that Henri is," said Diana as they snuggled down for the night, "ranting on about molding men's minds all the time. The cassis ice cream was sensational, let's have it every day while we're here." It had been fun, but she regretted the mad joy of the night before. Then they had been nowhere, free, between places and time. Now they were somewhere.

"Henri's strange," said Tom, unconsciously echoing Nick's words. "But you're so lovable." And he kissed the back of her neck, and fell sound asleep, the way he always did when he'd drunk too much wine.

The next morning was brilliantly sunny. Breakfast was brought to the room, huge bowls of cafe-au-lait and shiny domed rolls with white country butter and deep fruit preserves in small glass dishes.

Diana burrowed in against the pillows. Tom was in the bathroom. She sipped the warm dark liquid and feasted on the jam and bread. Something like peace or a silence before a voice is heard speaking began to grow. She wanted no one and nothing to intrude. She wanted to stay in the bed forever and be fed, by mysterious hands. The voices in her head, that noise like a continual static, died away. The tentative silence tantalized, deeper than speech but yet promising revelations into things remembered or known. She reached out, concentrating. There was a pattern, there was a vision. Something she needed to know, and, if she could keep still enough, it would reach her.... Tom appeared, got back into bed beside her and ate ravenously. He finished. He looked at her expectantly. They made love.

Afterwards she said reproachfully, "Hurry, we did promise the children we'd be there early today...." Tom smiled. He was picking his ear. "Just relax, there's plenty of time."

The roads were beginning to dry out-and the courtyard was bustling with activity when they arrived. The younger children were playing games in the dirt, the ornamental fowls were looking brighter, fluffier. Marianne had taken Jean-Pierre to town for his riding lessons. Henri was working in his study. The elderly somewhat feeble-minded woman in blue house slippers, whom they had observed the first afternoon they arrived, directed them towards the barn to collect Nick and Kit. Feeling stretched and sensual and ripe in her short suede skirt and black boots, Diana followed along after Tom. And then, passing the kitchen window, she turned, and saw, in a flash, Patrice and Jean-Francois at the sink drying dishes. Patrice was holding a dish towel, pointing to her and saying something to Jean-Francois, who laughed, and somehow Diana knew that Patrice had said, "I'm going to try to go to bed with her," or something like that. She remembered *"Le Diable au Corps,"* and she blushed. Patrice, when he noticed she was watching, hastily rearranged the expression of mockery on his face, and waved.

She was relieved when Patrice came out and announced that he had promised to take care of the children for Marianne so she could go to the dentist. They went off, just the little family, alone.

In the car the children were full of Henri stories. "He's mean to everyone," said Kit indignantly. "He always interferes when the children play. He hit Jean-Pierre again because he took a toy from Catherine, but Catherine had thrown the toy down; she didn't even want it, but he said Jean-Pierre had made her put it down."

If they left the children there for a few weeks, they would learn French in no time. The drama was irresistible.

On the way to Cluny, Diana got out the Michelin and read to them, the way Tommy liked when they drove so he could learn while driving. The history of Burgundy was satisfying. The Dukes all had memorable names, the Beautiful, the Fat, the Stupid. They were allied to all the ruling families of Europe in the middle ages, they cheated, killed, pillaged, and, finally, declined. But Cluny, the remains of the great monastery, founded in 910, which had homed St. Bernard, was a terrible disappointment. The huge complex of buildings, which had once risen like a powerful island of safety and order in the midst of the turbulence of those times, was mostly gone, the lines of sightseers snaked round an elaborate papier-maché construction of what had been. Everywhere the guides were saying exactly the same phrases at the same places. As one group entered the vast hall which remained, echoes of what had just been uttered floated to the ears of those hearing another part of the story until the whole became a round of banality and foolishness. As they tramped doggedly around the walls, Diana kept recalling the way, the first day, Patrice and Jean-Francois had come into the salon and kissed her hand. Empty places, empty gestures. She decided to be careful.

That evening they brought the children back to Henri's after dinner. They planned to sleep late on Sunday and arrive for the farewell Sunday dinner. Diana was already wishing they could go somewhere away from Paris every weekend. It was so good not to think. To see, to move, to eat, to sleep. But Tom had to dig into his experiment. It was already the first day of November. "They don't have Halloween here do they?" noted Kit. Did she pity the poor French children or was she homesick, Diana wondered. She told her the word for pumpkin: *"Citrouille."*

Last year Kit and Nora, it was the remission then, had gone

to the Bridges' for a party. Nora wore her wig to conceal the pale tendrils left on the now visible scalp. "I couldn't play with the others really," said Nora with a touch of bitterness in her direct way, "the wig kept slipping." It was pain, pain like a thousand knives ripping her flesh to hear that. "She wears a patch because she's had trouble with her eye," Diana told Gillian Bridges. A few people knew. The fear, the ever present fear, that Nora would know, and Kit and Nick. And how exquisite Nora had looked, her face framed once more in flowing blond hair, wearing the beautiful Pakistani sari, blue and gold, sent to her by Tom's mother from Pakistan, and Kit wore a matching one of red and gold, and held Nora's hand protectively. There was eighteen months between them. Kit had taken her first steps the day before Nora was born.

They arrived for lunch at exactly one o'clock the next afternoon. In the long dark dining room, a long narrow table was set with heavy white cloth and lovely crystal and porcelain. Of the Drouot brood only Jean-Pierre was permitted to the table. The elderly bonne shuffled around serving soup and later a minuscule amount of roast. Diana praised the wine, and Henri, who by now seemed madly happy to have them there, began at last on the story of academic tragedy and treachery Patrice had predicted he would tell. They shook their heads sympathetically.

The meal came to an end. They lingered over the coffee, black, thick, and bitter, served in old white cups with a worn gold rim. It was a good feeling to be part of the country, to be with people of the country. They spoke of meeting again, perhaps spending a few weeks there in the summer. Even Marianne looked slightly less tense, the little frown between her brows eased, perhaps because they were finally leaving.

"Your son is extremely intelligent," Henri remarked to Diana as they shook hands at the car, "and your daughter, well, she knows how to get what she wants."

Diana found that oddly touching, but as the car pulled away down the furrowed lane, they were all overwhelmed by the comedy of the past forty-eight hours. Patrice made a grimace. "He has gotten worse than before, I forgot how he was."

"But they were lovely to have us," Diana affirmed guiltily.

"Yes, yes," said Patrice hastily with the look of one caught out, "they are good people. And, of course, Just now they are rather sad, it is six months ago they lost one of their children, a four year old, of pneumonia. But I knew they would adore you both and the visit was good for them."

¤

Chapter V

Diana sat in the bathtub filled with gray filthy water where clots of gray soap with suds floated sluggishly. She hated bathtubs. Worse, her hair was still falling out handfuls and handfuls every time she washed it, every time she combed. It gave her a sickening, impotent feeling, the kind one has in a nightmare, like the nightmare of her teeth crumbling in her mouth. But this was worse because it was really happening. It had begun the week after Nora died, and she had mentioned it to people, hoping for reassurance, but no one had understood the terror, the icy terror she felt when she saw the long brown strands alive, but detached from her, float to the floor, or settle at the bottom of the tub. With repulsion she gathered them up and threw them away. She would have no hair left if this continued. She would wear a wig.

Her mind went back to the days before Nora died. Why had it seemed right and proper that Tom should go to Europe to talk about his experiments when the doctors had told them that Nora could die at any moment? Night after night Diana had slept beside her in a little cot, to bring her water, to administer the morphine which was killing her, to carry her withered emaciated body to the bathroom. Why did she accept Tom's leaving? Why had she been taught to accept, to bear, to submit? Wasn't she wrong to let Nick wall himself away after his first tears from the· fact of Nora's death?

And when Tom had been forced to tend Nora until the nurse came because she, Diana, could go no longer night and day without sleep, she had thanked him. Coming from the sunny horror of making the funeral arrangements, "Tom," she had said, "Those last few days, I couldn't have gone on without you, you're so much stronger than I am." He had given her such an odd look. "That's because I saved my strength for the end." What things she didn't understand! She stopped remembering, like someone who slams a drawer on unthinkable objects.

The days before Thanksgiving ticked away, like a ghostly clock. Last year this time, Nora had been going to school for a part of every day. She learned so rapidly how to read. Everything came so quickly to her. She won all games of concentration she played, because, as she said seriously to Diana's mother, "I never think of anything else when I'm playing, not even Christmas." There had been hope then for Diana alone; Tom and the doctors understood better this kind of tumor was always fatal. But the less reason to hope, the more one hopes, it is the last thing left. Last Thanksgiving she lived through knowing it was their last one, and not knowing.

"What will we do for Thanksgiving?" the children kept asking her, hopefully, humbly. She raged at her impotence, at her being the One to keep everyone's world intact. Was anything more intolerable than the death of a child? Her own mother had lost her mother. Lost, loss. Her mother had been thirteen in the great flu epidemic of the first world war. She had kept death vigil at her mother's bedside. She never talked about it, not the actual sounds and sights. Only that for a year afterwards she had strictly observed all the Jewish ritual for the dead, prayers, fasting. Diana had seen a picture of Sara taken at school soon afterwards, she was shivering, thin, hair flying wispily around her face, shoulders almost touching so stooped was the orphaned child, easy to see, in marked contrast to the round easy going fat-of-the-land look of her peers. "My mother watches over me," she told Diana, when Diana was a little girl listening to the stories of her mother's childhood. And hadn't Diana secretly believed that her mother was "watching over" her? It was another kind of mother love than Diana's, that of those women of Sara's generation and before, intense, hermetic, a hothouse passion, a singlemindedness which made it heroic, larger than life. Besides it Diana felt her own love for her children inferior, superficial, selfish. Not that she wasn't sure that she would die for them, only that she had no interest in living for them. It was right and natural, but secretly Diana felt she was cheating her children of that rich, unstrained cream of mother's milk upon which she had been nourished.

"Are you giving Tom what he wants, the way he wants, when he wants it?" That's what her mother had written to her when she was first married in England. How far short of those standards Diana fell!

On Thanksgiving day, Diana woke early in the morning, got the children off to school, Tom to work, and burst into tears. "Will there be a turkey?" Nick had asked. She was exhausted. There was no strength left in her, ceremonies were unimportant; why couldn't they leave her alone to grieve and grieve and grieve?

The cold grey of a Paris November crept into the bedroom. Even bed refused to be warm. She stared at herself in the large mirror over the small fireplace. Her cheekbones were hollow, her eyes bulged, her nose was swollen from crying. She looked like a tragic rabbit; when she wasn't smiling her face was so ugly with grief that it revolted and frightened her. She threw cold water on her face and called Sylvia for advice.

"But it's the easiest thing in the world," said Sylvia. "You just call a bakery, they're the ones that do it, and they deliver it with stuffing and gravy right to the door. I have a jewel of a place near me that's done it for years. Much easier than doing it at home, you'll see!"

Overwhelmed with gratitude Diana asked if she were free to

join them, "Of course," she said instantly, "and why don't I bring Adam Reiner, he's in town and he knows all about Tom and his outstanding work and he'd love to meet him."

"Wonderful," said Diana. She was terribly curious to meet Adam Reiner who figured in her aunt's stories as a strange love totem, the one she'd had a crush on but whom Sylvia had stolen from her. Adam married someone else, but all these years Sylvia had kept up a warm close attachment to him. She had always visited him on her frequent trips to the States.

That will help swell the number at table, thought Diana. For so many years they had sat down with twelve and thirteen. She grabbed her coat and got her little marketing basket on wheels down from its hook.

Downstairs in the lobby she ran into Patrice and hastily invited him, "After all, you're like a member of the family," she said. And remembered one second later she'd have to telephone Sylvia to bring wine glasses or they wouldn't have enough. And remembered, meeting Patrice, of the time she had called him at *Cité Universitaire* and found out, from the receptionist there, that he didn't live there. When she had asked him where he was living he had said; "Well, actually, upstairs in the *chambre de bonne* above you." "Why didn't you tell me?" she had asked. He shrugged. After all, Diana had thought, it is none of my business and he probably needed to save money and didn't want to talk about it.

Back at the apartment, she unwrapped package after package, fruits, cheeses, flowers, wine. In the living room, still without a comfortable reading chair, she put mimosa into her favorite vase, an old pottery earthenware with a simple green glaze around its neck. The mimosa with its hard tiny gold balls stood out from its elegant thin green leaves like a jeweled plant of a goldsmith's devising. She called Sylvia who promised to bring the glasses and, rather gingerly, to bring anything else that was needed. Sylvia's voice in her ear, like nothing she had heard before, now gushingly sweet, now icily metallic, now imperative and ruthless, there was no way of knowing which way that voice would turn, rage and hate lay so close behind its fluting tones.

She greeted the children at the door with the news, "We're having cousin Sylvia and a friend and Patrice for dinner. "Why Patrice?" murmured Nick, resentfully. "He's always here." "But," said Diana, "he's done so many nice things for us, and we're supposed to share our holiday with less fortunate foreigners," she joked. "And the best is that the turkey is going to arrive after the guests, all cooked and ready to go, delivered by a *boulangerie*." That had the desired effect.

Excitedly the children set the table, and Nick helped her drag in the two lauriers, her pride and joy, and place them, two green courtiers, on either side of Tom's chair. At precisely seven Sylvia arrived, beautifully coiffed, wearing a simple black dressmaker's suit with a heavy gold Aztec pin, patent leather shoes with a gold buckle, and a lovely bright red coat. Behind her was a small slim older man who resembled both Ed and Arthur; dark deep set eyes slightly bulging brow, jowls, stooped, but his manner unlike Ed's was refined, delicate, soft-spoken. And Sylvia was transformed from her usual combative self into someone Diana had never seen before, She glowed with pleasure and pride.

They sat down on the dining room chairs dragged into the living room, With every creak of the elevator the children drew breath thinking it was the turkey. Tom's key in the lock was a dreadful anticlimax; Patrice's appearance several minutes later, with a huge bouquet of chrysanthemums, was almost infuriating to everyone, except Diana, who felt, seeing his blue eyes sparkle, how much fun it was that he was there to be their friend and what a difference his presence had made to their stay so far. There was nothing to do but make jokes about waiting for Godot, *"le jour de merci donnant,"* and the Pilgrims.

And then at last, the annunciatory creaks of the elevator grew louder, the clang of the heavy door shutting, the shrill ring of the bell. The children threw open the door, and there stood a dark-skinned man in a blue smock holding a gigantic turkey in a covered pan. He bowed courteously, asked to be shown to the kitchen, unwrapped the bird onto the waiting platter, poured the gravy into a sauceboat, handed Diana the bill, took her money, wished her a "bon diner" and disappeared like a dream.

Triumphantly Nick bore the bird to the table. Kit with Tom's help lit the candles. Then Nick, with Tom's blessing, carved, something he loved to do, and Tom detested. How nice for him, thought Diana watching the scene, to have had a father and a son who like to carve. Another part of her wanted to weep watching this scene without Nora. Why were they pretending to be happy and to have forgotten? Why weren't they mourning and weeping? The other mind said, no, life is to go on, your grief is self-indulgence. She sent up a prayer for all those not at the table and put everything from her mind.

Adam on her right murmured questions to Tom about his work. He seemed most excessively mannerly. The dining room was in total dark except for the candlelight flickering. The children looked rosy and happy, the penumbra covered Patrice's timidity, which in a situation like this one was clearly very great. And Sylvia listened to Adam and Tom with a muted voraciousness of manner so unlike her usual self.

What do I really know about her, Diana thought. That my mother once said, in shock, "She left a child with a fever to go to a party!" That she spent months away from Ed, to travel to the States, to study languages in Italy. That she once asked Stella Field, how much love do you give a child? That she had sat by the bed of her brilliant beloved younger brother who died of cancer in a hospital ward where the other patients tormented him because he was a Jew. That her mother had committed suicide after that.

The bird was demolished; the chestnut stuffing evaporated. Tom got up to uncork the champagne for a grand finale, and Sylvia turned to Adam cooing, "Ah. champagne, we didn't know anything about champagne then, did we Adam? You never had champagne at my house, did you?"

"No, Sylvia," he replied gently, "No."

How ridiculous Diana thought, she's acting like an ass, a child. Every atom of Sylvia's being was transfigured by what, her love, her desire for this Ariel mincing fellow so unlike Ed's gross Caliban? What did Sylvia need? Diana needed Tom the way blind newborns nuzzle the flank and teat of the mother. She watched Tom at the head of the table radiating pleasure. She married him because she could trust him and his passion for her, and she couldn't trust herself. He never wanted to be without her. But she was often happy and relieved when he went away. Was that the mystery at the heart of her life? A golden child was eaten to a skeleton before her eyes; there was no future only a present that became a past. Your children were taken from you transformed into strangers more estranged than dear friends, gone from you that time when they are still a part of you held on hip and thigh, knee, nestled in the lap. That time gone when you are the world for them. Wasn't this the world, the only world, where women were permitted to feel like men, in control, looked upon like gods, the givers, not the receivers, o£ love. Was that why some women loved child-men, she wondered? She could never do that.

The dinner was over. Everyone rose to help clear the table, then marched about the rooms to wear off the effects of dinner. Diana and Sylvia washed up the wine glasses quickly so she could take them back. With the crispness of the old Sylvia she remarked, "You're not really set up here for giving parties, and I'm sure you're planning to entertain. Why don't you use my place?"

Diana felt her shoulders sag as if a great weight had been placed on them. She saw herself rushing to shop, to unload bundles, to worry about getting everything hot to the table, and the long trek down the icy corridor to the dark dining room. The guests would sit on the fragile gilded chairs in the petit salon, and they would admire the décor, and the men would talk easily and interminably about work, and the women would find some kind of common denominator as they always did in their shared condition of womanhood. And at the end, couple by couple, they would leave, and, couple by couple, they would pronounce on the others in the walled fortress of their bedrooms.

"You really must have people in; it's the only way of getting to know them, you know, and the French aren't easy to get to know," Sylvia warned.

Who should know better than Sylvia, thought Diana, who had lived in Paris for twenty years and still didn't number a single French person among her close acquaintances. And not for lack of trying.

"Well, we could take them out to dinner," Diana offered weakly. She had no enthusiasm for it. None. Tom should worry about things like that for a change, she thought. All of their married lives she'd been the one to do it, attracting people, entertaining them, amusing them, now he was the famous man with the work that was being talked about. Why aren't the French running to have them in? She thought angrily, it's because he's so incapable of being friendly to people. They interpret his silence for standoffishness and they leave him alone. And she decided that she hated the French.

"Do think about it," said Sylvia, giving her a French embrace, a kiss on either cheek. Then, to Tom, "It was absolutely thrilling to learn of your marvelous advances in science. We must get together as soon as I return from Luzerne." Like a great winged bird she spread her arms wide and bent to let the children embrace her. Tom beamed at her retreating form. Adam Reiner, in his sober raincoat whispered his thanks and farewells.

With a sigh, Diana shut the door behind them. The tiny kitchen was stacked with messy plates. "What a magnificent feast," said Patrice, who had been so silent all evening, as he followed her into the kitchen, and companionably took a dish towel from the back of a chair. "And your cousin is an amazing woman, she is so intelligent, not at all like the wives of most high officials, and she is so elegant, and she knows so many famous artists, what a chance for you to have her here."

Really he's an impossible little toady, thought Diana bitterly. She couldn't stand the way he was spilling those speeches out so that Diana would repeat them to Sylvia. Did he think that could do him any good? She was almost sorry she invited him. She much preferred him when they were just joking and fooling around *"en famille."*

"And Tom," he went on in the same unctuous voice, "I had no idea he was such a great man. You must be very proud, Diana."

There was silence while they washed and dried mechanically. The great man appeared and yawned. "I think it's too late to make a movie, Do you need some help?"

"We're finished," said Diana. Patrice understood.

"Well," he said, bowing, "thank you again," and he let himself out by the back door and disappeared up the stone steps.

"Why didn't you leave the whole mess for Agnes?" asked Tom, as he patted Diana affectionately on the rear. "When will you stop cleaning up for the cleaning woman?" It was Tom's firm conviction that Diana did only the things she wanted to do and that she wanted, for some inscrutably feminine reason to pick things up from the floor, and pile papers to one side, so that she would look neat for her cleaning woman. Her explanations had never prevailed. Regally, Tom threw his things to the floor, strewed them on surfaces, so did Diana, but she, unlike he, was overcome by the disorder it produced, dragged into the chaos, obliged to tidy up.

But later that night she wondered why she hadn't? Cleaning up dishes in the sink was exactly the sort of thing one always paid the concierge to do in French life. Except that she hated the concierge. Indeed, since Diana, to *Mme. Guillemin's* amazement, had procured herself a cleaning woman through her own devices, they only nodded icily to each other in the hall. And Agnes, a heroic figure, too big even to squeeze comfortably into the elevator, was impossible for *Mme. Guillemin* to stare out of countenance.

In four hours their tiny apartment, like a doll house in Agnes's huge capable Breton hands, shaken out, vacuumed, washed floors and all, polished and all the children's clothes washed and left to dry on racks in the bathroom. Agnes was a mother of six, the youngest a year younger than Kit, and she had an unshakable conviction that Paris was filled with white slavers. Stories of missing children sent round the corner to buy a loaf of bread were uppermost in her mind. She was shocked beyond measure that Diana let Nick, a mere ten year old, travel on the Metro. In fact, that had become Nick's pastime. All day Saturday he spent on the Metro taking as many correspondences as possible. On the big Metro map they had posted on one wall Nick was busy circling the stations he had visited. But Agnes warned that there were men, their pants, they drink, little boys.... There would be a pause. Perhaps a foreigner like Diana was naive and didn't understand the ways of a big city like Paris. At any rate each week, she warned Diana like one trying to convert, but tactfully, convert her to all the proper fears a French mother should have for her offspring. A proper French child was one who withdrew screaming from the proffered hand of a stranger.

Agnes herself lived under such a rule. After she had worked for Diana for several weeks she confided to her, *"Mon mari, il est petit comme vous, Madame."* She smiled a broad smile that showed her small yellow teeth with their gold fillings and her sagging chin, "But he is terribly jealous. He wanted me to stay in the apartment and not work, just stay at home. He works hard, he has two jobs, and he doesn't drink, like some of them, you know, but he does have a terrible temper...." She smiled again and shrugged "But what do you want, there's always something." Her tiny head perched out of proportion on her huge body. She had round brown eyes and a wide pug nose.

"Mon pere m'a donne un petit mari, quel homme, quell petit homme...." the refrain ran in Diana's head every time she saw Agnes. She tried to imagine him in their lovemaking, crawling over Agnes's vast good natured expanse. What was it in Agnes that made her stand for beatings, when she could undoubtedly have battered him to death with her fists? He was so jealous of her, fearing that she might grace a sheik's harem. And he had bred six children on her all with ears which stuck out like pitchers. But his beatings to her were no more than her periods, something endemic to being a man; something over which they and you had no control.

On the afternoon when Agnes came, Diana left the apartment. There was no room in it for both of them, they were of the same species, but she was a lap dog to Agnes's St. Bernard. Down, down, down the turns of stairs she went, smiled and nodded at the bottom with what she hoped was the proper amount of middle class condescension at the lurking *Mme. Guillemin*. Agnes had reported to her that the concierge had intimated she wasn't welcome in the building but that she had responded that was for *"Madame"* to decide not the concierge. But Diana laughed at her sham "grown-up lady" performance. She knew *Mme. Guillemin* wasn't the least taken in. Patrice had quoted *Mme. Guillemin* as characterizing her as *"farfelue."* It was a difficult word to untangle, having the contemptuous connotations of female egghead, bluestocking, visionary, not of this world. With her long hair and her soft girlish voice and her small stature and her way of dressing, very few people called her *Madame*. No one took her seriously and she didn't take herself or anyone else that way. Sylvia, now she was a different story! When she appeared saleswomen bowed and salesmen cringed. She beat them at their game, had style, and was ruthless down to the last sou.

Today she was following Sylvia's advice and going to see the monument built for the French Jews and others; who were taken off to Dachau. Outside everything was covered with a misty shroud, light and fine, but stronger than any attempts of the sun to break through. The monument was at the back of Notre Dame. There in the shadow of a great Christian monument to God's love and mercy, in the shadow of the all-encompassing compassion of the Holy Mother, here women, children, men had been rounded up by a willing French population and sent to their death.

But when she arrived at the back of the church where the Ile points itself like the prow of a boat, Diana, at first, saw nothing, only a stone wall; low, which faced out on the misty river. And then she spied a set of narrow steps which led downwards into a tiny enclosed courtyard. Carefully, for the steps were very steep and covered with a fine moisture, she descended step by step and entered the courtyard. Directly ahead of her there was a door with a grill in it through which one could see the river slowly silently flowing by. Was that it? she thought, the memorial?

The river running free behind the grill in the door? And then she turned her back to the river and saw an entrance carved in the rock. Heart beating, she entered. All was silent. The walls were engraved with names. and there were a series of small cells with bars across them, and through the bars on the cell walls were the words of poets and writers, chiseled in the marble. Silence, silence there in the underworld, and the blood in one's ears pealing like distant bells.

On that day then there had been the sight and sound, the banality of a just plain day, and unbelieving people with possessions, family, moving off to their end on a more direct route than most take. It should have been thunder and storms and portents at midnight, but it was only a gray, November, chill early morning.

She began to weep and slowly, like someone whose arms and legs are manacled, exited through a different door and ascended the second staircase. Death, death, everywhere.

Now the fog was covering everything as she crossed a small bridge that led to *Ile de la Cité*, and the Styx flowed uncaringly beneath her feet. The old narrow, crooked medieval streets gave off a fragrance of burning wood. Tom had heard of a tiny place famous for its homemade ice cream. She decided to find it, she could tell them about it that evening.

"Ah, ma pauvre Diana, of course Leon Blum started the war, every school child knows that!" It was the voice of *Mme. Freilander* as she sat bolt upright in her chair, dressed in her unchanging plain black mourning dress with a thread bare sweater about her shoulders. *"Ah, ma pauvre Diana."* How many times did her youthful American ignorance cause that affectionate belittlement to burst forth from *Madame's* thin firm mouth.

She found, to her amazement, the shop. It was so small

and shabby, one might have taken it for an ailing grocery store where no more than a few bottles of vin ordinaire and some dusty packages of semolina are sold. Inside there were only four or five tables with old bent-wood chairs drawn up around them. Behind a long sink was a middle-aged monsieur and a woman, probably his wife, frizzy haired, pasty-faced. They were having a desultory conversation with a plump elderly man wearing shabby black suit and a beret.

All three of them stared at her. She looked at the list on the wall of *"parfums"* and decided instantly to have cassis, now her favorite since the trip to Cluny. The woman brought it over, Diana thanked her. They went back to their conversation. Perhaps they had been here on that very day when all those men and women and children had filed off, heads filled with comforting notions as to their final destination. So many long journeys filled with so many illusions. And how did *Mme. Freilander* feel about the Jews, her own son-in-law having spent years in Buchenwald and returned with tuberculosis. She had been a courier in the resistance but had great pity for the German soldier whom she always described as *"très correct."* *"Pauvre Mme. Freilander"* in her turn, thought Diana, remembering the phone conversation she had once overheard between *Madame* and a friend. "Well, what do you want," *Madame* had said about her husband, "he's not a bad fellow, but he is a Belgian!" Tall, bony, with a long monkey's face and a yellowed tobacco stained simian smile, he would sit at the dining room table in his white undershirt, leering at Diana and her roommate, Jessica.

The dark wood stained greasy interior of the little shop with its dim lighting brought back that year, the classic "Junior Year Abroad." Memories of climbing the dusty stairs after an evening out, trying to open the big front door quietly, and the feeling of loneliness and anger if she arrived home before Jessica. She had been betrayed by her, there was no doubt. The year before, they had roomed together, and for Diana it had been like coming in from the cold of Freshman year in a house where she had fought with her first roommate and then gotten a room to herself. But Jessica adored her and admired her and mothered her. Her love made Diana feel that she could do anything, and that year she won a poetry prize and for the first time got all A's. In that little world of a women's college, Jessica's fabulous beauty wasn't something to take her from Diana the way it was in Paris, where every boy and man who saw her wanted to sleep with her. *"Celle-la, c'est une Bovary!"* Diana remembered hearing a male French teacher remark as he watched Jessica make her way from a concert one night at school. And Diana looked and noted with a new vision Jessica's tall voluptuous body with its graceful willowy waist and her dark coal eyes burning legacy from an Indian forebear in a heart-shaped face that was suffused with a dreamy tenderness.

In Paris Jessica had soon found a lover and spent most of her time with him. Now she was married to a staid businessman, and she and Diana had seen each other a few times over the years. She remained just as beautiful, just as loving, just as mysterious.

Diana let the cassis ice cream melt on her tongue. What a different love it had been, that loving relationship where Jessica had given to her, encouraged her writing, believed in her, tried to cheer her when she was depressed. They each had their dreams, Jessica was going to be a painter, Diana a writer, odd dreams, so very dream-like. Everything had turned one hundred and eighty degrees as Diana became Tom's Jessica. The love Tom and the children gave her was a love that drained her, that acknowledged her by the act of taking from her. Was this the bond between mothers and daughters, that only one's mother mothered one and understood the tiredness, the strain, the effort to keep the household, the responsibility for everyone's happiness needing to be woven from the very nettles of daily existence as the heroic sister of "The Twelve Swans" had redeemed her brothers from enchantment by weaving nettle shirts with her bare hands? But this was the only life a mother could see for a daughter. What else was there? In the days when the householding was over, then women were permitted to rest, and better yet, encouraged to disappear, the interfering mother-in-law, the unwanted mother, the aging wife, the doting possessive grandmother, who wanted these unnecessary women, hated the most by the people who needed them the most. But when your child is taken from you, what covenants are left? Her mother's voice said, but you have Tommy and Nick and Kitty, you are still mother and wife, you must continue to live for them.

Outside, from the damp ancient streets, the country smell of burning wood drifted and hung over the glistening wet cobble stones. Diana was transported by its fragrance to Christmas vacation of her junior year, to her luxurious dark bedroom at Becheron, tucked into silky sheets. She remembered the taste of morning *café-au-lait*, fresh bread, and huge cherries in jam, and Odette, Caroline's wiry small maid, leaning over to make the fire in the fireplace causing it to crackle and sigh. It was the end of December, and across the house Caroline Richardson was waking in her bed of new widowhood. Diana brooded on the word widowhood. She had often imagined Tom's dying, in a vacuum, of course, no bedside scenes, no anything, just, Tom would be dead, and she.... There was no story to follow, even, just the possibility of another story. She remembered her shock of surprise in the library at school, shortly after their marriage, when a tall handsome boy had appeared looking for someone. She had begun instantly, as was her habit, to imagine a story about him and her, a story which always had as its finale their marriage. With a start she had aroused herself, she was married, she had laughed to herself. And that was the end of all stories.

And now thinking back on it she realized dimly how different Caroline's history was. Caroline had come to Paris a young girl, a painter, right after the first world war, she had lived with a fellow painter, had a child by him, who died but she had never married him, not even when the child came, a child who lived to be twelve. In her fifties, and now Diana saw herself again as a twenty-year old gazing at sixty as at the very end of life, only then did she "marry." And then after no more than ten years with her husband, a sculptor who was famous and loved, she found herself a widow. Diana had heard it all, all of that story at the side of the fireplace in the salon, seated on a cushion at Caroline's feet, watching her huge pansy blue eyes in her wrinkled elegant face. But it was a story from another world.

"You have the eyes of a poet," Caroline had said, "I've known them all." And she had, she'd known every famous author, painter, poet of the twenties and thirties, but there was no one left for her but a few very old faithfuls. The crowd, which would have been there at the little chateau on Christmas holidays, was reduced to Diana, whose parents had briefly known Caroline and her husband. On New Year's Eve the servants had crowded into the salon to wish *Madame* a Happy New Year and to receive their New Year's money, Caroline had turned to her afterwards with gratitude, "I'm so glad you were here. I hate doing that sort of thing." And indeed, it had seemed to Diana somehow medieval. As had the scene in the kitchen when she had to chat with Odette on her way out for a walk. There were all the black garbed women, making soups, plucking fowl, preparing the delectable things which the two of them ate. They would nod respectfully. They were glad that she was there. It was *"triste"* for *Madame*, But they were worried about their lives. When the old king falls... Caroline's affairs were, of course, tied up in terrible French law suits with Latin descriptions like curses on them: *usufruct,* right of the second wife, etc. She had been hated by the two sons of her husband's French wife. "She cared nothing for him," Caroline had said, "just for his money and fame. She was very beautiful and very cold"

Then, Diana had understood only the drama of Caroline's

life, but now, from a distance, she discerned a thread she had ignored. Caroline thought of herself as a painter first and always. When Diana and Tom had tea with her on a brief visit to New York, she flushed with pleasure telling them about her painting. "I painted an apple recently," she said; "It was the best apple I have ever painted." Her eyes had flashed irresistibly child-like, blue as ever.

¤

Chapter VI

The year was turning its way to darkness. Days stayed a heavy leaden gray until early dusk brightened the boulevards with artificial light. In the mornings Diana lit the tiny oven to warm up the kitchen, when she made the children's breakfast. Without the light the apartment seemed raw and neglected. After months of waiting and hoping, Diana received her poems back from the magazine she had sent to. Again, they had "almost taken" one of them. But she was far away from all that. It was an effort to keep her eyes open at her desk. After a bit, like a gas, sleep came creeping over her, and she would stumble back to bed, guiltily, furtively. She was emptied of everything, desire, energy, will. But she always got up and dressed herself before the children came home, stronger for their needs than she could be for herself.

One day Patrice, who dined with them almost every night, invited her to come to lunch with him at a small restaurant in the Parc Monsouris. Mist hung all over the city and in the park, it swathed the bare trees, benches, and the lake in an artificial, theatrical air of melancholy.

"You must come to Saint-Tropez for the Christmas vacation," said Patrice, for the hundredth time. "Paris is dreadful at this time of year, unhealthy, very unhealthy." He turned and glared at the couple at the table behind them who were both coughing. Their waiter was sneezing a few tables away. Diana looked at Patrice gratefully. He was like the children. He roused her, got her back on her feet. Yesterday he had dropped in to watch a program on television with them. Tom was away in Germany for the week. Patrice had sat on one end of Kit's bed and she on the other. Diffidently he had reached out and stroked Kit's hair with his thin nervous intelligent hand, and Diana had been touched and warmed, as if in some disembodied way his hand were stroking her through the medium of Kit. She had looked away to disconnect herself from that feeling.

"Right now at Saint-Tropez it is no less than 80 degrees, I assure you," Patrice went on. For the last few weeks that had been the wedge, the official contrasting of the temperature there and in Paris. Diana tried to imagine the family house he talked about, but couldn't. It was not far from the water, one could see the water from the dining room window. There was a little house behind it where Patrice would stay, and she and Tom and the children could have the big house to themselves. Nearby was a peasant family who always brought them eggs and rabbits. For Kit he endlessly discoursed on that old peasant woman and the eggs and the rabbits.

Now, looking at Diana he said with concern, "You should get away, Diana." "You are not looking well, the sun is what you need." How infinitely touching Diana found it, that he should think of her. Nobody ever thought of her, except her mother. Tom once must have thought of her, but that was only until they were married, after that it was her job, to think of herself, which meant thinking of him and then, later, the children.

"See," Patrice said, and he fished a color snapshot out of his wallet. "Here are my mother and father on the beach with Isabelle, my sister, last summer. You see, she is a bit weak because she has had a brain tumor. But she is better now. Except that she still goes to the hospital for treatments."

Diana grew cold. She saw a delicate smiling face and that purity of bone she thought of as Nora's: the flesh was being taken away and only the spirit left to shine through the bone like the light behind a translucent piece of shell. On either side the mother and father, middle-aged French people, attended her. She looked hurriedly away. She could never tell Patrice about Nora now, not that she had any desire to.

"She is so good and so thoughtful for everyone and so intelligent," Patrice was saying. "She is a much better person than I am. We were very worried, of course, but now things go better."

Out in the corridor, the patients lined up for radiation therapy in their beds, most of them so old their yellow faces and gaunt limbs already had the waxen look of death. Their bony legs with knobby protruding toes and talon curved toenails lay exposed where the sheets had slipped away. Seated in the waiting room, Nora and Diana would wait their turn with coloring books and books to read. Nora, fearless, would enter the room, the white quiet room with the huge nose cone of a radiation machine pointed down against her temple, over her stomach. She lay quietly on the table, able to remain motionless and interested, while the mysterious rays destroyed her tissues in the hopes of arresting the cancer. Then they would walk down the corridor past the never diminishing line of those waiting bodies. Did Nora see them, Diana wondered?

There was nothing to say, they would live through it all; the hope, the lies, the hope, the hope that swelled in proportion to the reality that loomed nearer each day.

"How is Michelle these days?" Diana asked changing the subject.

"They are all in the greatest excitement. Her older brother is getting married in Iran, and the whole family is flying there at Christmas. That's all they can talk about."

Listening to him, Diana remembered all the boys who were students at *Science Po*, all fils de papa, all hoping for no more than the most prosaic of sinecures to see them through the rest of their lives. They all had hungrily eyed the American girls who were pretending to take the courses there. She remembered the one who told her that he was related to the Princes of Grimaldi and she had believed him and repeated it all to *Mme. Freilander*, who had promptly looked it up in her equivalent of Burke's Peerage and proved there were no such descendants. Now she was amused to think how easily taken in she had been. But perhaps that was because it didn't seem very important to her, one way or the other.

"Listen," said Patrice interrupting her thought, "'why don't I get tickets for the three of us to go see Gabriel Bourdet, the director everyone's talking about. I told you during the événements he does *Teatre de banlieue*, goes into the suburbs where the workers live, and puts on productions there. He's opened up his theatre again and he's doing Don Juan. We must all go."

Last night he and she had gone to see a movie together. *Mme. Guillemin* had looked at them oddly as they came laughing and chattering down in the elevator. Sitting beside him, occasionally turning to share the scenes, without the counterweight of Tom on the other side had seemed a bit odd. They were laughing together. They were in the dark together. Everything had a different flavor. Was it strange for Patrice to take her out to the movies, and then afterwards to a cafe as though she were his date? But it wasn't like that. It was far, far from that. But why did she lose Tom's scarf in the movies? She hadn't even noticed that it was gone until they were on the Metro returning home. The carelessness, the unthinkingness bothered her. Wasn't she thoughtless about others?

The morning of the day Tom was due back, Diana arose full of an unaccustomed energy. The children disappeared as in a dream, and, rather than return to bed as she usually did, she rewarmed a breakfast cup of coffee and sat at the desk; holding the warm cup in her hands, letting the warmth flow through her with the silence, and she stared out of the window. Lines began to lift themselves out of some dark recess in her head. She said them softly to herself, then quickly wrote on the empty paper in front of her. "My first letter A she is." It was a poem about the painting she had seen a few days before at the *Jeu de Paume*, the grand portrait of a woman by le Douanier Rousseau. The long narrow canvas was almost entirely filled by the figure of a woman dressed in black, at her feet a small kitten, and, bordering the garden path on which she stood, stiff daisies and pansies were lined in orderly obedient ranks. Her mutton shop sleeves puffed shoulders like the wings of an angel and the stiff shape of her dress stood out from her narrow waist like the kirtle of a Cretan Venus. Here, thought Diana staring at the picture, le Douanier has captured in one ikon the three-fold power of the woman, angel of death, mother, and Venus, it was all there in the chilling sinister robes, the sexual silhouette, in her evident empire over all nature and living creatures. Diana understood woman, the first principle, the first letter to be learned in life in all her terrifying omnipresence in the life of man.

The poem flowed on the paper as though it had already been dictated and memorized by Diana, but once she had written it out she began to see ways to improve it. It was so quiet in the room she could hear the noise the parakeets made as they sidled up and down on their bar. Occasionally they burst into song, but mostly they pecked at the lettuce suspended from their cage tearing at it with their beaks until it hung down in ribbons. When she finished the first draft of the poem she stared out at the sky. On the seventh floor, she and the pigeons marked the incessant change of light and dark. The clouds passed overhead now coquettish and amorously breasted, now pearl gray, now smokey blue, now rose, as *"cuisse de nymphe,"* and then, without warning, turned to a slate-grey military-heap of cannon balls. The clouds gave way to rain, first violet, then smutty black. It was the black light of meanness that put her in mind of the back streets of French existence. Back where one enters little shops to the warning of a dispirited bell that calls the owner from the back room, a sallow angry presence before your arrival, who waits on you sullenly, haughtily makes change, and disappears to continue passionate brooding on ancient wrongs. And then, as suddenly as it came, the rain would dissolve, and the sky would lighten, beginning to play with the line of roofs like a huge cat, and finally, as people were rushing home from work, with all the swagger of a master showman, it would unveil a magnificent sunset; a grand finale before the night. Was it any wonder Diana thought that the French were capricious, frivolous, baroque, and full of spleen?

She had stopped thinking of the poem and let herself be carried away on the broad back of the silence and the light. Why, she wondered, did she never miss Tom when he went away? That was painful to think about because it must be connected to her selfishness, or, equally painfully, to a suspicion that she didn't love him as she should. When you loved someone you never wanted them out of your sight, so she'd read, and so she'd observed with her mother, who never wanted to go anywhere or do anything without her father. And that she knew was the way Tom felt about her. But when the children were younger she'd always been relieved when he was away, because she was so tired and he had been another burden, another responsibility. If he was unhappy about his work, she was depressed, a worse depression than his, because it was out of her control to change things.

In the room the sunlight made dazzling prisms on the beveled edge of the mirror above the fireplace, and then suddenly, like a hand over a face, a cloud would cover the sun and leave her in shadow. How had it happened really? Tom had been shy, unsure of himself, a boy more timid than Patrice in social matters. And she had been self-confident, adventurous, assertive. Now Tom was a man, respected, listened to, admired. It was his life, his decisions, his wishes, that were important. She entertained, and was loved, and made the home, and he did every thing else. He could, in fact, do things, and she could do very little. She depended on him for so much in ways she never could have imagined when they got married, when she was a girl and he a boy. How had she appeared to others? It must have been different than the way she saw herself, because an old admirer had written "Marriage is not for you, you're not a domesticable animal." Why had she thought she was? Right before they learned what was wrong with Nora, tired out then from the nights by her bedside, Diana had taken her mother aside. "As soon as Nora's better," she had said through almost clenched teeth, "I'm going to have to do something about getting time to write. I'll die if I don't." Her mother, she remembered, had flinched. Fear of such violence, disapproval, or concern for her daughter, who might be making a demand that couldn't be fulfilled without pain for others as well as herself, was that why? Was there such a thing as a punishment for desiring the wrong thing? Did her mother think she had been punished for daring to wish for something other than the health and well-being of her family?

She could feel the energy ebbing from her like the ebb and flow of light in the room. Her mind turned to Kit, who had returned home from school in tears yesterday. "I want Nora," she wept, "I want Nora. I have no sister now. I'm jealous of Brigette. She has her sister, Marie Clare, and she looks like Nora, she has blond curly hair." Diana held. her and rocked her. How could she for a minute have forgotten the amputation which Kit was suffering, Kit who had no memories apart from that little other self, eighteen months younger. The warp and woof of their lives had been knitted, second by second, together; they shared secrets, shared games, shared terrible rivalry for Nick's all important love. "Her little hands were so smooth that I used to think she put talcum powder on them," she said to Diana, when she bathed herself that night. Where had the children buried the little body that had turned to ash? It would lie in the cellar or up in the breathless attic with so much else over their long years of "recovery." But to look too long into the vortex of that shared grief was too frightening for Diana. If she stumbled and fell they might all fall. All she had to offer Kit was a humble, "I know, we can never stop missing her."

When Tom returned from Germany, he was refreshed and more like his old self than he had been for months. He had given a seminar which had been received with the greatest enthusiasm, he had talked shop for eight days straight with Hans his colleague on the last brilliant set of experiments. He feels as though he exists again, Diana thought. What was power and intelligence and creativity if it went unrecognized, uncared for, unthought of, by those around us. Weren't people like Bishop Berkeley's chair or table, when no one was looking at them, who was to say they went on existing?

Over the years Tom had acquired viewers, so that there were always people who could testify to his existence: students, technicians, secretaries, colleagues, herself and the children. But here he had been deprived of his retinue and lived in the obscurity of an exile. His stomach ached continually, and Diana wondered if he were not developing an ulcer.

But if he was a god in disguise to the French, for her he had become an un-god. Or had she grown up? Or was it the same thing? No longer could she turn to him as she had so many times in the past to ask, "Will it be alright?" about some situation, trivial or grand, and receive the comfort of his reassurance. He had failed to save Nora. He was exactly like anyone else, as helpless as she was. There were no more protectors, magic workers, parents. He had been the last of them, and he had been discredited.

Despite his good cheer, a few days after his return the stomach aches started again, not really stomach aches as much as continual indigestion. He had seemed delighted about the tickets to the *"Teatre de Banlieu,"* but when the door-bell rang the night of the play, he was not feeling well. Patrice, entering with a broad smile, was instantly solicitous when he saw Diana's tense expression. "Tom's not feeling well," she said quickly, "We're not sure that we can make it."

Patrice sat down circumspectly while Tom looked up briefly from his paper and smiled at him. "How are you?" Patrice asked, and Tom smiled again and mumbled, "Fine, it's nothing." The minutes ticked away. Nervously, her stomach tensed now, Diana sat sipping her dinner coffee. Patrice looked at a magazine. Seemingly unconcerned, Tom read on. Diana thought she would scream. He never worried about time, about being late, but since she was a child she had never been able to stand the thought of not being on time. The minute she knew she had to be somewhere or to do something she could hardly do anything else. She was eager to see this play, and it didn't seem possible that he wouldn't pull himself together, but he'd have to hurry, the last train left the *Gare Montparnasse* at seven thirty and it was only half an hour until train time.

Patrice began to fidget a bit. Diana felt embarrassed; he might miss the play if Tom didn't hurry up. She wanted to shake him and say, can't you see we're waiting for you? Waiting for him, like a god to render his decision. "What do you think, Tommy?" she asked in as unstrained a voice as possible. It was the last night of the play. Their last chance to see the production. Slowly Tom looked up as though he'd forgotten what it was all about. Diana held her breath.

"I don't guess I'm really up to it," he said reluctantly, "I think I'd better stay home." There was a pause. Patrice looked unhappy. Time was racing on.

It was unfair, Diana said to herself. "But why don't you and Patrice go without me?" said Tom.

Like a violent wind smashing its way through a house scattering papers, knocking pictures from their place on the walls, and blowing lamps from tables, images and emotions rose together in Diana's mind. The most fearful one was Tom sitting in his chair as the door shut behind them. That was unthinkable. What kind of a person was she, what kind of a woman, and adult, was she if she couldn't give up an evening at the theatre and be with her husband? Her mother would never for an instant rather be anywhere than with her father. It was one thing to go out with Patrice when Tom was away, but to leave him in the house and go off with someone else. No, that was unthinkable.

Her heart was thudding. She rose slowly, but began to move more quickly. "You're sure you don't mind?" she said. She wasn't her mother. She wanted to go out. She wanted to so very much that there could be absolutely nothing wrong with it; it was natural and what was natural was good. Even her mother believed that. She raced for her coat. Patrice stood up. "It is so bad that you don't feel well," he stammered. Tom had sunk back in his paper again. He just nodded.

She pulled the door quietly behind them and together they got into the tiny elevator. Diana stared at the floor. When they arrived at the lobby they raced out, happening on *Mme. Guillemin*, who stared at them in astonishment.

"Do you think we'll make it?" Diana asked Patrice.

The sour wet smell of the Metro hit them as they dashed in and found seats. At this hour the Metro was filled with couples holding hands breathing garlic into each other's mouths, staring at one another in the blatant sexual way of the French, managing to be both haughty towards others and intimate with themselves in public. A girl in a short skirt and tight skinny sweater was plastered to the side of a dark, oily-haired man in blue jeans and sweatshirt. Only after she had stared at them for a minute did Diana see the woman's hand, like a snake, caressing the man's bare skin under the sweatshirt. And all the while the woman stared straight ahead, her other hand holding on to the pole. Patrice smiled down at Diana.

Time was ticking away. The *Gare d'Austerlitz*, huge, shabby, ribbed like a beached whale, smelled of piss, tears, arrivals, stale bread, and departures. The big clock on the wall showed 7:20. "Quick," said Patrice, "it may be leaving now."

He started to run, and Diana ran after him down the corridor, listening to her boots ring out on the slippery damp passageway. Her heart began to pound. She loved the feeling of running and the disapproving looks of the men and women whom she passed. But then the blood began to burn in her throat and chest, her breath cut her like a knife and her legs began to grow heavier and thicker. "You are thirty-six years old," she said to herself and saw Patrice looking back over his shoulder at her with an enigmatic smile as though he could hear her thoughts. She was frightened, the running had become a challenge, a test, a proof. Patrice was pointing, now, the train was starting, as in a nightmare, to pull out. Patrice leaped on, extending his hand and pulled her into the little metal passageway between the cars. The blood was tearing in her veins.

"You are so swift," said Patrice flatteringly as they lurched to seats and sank into them facing each other, drunk with triumph. Diana felt his blue eyes stare at her intently, it seemed to her they were glinting with a kind of pride that she was with him. She grinned back at him and crossed her legs demurely. They were giddy and laughed at everything. Meanwhile, the train rocked and clacked along the rails and passed through one drab station after another.

Sodium lights shed their angry raw light over the deserted boulevards. In the identical stubby square boxes where people lived and slept most of the lights were already out. These were the immense *cité dortoirs*, the quarters where the workers were billeted in the service of a vast inexorable force.

Patrice continued to grin at her and in the dark pane, which reflected them back to themselves, she caught sight of a young woman, hair curling around her shoulders under a fashionable fur beret, a young woman whose heart-shaped face dimpled in a gay mocking smile and whose round tortoise shell glasses accented the childlike impishness of her features.

The dusty odor of the train seats, the sound of the wheels in the night, a window opening letting in a scent that she remembered from long ago. It was the smell of adventure; it was the smell or being on one's own, of not knowing what would happen next but of a world filled with immense possibility. It was a fragrance distilled from an essence of self – a long forgotten self that was accountable only to itself. It was all there, pressed and preserved like a dried rose from the days of her year abroad, the only time she had ever "been on her own." There was nothing more natural in the world than sitting there with Patrice, did her feeling of guilt come from convention, a convention that was not even of her time, but of her mother's? Or did it have some other source?

Later that night, when she tiptoed into the dark apartment and got into bed beside Tom, she felt to her relief, as he wrapped his arms around her, that he seemed to feel what she had done was perfectly normal. He forgave her.

A few days after the theatre Patrice dropped in at his usual afternoon hour and told her that he had been invited to go to Iran for the wedding of Michelle's brother, and that he might not go to Saint-Tropez after all. To Diana all this familial flying about seemed glamourous and exotic. Tom had told her that Hans and Lucy would probably be in town at Christmas, and it seemed likely that only the children would be disappointed if they didn't get down there. There was always Easter, after all. But then, a few days after that, Patrice appeared and said, no, on the contrary, he and Michelle would be going down together and that she was longing to meet them and have a chance to play the hostess for them. There was a pause and he added that since the family was so respectable they might even have the illusion that she and Tom were chaperoning Michelle and himself. Then he told her once more what the temperature was in Saint-Tropez at that very moment and begged her to go and get their reservations in *couchette* because everyone, but everyone, left Paris for somewhere at Christmas, and it was imperative to get space.

Tom listened to all of this with only half an ear, and was neither for nor against the idea. "Aren't you curious to see Michelle?" asked Diana. She had bought a pair of shoes in the fall, which she wore everywhere, and the first time she had worn them Patrice had exclaimed in delight, "Why Michelle has a pair just like those." Diana imagined her as blonde, shy, and lovely, probably adoring Patrice and hanging on every word he said. What was that curious story he had told her one day about how they had come to be engaged?

"I had broken up with another girl, and she saw that I was very unhappy, and she agreed that we should be affianced." It sounded so strange. Who could know what it meant? It was clear that nothing would happen until he and she both took their respective exams. The world was not so wild in France among the *bourgeoisie* that mere students could marry.

With only two weeks to go until Christmas, Patrice began to talk incessantly about the presents which he was getting for the family. He had found some things for Kit, wondrously Kit-like, at an antique store and something clever for Nick and records and books for her and Tom. Diana decided to bring their little record player so that they could listen to music. She began to worry about what she should buy Michelle. She had already picked a present for Patrice, a very famous book on politics and the law in America, which she was sure he would want since he was an enthusiastic student of politics in The States.

Patrice was leaving a few days before their departure, and the night before they all had dinner together, and Diana gave him a small suitcase and the records to take down for them, presents, and some items for the house. They said goodbye, and Patrice said he would call them as soon as he got there to report on the weather.

The next morning the phone rang very early. To Diana's sleepy amazement, it was Patrice's voice, high, excited, and speaking in English. He had left the house at five in the morning to catch his six o'clock train, put all the bags down in front of the apartment house to fetch a taxi, and one second later, when he returned, they were gone. He had reported it to the police, who had merely shrugged and told him it was the Arabs, by which they meant the Algerians who, in blue smocks, swept the gutters clean with medieval brooms early in the mornings. It was so unbelievable that all Diana could do was find it funny. She tried to pretend that she was upset and told Patrice that she would go later that day to the Central police lost and found department and make out a full description.

"Tommy will be so angry when he hears this," moaned Patrice, "and all those special things for Kit gone, and I can never replace them and your record player. I am a fool. Promise me you will come."

Diana tried again to reassure him. She climbed back into bed where Tom was sleepily wondering what all the commotion was about. When she told him, his reaction was the same as hers, he burst out laughing. "That kid is nuts," he said, "Why the hell didn't he leave the bags inside the lobby, at least?"

"Nick would never do a thing like that, even at ten," murmured Diana. It was funny because it was sad. Patrice tried so hard to "get things his way" was the only way Diana could think of it. He was so conscious of how people used each other, and how they schemed to get what they want, and, like every Frenchman, he had been brought up with the cardinal rule, *"Il faut se défendre,"* "look out for number one." And then he did something so childishly unthinking, incautious, and imprudent, that you could only laugh at him. But suddenly she no longer wanted to go down for Christmas. Later that morning when Hans and Judy called to say that they would definitely be in Paris for the holidays, Tommy and she decided to stay in town.

Only Kit was unhappy with the decision. "You see," she said immediately, "Patrice will think we're not coming because of the suitcases, and he'll feel he failed us."

"Well, that's not the reason," said Diana. "Daddy's just getting started in his experiments, and Hans and Judy are coming, so it will be more fun for him if we stay here. And Patrice will have Michelle and he won't be lonesome."

When Patrice called, she broke the news to him as gently as she could. "Perhaps you will change your mind," said Patrice, sorrowfully. "I am so lonesome and the weather is so beautiful here."

"Well, you will have Michelle soon," said Diana cheerfully, and then she added the big gun, which she knew would silence Patrice, "And besides Tom is just starting a big experiment."

"Ah well, if it is Tommy's work then that is the most important thing," he said obediently. "But if you change your mind, just call me, and I'll have everything ready for you."

A few days later they got a postcard from him. "Dear Fields, the weather is marvelous, blue skies. My neighbor has two little rabbits. I am a bit lonesome, Michelle couldn't come, she has gone to Japan with her family. I am getting a lot of studying done. Best to all, Patrice."

"Japan?" Diana said to Tom. "Did he say anything about the family going to Japan? Tom shook his head. "They do seem to be a pair of star-crossed lovers," he remarked wryly.

Communication with Saint-Tropez stopped. And then, unexpectedly, the phone rang one day, and it was Henri Drouot. Diana was pleased to hear from him. She had written only the briefest of thank you notes, never mentioning the loss of their child. She had felt inhibited by her lack of correct French, and by the fact Patrice might have revealed something they would prefer unspoken. Now Henri said that they were in town to settle Jean-Pierre with Marianne's mother, and they were anxious to see her, and could she come to their place at eleven the following morning?

Henri's mother-in-law lived one Metro stop from the Fields in a row of big grey apartment buildings which faced an empty lot– what the French call a terrain vague. It was a sad street, the sort which depresses as soon as one sets foot on it. The building itself was no cheerier. Diana entered the dark vestibule and walked up the two flights of stairs, which were covered with dusty brown carpeting. For once she appreciated *Mme. Guillemin*. On the door on the right was a small brass plate marked Levy. Her ringing produced sounds of running feet, and then a bolt was thrown back, and there before her stood Henri, pipe in hand, his thin face punctuated with a sharp gallant smile.

They shook hands, Diana felt filled with an unexplained goodwill. Perhaps it was the pleasant feeling once again, of having made French friends, of knowing people of the country, of relationships, or their possibilities.

Following Henri she entered a salon crowded with furnishings: a sofa under a huge portrait, a coffee table in front of that, several large stuffed armchairs, behind them, near a window, a small grand piano. The effect was one of clutter and darkness. As she entered the room a gross thick set man in a dark suit rose slowly and upon being presented to her by Henri, who danced around him like a small fly, he extended a thick pudgy hand. *"M. Volker, un cousin de ma femme; Mme. Field,"* said Henri. M. Volker looked at her from the small depths of brutish brown eyes, which reflected a steady amour-propre that seemed connected with the air of prosperity he exuded. *"Il faut partir,"* he announced in gravest tones, "*Appelons les enfants.*" Henri disappeared instantly and returned with Jean-Pierre, who was dragging his feet, and another child about the same age and size but built along the solid piggy lines of his father. The men stared down at the boys like policemen in charge of two incorrigibles.

In the same direction from which they had emerged, hurried footsteps were now heard. Marianne entered looking more haggard than ever. She barely smiled at Diana as she extended her hand. Over one arm was a coat. "In case it gets cold," she said. Jean-Pierre made a face. And suddenly Diana knew that she was witnessing a terrible, painful family tragedy. Now there were a round of serious handshakes and last minute exchanges of regards for other members of the family. In every way, by tiny movements of his thin body, by winks and smiles, Henri seemed to be impressing on his cousin-in-law an intimacy, a bond, which Diana could see M. Volker was far from acknowledging.

Marianne knelt down and embraced Jean-Pierre. *"Sois sage, mon cheri,"* she whispered. There were silver hairs, stiff and wiry, among her chestnut curls. Cousin and children moved off. The door slammed heavily behind them.

Diana could feel her heart wrenched for Marianne.

Henri sighed, and motioned her to sit down. "Some coffee, some tea?" Diana asked for coffee. "Marianne, bring something for us," commanded Henri, but a shade less crisp than formerly. Obediently Marianne disappeared like a genie. Diana felt in accord with Kit who when she had been invited to come and see Jean-Pierre and Henri said, "Certainly not, he gives me the creeps."

"Well," said Henri, clearing his throat, "how are your fine husband and your children?" As soon as she had murmured the appropriate phrases, he hastily began. "We have come here, Marianne and I, to settle the boy in with Marianne's mother. You see the doctors think it best for him not to be at home with us for a time. He is a very sensitive child, very nervous, and I perhaps ask too much of him. Here he will be able to study and be tranquil. Naturally, all this is very hard for Marianne, and for me, but we think it the best way. He will see us on school vacations. Marianne's mother is a very good person and he has many cousins among Marianne's family, mine is in the provinces.... and her people are good people." He sucked reflectively on his pipe, looking at Diana thoughtfully over it with his dark brown round eyes, eyes like a sparrow, liquid and shiny.

Marianne returned and placed a tray on the little table. Coffee from a silver urn was poured into old delicate porcelain cups Marianne had handed round. It was Nescafe. The three of them stirred, sipped. Marianne looked down, silent. Henri puffed, tapped the bowl with wiry fingers.

"How are the children?" asked Henri once more. "How is their French progressing?"

Diana murmured something non-committal. They were, in fact, dissatisfied with the progress the children were making.

Henri cleared his throat again, "It would be very kind if some time you and the children might see Jean-Pierre. Your boy would be a good influence on him. He is very *solide*, your Nick, more at ease with himself. Marianne and I would be happy if that should happen, Jean-Pierre needs to be with others who can guide him and set a good example...."

Diana felt touched, flattered, and revolted all at once. His terrible need to mold, to subjugate, to impose himself on his children like so many little subjects had driven one child away already, and yet he couldn't be at rest. How typical of him not to see that Nick was three years older than Jean-Pierre and that they would never be at ease with one another. But no, it was not the French way to take these things into account. Children were to be bent and twisted, pruned and raked, until they lay flat and conforming to pattern rather than their nature. But, of course, they weren't plants. But a second later she laughed at herself for her prejudices against the French. What child anywhere wasn't being formed in conventions that would warp and deform them? Not mine, she added hastily to herself. But then what about the things which society did to them, and death, she added, and my mother, she added and all our mothers. Everywhere society was a schoolroom, schooling people for its own inflexible purpose: the hive of soldiers, workers, and mothers.

Suddenly Henri looked at his watch. "Let us go into the bedroom," he said, "we can talk while I make some phone calls, our time is short here. Marianne and I must leave tomorrow, the others are waiting for us." Diana followed them down a dimly lit corridor until they turned into a bedroom with two old twin beds cluttered with suitcases. They sat on the beds. Diana was offered the sole chair, faded and misshapen. "See if you can get Marie-Therese," Henri said to Marianne and she began to dial a number. "It's busy." He nodded. "You will try it again." Diana shuddered at that way of speaking. How lucky Jean-Pierre was that someone had seen what was going on.

"By the way," said Henri, "do you ever see the young Montcheval, these days?" Diana gave a start. It seemed that Henri must know that Patrice practically lived with them. But he went on, as though ignorant, "One doesn't want to see too much of him, he has a way of fastening on and one ends up by feeding him every night, as we did, eh Marianne?" And now even Marianne grinned coarsely as if at some long shared family joke.

"We do see him a bit," Diana acknowledged, fascinated and curious.

"And then," said Henri, going on as if it meant nothing, "he is a very sick boy, I'm afraid. His poor family has grave worries on that score. He's a *mythomane* you know, a very *grand anxieux*. Would you believe he has it fixed in his mind that the young daughter of friends of ours is in love with him? He has absolutely terrorized the poor girl. Not only doesn't she not love him, she detests him. She makes one excuse after another when he asks her to see him. The family is going to cut off their relations with him completely, I think, difficult though it will be, because Patrice's family encourages this, I think. The mother is, you know, terribly snob."

Diana felt her cheeks growing hot. It seemed impossible that Henri didn't know how close they were to Patrice, that he didn't mean every word especially for her. She saw her whole relationship with Patrice (what would she call it anyway?) turning to something horrible and calculating. Had he not, indeed, "fastened on them?" But that was Henri's way of seeing things. The French thought so much more of a dinner than an American did. She remembered at home people had often said similar things to her about a close bachelor friend of theirs, who for ten years had eaten off and on at their house. But I like it, she would explain. He amuses me. Perhaps, she saw now for the first time, she always needed to have some other man around besides

Tommy, perhaps Tommy wasn't enough. Before she married him, she had seen that she didn't love him the way her mother loved her father, he did not enslave her with his love, and that, of course, had seemed to her the only real love, but she doubted that she would ever feel it.

Things were different in her marriage. It was Tom's way of loving that was like her mother's. But yet, being a man all other things were permitted to him, to love his work, to work all the time at it with no qualms that he was neglecting them, to make all the decisions – if he wanted to – to leave them to her if that were easier. And yet he loved more, she felt that, she would always feel it, it was that which gave her her power and her vulnerability.

With the same malicious gleam in his eye, Henri was still going on. "Patrice was ill for a year right before he had to take the bachot. He had a nervous breakdown. That was when he was so attached to the Pontmarres at Cluny, ate there, slept there, you know, before it was our turn, eh, Marianne?"

Diana could hear them. "And then these poor, naive Americans, such babies you know, they fell for every word he told them. You know, I think the woman had her eye on him, I wouldn't be surprised." She grew hot and hotter.

"Oh, he does completely wild things. He disappeared once for two weeks, no one could trace him; he was supposed to see our friend, they of course cabled his family, everyone was wild, they thought he'd been killed. He never told us where he'd been. Yes, *ma chère Diana*, he lies, he's a dreadful little opportunist, comes and stays for months and then goes off and isn't heard from for two years."

Diana felt the venom drip from Henri's lips. She didn't dare ask him anything for fear of revealing that she had been taken in. She tried desperately to look "normal."

Speaking for the first time Marianne said severely, "Just don't encourage him if he starts coming around or you'll never get rid of him."

"What this country needs is licensed bordellos, said Henri bitterly. "Young men are driven wild, it's a shame!" It was so unexpected that Diana wanted to laugh, but she suddenly remembered the words of a friend of theirs who had married a French girl. All middle class French guys are horny – they can't get it from the girls they're going to marry – it's rape or nothing."

"Yes, I just spoke to the Giret yesterday, they are quite upset about Patrice...." He stopped abruptly. Marianne, who had been patiently trying to get Marie-Therese had at last succeeded. She passed the phone to Henri. Diana had a moment to recover from her confusion.

"Ma chère Marie-Therese," Henri began, purring like a cat, "it is to you, only to you, that I can confide our precious Jean-Pierre. Don't break our hearts and say that you're all booked, only someone of your *"hauteur,"* your *delicatesse*, your sensitivity, can understand and bring out the best in our poor boy. He has talent, we know. He needs the direction that only you can give, *ma chère*.... "

Diana listened in embarrassment. All of this to arrange piano lessons for a seven year old! Was this what Patrice's life had been like as a child? If it was; was it any wonder he lied from time to time? How would a child grow confronted always by the sinister presence of grownups directing, imposing themselves, inserting themselves, into every breath you drew. She watched Marianne for some sign of her feelings. On her face was indeed; a strained and distant expression. Diana's thoughts returned to Patrice, she recalled the tense look on his face the first time they had seen him at Cluny. The Drouots had put a good face on their visit, when they were together, but privately, with Patrice, they must have been filled with rage. He had not written for two years and suddenly he had arrived with an entourage of four. Or, at least, that's what Henri was saying. But why should she believe Henri, she wondered, as she listened to him make his final meows to the all desirable Marie-Therese. Maybe Michelle was afraid to tell her family how she really felt about Patrice, seeing that they didn't approve.

Henri had finished his conversation. Diana decided to hazard one question more. She felt disloyal to discuss Patrice with someone who was so obviously his enemy. With a deep breath, so her voice wouldn't tremble, she asked, "Oh, are the Giret in town for Christmas...?" Henri looked surprised. "Yes, of course."

Stiffly, she got up from her uncomfortable chair and took leave of them. Already Henri seemed weary of her, weary of everyone, that fatiguing world which must be threatened, cajoled, rebuked, manipulated. Falsely she promised that they would try to see Jean-Pierre. Henri bowed and shut the door firmly behind her.

Out on the street the light struck her eyes as though she had been emerging from a dark tunnel. She raced to leave the street behind her, to return to the sanctuary of her windows, her sky. Of course, what Henri had said must be true. Patrice's words, "Michelle has gone to Japan with her family," seemed the words of a true madman. *"Mythomane."* She tasted the word on her tongue, rolled it around her mouth. How grand and mad it sounded. A *mythomane* suffered obviously from *mythomanie*. She remembered his excitement when he had reported so many months ago, it seemed, that Michelle was going to the concert with him, and how downcast he was when he related that "she had gotten sick." Never once had they seen Michelle in all the time they had seen him so frequently. Hadn't Diana once asked him "But when do you see Michelle?" and he said, "Oh, I see her every day after she leaves the *lycèe*." But that was impossible because he was at their place almost every afternoon, and many evenings as well. And that impossible story about the wedding trip to Iran. She shivered and she laughed. She and Patrice suddenly struck her as being alike: he constantly wanted to see her poems, but she hadn't any to show him, and she wanted to see Michelle, but he had no Michelle to show her. They were both great pretenders. Or looked at another way, she had written a few poems and he had seen and known Michelle, and each was filled like a person suffering from a false pregnancy with the desire to enlarge upon that meager reality. But on the other hand she had never encouraged Patrice to believe that she was a "poet," he had blown that up for himself, taking for granted that she was more than she was because of her age, she supposed. Whereas he had actively lied to her. But why?

And then again she thought maybe Henri didn't know the whole story. But that night, when she told the whole thing to Tom, he said, "That kid is crazy." And, of course, she agreed with him.

¤

Chapter VII

Christmas had come and gone, another terrible way-station of the year, with memories of their always immense Christmas tree, decorated with old family hangings; of the children and herself stringing popcorn and cranberries; of the faces rosy and excited of the first one then two then three happy children gazing up at that glowing pagan idol of a tree. And the memory of Nora's voice that very night of Christmas Eve screaming in pain, "My leg is killing me." It was the beginning of the end of the remission, the months from September to December.

Forlornly, the four of them had gathered in the dark December morning around the little laurier and opened some few presents. They had a call from Diana's mother and father. Diana could feel the pain in her mother's voice, the worse for her habitual efforts to deny any thing painful or bad.

Now it was New Year's Eve and they were at a Reveillon Souper at Jerry Berg's, Tommy's only friend at work. Jerry was a thin, slight hook-nosed American Jew from Wisconsin, and he had married a French girl, Catherine, of good family as they say, that is very Catholic, very antisemitic. She was clever, rebellious, dark, and vivacious. They were living on the seventh floor of a tiny old building on the *Rue Mouffetard,* and the narrow treads wound round the ancient stairwell at such a precipitous angle that one arrived completely dizzy at the top and risked a broken ankle, at least, on the descent. Diana admired Catherine as she thought of her doing the stairs several times a day with laundry, shopping, and airing of the Berg offspring, a male child of amazing proportions and liveliness named André. The tiny crowded rooms of the apartment were chaotic. The kitchen was almost impossible to move in because of the vast quantities of as yet unreturned bottles, and through all the confusions André rampaged, pulling down, tearing up, chewing in, inexorable ur-baby.

At last he had fallen asleep from sheer exhaustion and been carted off, and the four of them had sat down to a large disorganized meal of charcuterie, oysters, white wine, cheese, and fruit. Diana was grateful to the Bergs for the invitation. It was the first evening at the home of friends, since they had come to Paris. Jerry was a funny, restless paranoid, who told long stories of the Byzantine workings of the lab. He was also very much a parlor Marxist, and when they finally got up from the table and moved to the living room – separated by a simple arch from the "dining room," he held forth on the position of the communist unions vis-a-vis the students during the uprising, and pointed out the correctness of the position of the communists in refusing to ally themselves with the students.

Catherine got out her knitting, and Diana and she took to one end of an old sofa to talk over children. She had invited Nick and Kit over for tea one day, after taking them to the Tuileries. Both of the children adored André, whose every act filled them with amazement. And Kit had fancied herself as adjunct 'babysitter' for him.

"Nick," Catherine reported, "was very serious and careful of André. He looked out for every possible danger, took things away from him that were too small, got him to sit down in the stroller so he wouldn't fall out, and very attentively watched me give him a bath and feed him. I know he could do it better than I can. And Kit," and she began to giggle. "For a while she wanted to feed him, but then she lost interest and started to play with his toys, and then she got hold of one of his pacifiers and sucked on it very happily, and for the rest of the time she played with his blocks and stuffed animals."

Sitting there, her hands folded in her lap, Diana watched Catherine's quick fingers flash needles and wool, and she wondered at the changes in her life. As though some one had taken her up to a high place and told her to look back, she viewed all the small incidents of her past stretched out behind her. She remembered so well the first child, the days filled with him, herself then, evenings like this one, the cheerful "occasions" of the small life lived in academe among congenial people, all young, sharing, the women, their world of watching husbands progress in careers, themselves having babies, tending to them. Now suddenly the babies were there and turned to children; the career was established.

I'm bored, she thought, I'd be having much more fun at home doing the dishes with Patrice. This wasn't her world anymore, the world of the men talking about work and politics, the women about husbands and children. Was it Nora's loss which had smashed that world forever, or would it have happened anyway? It was more fun with Patrice she realized, because he was seeing her, looking at her. Here she was once again part of a unit, an appendage of Tom's, a wife-mother fixture.

As though she had heard Diana's thoughts Catherine suddenly asked, "How is that strange boy, your *fils du propriétaire*?" She had met him once, when she and Jerry had stopped in to the apartment, and Diana had seen that Patrice had recognized her instantly for what she was, jeune fille de bonne famille, and had pranced (or so Diana thought) about her accordingly.

But hearing him referred to in this offhanded contemptuous manner rankled now. Was there something about Patrice which everyone saw at once except herself? Sternly she reminded herself that even if he was strange it wasn't important one way or the other. She was grateful for all he did for them, for her, which was to distract her.

"Oh he's alright, he's invited us down to Saint-Tropez for Easter." Diana said casually, unexpectedly trying out the idea to see how it sounded. But still she was nervous at the thought of seeing him after Henri's stories. I need someone I can joke with; she said to herself again, that's all. And she remembered the way Patrice had looked at her when he said one day, "I want to have a daughter like you," and she was amused but a touch chagrined that he hadn't said wife. Or the time he said, when they went down in the elevator together, "You are cruel and capricious; that's why I like you," and his eyes sparkled as he said it. Diana thought about these words often, not because she found them important in themselves, but for their strangeness, their uniqueness in that they related to her alone. They were testimonies to her existence, an existence she was as avid for as a mirror.

A few days later when the children came clambering home from school and burst open the door, Patrice was behind them smiling diffidently. Diana felt a start of pleasure and couldn't restrain a smile. "The children found me on the stairs," said Patrice, "and invited me to come in." It was clear he felt ill at ease, and Diana wondered if he had been keeping away because of embarrassment over the stolen suitcases, which he couldn't pay them back for, or if he did see Michelle every day, had she told him about Henri? She smiled back and when he said, "You are going somewhere?" seeing she had her coat on, she answered, "To the *Théâtre Palais Royale* to get some tickets, want to come?"

The children flung themselves on their beds to read, and together, Diana and Patrice went out into the fine spring air of the January day. It was good she felt, so good to have a companion again. They picked up the tickets and decided to walk over to the *Palais Royale*. There the gardens were quiet, it was Monday, and most of the shops were closed. Along the garden paths, navy-blue prams on high wheels looked like gigantic bugs. Nannies and mothers sat knitting, reading, talking and keeping a watchful eye on their charges, the pale-faced city children, who ran up and down the paths and played near the fountains, which rose and fell in their own knit and purl of light and water. Everything was framed by the splendid 17th century loops and columns of the arcades. The footsteps ringing out under the voûtes, the sound of running water, the attenuated voices of the children calling to one another, the tiny pecking of the pigeons grazing over the hard dusty ground swelled to a vibrato, which accompanied the water-color delicacy of the sky overhead and the dreamy look of the figures enclosed in the courtyard.

Diana and Patrice sat on a bench. "Did you know that Colette lived here?" Patrice asked. And they both gazed at the elegant facade and long windows, which looked down on the gardens, as though they would catch her peering down at them, her celebrated frizzy hair and long feline eyes staring intently, as intently as a cat, to see what their hearts were up to.

"When you come to Saint-Tropez at Easter," said Patrice, "I will take you to her house there, it is not far from our house. In the garden is a magnificent cypress."

Diana remembered that somewhere Colette had warned never live in an apartment higher than the first floor, it cuts you off from humanity and leads to the sin of solitude. Wasn't that the sin she longed to commit every day? Seated at her desk at night she could see herself hanging against the velvety black of the Paris evening, behind her, to one side, the terra cotta statue of a Chinese peasant astride a little donkey on the mantelpiece made his endless journey into the dark with her.

In front of them now a big man, bulky in a winter overcoat, came poking along using a black umbrella as a cane. He was talking to himself loudly in two different voices. One was high and irritated, the other low, rumbling, and violent. Fascinated, Diana imagined his coat, like a pupa case coming apart with a great ripping motion and the two people who lived inside him splitting asunder into freedom.

That's how they all were, two people at least, weak and strong, angry and contented, noble and despicable, in one miserable shell. In that man the struggle was coming to a final resolution, which might be annihilation. Two people were struggling in her, one who had been overtaken and engrossed by the other. Now that person wanted her time, her day. High in the air Diana caught sight of the three-quarters moon, a chalky white thumbprint on the pale blue sky. She felt a bit as though she were on the moon and laughed to herself remembering, *"Ma chère Diana, tu es dans la lune!"* the phrase *Mme. Freilander* always mocked her with.

Without stopping to think about it she said dreamily to Patrice, "You know, Henri was in town at Christmas." He shrugged. "Apparently," she went on, "the Givret didn't go to Japan for Christmas." "Yes," he said. "They didn't want Michelle to go to Saint-Tropez." She felt too embarrassed to really ask why he had invented those stories of Japan. He was obviously a liar, and, if she knew it, it was cheap to force him into more lies.

"Henri hates me, you know." Patrice said in a conversational tone of voice. "You see, I used to admire him so much, and I was so very much under his influence, and in a way I was even a disciple of his, and he needed that admiration, and then I said I would help get him a television program devoted to his work, and I thought Givret would help, but when that didn't work out, he believed that I had betrayed him, not that it was just because I was too young and not clever enough to do it.

"Now to get back at me, he tells people that I am *non fréquentable,* that I had a nervous breakdown...."

Diana blushed. She felt that he knew everything that Henri had said to her.

"All it was, really," Patrice went on, "was that I had contracted some kind of amoebic blood disease, when I came back from a trip to Mexico, and it left me worn out and for months and months. I couldn't do much of anything."

"You see, Henri and I were at one time really like a monarch and his court." So I am Henri, Diana understood. "Why, he authorized me to do anything, absolutely anything to get him on television. He even knew that the head of the programming was a great queer, and he told me, I was then only sixteen, to be as charming as possible. Now he'll stop at nothing to wreck my plans. He couldn't stand it that I liked the novels of Nathalie Sarraute and Robbe-Grillet. And he's madly jealous of his wife because he feels inferior to her." His voice grew more agitated.

"But Michelle and I will win in the end. We are going to persuade the family that we will get married at Easter. You see, I have very little confidence in myself, and Michelle, well, she is very much under the influence of that crowd in the sixteenth. If she doesn't marry me, she'll just grow up to lead an ordinary *bourgeois* existence, but she isn't really like that, she is sensitive and good. She is very good, not like you, Diana." He laughed. "We have everything planned. I will finish my ENA, and then we will go to China and travel throughout the Far East, because I want to specialize there, and perhaps I'll be in the foreign service."

Diana sat very still, a part of her numbed by this tirade. This was more than she wanted to know about Patrice. She was covered with the grime of his vehemence against Henri. There must be truth and lies on both sides. All the knowledge she gained only put Patrice further and further away from being her friend. She wanted to know him, she needed to know him, only in relation to herself.

On the path a woman knelt down by a rosy-faced toddler, who held something in her extended hand for her mother to see. The mother began to talk to the child, gazing up into that beaming countenance with worship in her eyes. When she looked away from the child, her expression was dazed, unfocused, as though she could see nothing besides this radiance that she had produced. And Diana remembered the many times she had crouched in front of her children and wondered why the world didn't come to a standstill and kneel there with her. She looked at Patrice. He could never know these things. He was holding two pieces of gravel in his hand and bouncing them together.

"I'm afraid," he said bitterly, "the only difference between me and Henri is twenty years. Everything I do, I always ask myself, would Henri do this? And then I do the opposite." His face was pinched and drawn as he said those words, and Diana was shocked that he understood himself so well and so little. Oh there was more to the story she knew, and if she were more skilled she could get it from him. Maybe Michelle did love him?

Suddenly she remembered that Agnes had said to her one day that Patrice had come when she was out and had come into the kitchen and asked her (and here Agnes had mimicked his precise French) "Do you want me to help you Agnes?" She said she thought he came when no one was in the house. "When you are away, I find cigarette butts in the ashtray, and no one in your house smokes. Maybe," Agnes suggested with a wink, "he comes to use the bath or the telephone." Diana had put it out of her mind. After all, where would he have a key?

Now looking at him, he no longer appeared charming. He was sallow complected; there was a red pimple burning on his forehead. Thank god, Diana thought, I'm over and done with love, that adolescent love which torments Patrice and Michelle, the madness, the dream world, the pain of the unfulfilled wanting. A mannered, affected, mincing strange boy, that's how he appeared to everyone.

There was a silence. Patrice said defiantly, "I didn't mean what I said about not having confidence in myself." Diana said falsely, "Of course, of course." The sound of her voice seemed to shock Patrice. "I've been talking too much about unpleasant things," he murmured. "How is your work going? If you come to Saint-Tropez, I promise you I'll take care of the children and you and Tom will have time to yourselves, and you will have time to work." Diana smiled in spite of herself. Perhaps there would be a beautiful room where she could lock herself up and write and write and write. It was nice to think about anyway. They both rose stiffly from the hard iron bench, stretched, and walked off under the darkening arcades.

¤

Chapter VIII

Diana sat at her desk. Everyone was gone. The apartment was oppressively silent, she was in prison or being punished. Was it the way Tom had left saying, "Well, get some writing done," that instantly made her resentful and contrary? Was she afraid of expectations which she couldn't fulfill, or angry that he made it seem so mechanical, and that he was, by merely noticing and mentioning what she was trying to do, thereby taking control of her. Often she had told herself she couldn't write if she had anything else which she had to do the same day. Now she longed for an appointment, an errand, an unexpected phone call, anything but this vast bleak expanse of time which stretched everywhere without interruption, without vision, arid and mocking. Did she think she was a writer? Then let her write.

But how was she to feel like a writer? To be a poet was like having grace. The spirit descended or it did not. Who was to tell you that you were a poet? She thought back to two years before when she had been accepted into the workshop of Alfred Livermore, the celebrated poet of the day. He was tall, in his late forties, with a funny pug nose and square face with jutting chin, and known to his intimates by his old boyhood nickname, "El," short for Jehovah.

She had been awed that she had been accepted after only a year or so of writing secretly, showing her poems to no one, snatching a few hours a week now that they had an *"au pair."* Nora was two, and the children were old enough not to need the attention of two adults, full time. She didn't think of herself as a woman in her thirties. She was terrified by the easy critical aplomb of the graduate students, and the cheeky ease of the undergraduates. Everyone seemed to know what to say about the poems which were read. But at the same time they all waited carefully for Livermore to express an opinion first and then they would concur.

In the narrow windowless room, where Livermore had open conference hours, there would be as many as twelve or fifteen around the plain dark table. At one end he would be draped sideways in his chair, long legs crossed, one arm flung over the back of the chair, one hand holding the other. In his deep aristo-southern drawl he would read their poems aloud. He said "verrah" for very, "Ah" for I. He had a way of saying, "Ah think this is verrah good, it's perfect of its kind," which managed to be like a kiss and a slap at the same time, "of its kind" operating as a wry gloss on the exhilarating "perfect." Then he would go over the poem carefully, line by line, starting with the most pleasant thing he could say and working his way backwards into the truth. Some mornings he was too bored or too manic to do this, and then they would have feverish rambling, "Ah had a dream last night, William Blake and Shelley appeared to me...." or anecdotes about his wife, the eminent literary critic. Actually there was only one anecdote. "Mah wife, Sally Beveridge, the critic, has absolutely no use for poets," he would grin puckishly. "She says 'Maud Miller on a summer's day' is the greatest line of poetry evah written." Or he would tell how his unique child, a girl, Eliza, had put some famous drunken poet in his place when she was only eight years old.

The only women poets he spoke well of were Marianne Moore and Elizabeth Bishop. Of men, well, he had his contemporaries but, one felt, no peers. He admired Philip Larkin and Neruda and Mandelstam. He would ask classes curiously whether they thought that Bob Dylan's lyrics were poetry. Curious, and perhaps wanting to reassure himself that he wasn't going to be threatened by a new voice, because he had come now to speak along with those who were in opposition to the war in Vietnam and was on the way to becoming a political figure as well as a famous poet.

He didn't of course take anyone in the class seriously. But he loved any nugget of information which he could get, an odd word; a stray fact; Diana could see him salting it away. His favorite bits of advice were "load the line" which was accompanied by an outwards pushing gesture of his shapely hands and "murk it up." He doted on a small fragile blond who wore crotch length skirts and huge granny glasses and brightened up with her arrival in class. "To have your own voice" was the greatest accolade one could win from him, and once he said to Diana about a line, "That's a very Diana Field line," and she was stunned to think that there might be such an independent entity as "Diana Field." To her it seemed that the younger poets around her were all obviously able to blossom into whatever they choose, and there were two women, middle-age like herself, who had already won prizes as poets. But she. where was she but in a unique limbo? Four poems in three magazines did not make one a poet. And then Nora's illness had carried her out from that sea of exploration, out onto a broader ocean.

What was it then to "be" something, an identity that one forged for oneself, not a being which was decreed in relation to others, daughter, wife, mother, it was that, which was more mysterious to her than sex had been when she was an adolescent. Sex, after all came into your life willy-nilly, it was a given.

Behind her, only dimly sensed, was the fear that a fourth identity was fatal, to want to do what her father did, not to be as her mother, would be to break the ultimate sex taboo, to claim for herself a right to work. It could only result in pain and destruction to all who loved her, and destruction of a self which she had constructed only by keeping another self out. How could she admit that there was something she wanted more than Tom's love or that of her loving the children?

An offhand remark of Livermore's, repeated to her by a friend, floated into her mind, "Isn't it funny that the great women poets were either divorced or Lesbians." Was a woman poet different than a male poet? Did a woman have to pay a special price before she could write, something which involved a blood sacrifice? Yeats, William Carlos Williams, her own Wallace Stevens, her idol Rilke, they were to be allowed a tranquil life and greatness, but a woman who knew that could only be mediocre? What sort of viciousness lay behind Livermore's quip, he who had been divorced and knew only too well how many male poets were homosexual. It was another way of looking at women through a prism, which framed them in "strangeness" and denied their ability to do unless they were in some measure "denatured." What frightened her in his remark was its congruity with her own fears, Why did the littlest mermaid give up her tongue, her right to utterance for love? Why did she leave her element to walk on two sharp pointed daggers over the dry arid land, for love? Why did love mean renouncing something vital if one were a woman?

Across the way three pigeons preened and strutted along the old gutters of the apartment house. A hand came out from one of the *Chambres de Bonne* and put food into the canary cage which hung outside its peaked window. Its chirping brought back the chirping of the birds as she stood that April morning staring at Nora; who lay eyes closed, a bubble in her half opened mouth. Outside, the huge sugar maple, which in summer shaded the whole back yard, was opening its hard tight buds into small wet parasols.

The day before the whole family had watched on the news the shocked and grief-stricken faces of Blacks, as they heard about Martin Luther King's assassination. The ghetto in Washington, D. C. had erupted into flames with looting up and down 14th Street. Morphine. A bullet. Death, violence, loss. She called her parents to tell them about Nora, and they weren't sure they could leave the city, the airport was shut down.

They brought Nora to the hospital for an autopsy, Diana in the back seat, holding her stiff lightness, shrouded in a blanket across her knees. They drove down Longwood Avenue past the hospital where Nora and the other children had been born. The Indian doctor who received the body, a gentle man who had given Nora much of her chemotherapy, shook their hands solemnly and said, "I hope I'll see you again." The poverty of response. She turned her mind off.

At college, even after she had won the Poetry Prize in her sophomore year, she didn't think of herself as a poet. Poetry had come too naturally, it seemed, for her to believe in it. Or was it simply that she hadn't wanted to face up to the work and competition, the reality of her desires, by taking herself seriously? She remembered a conversation with one of the French teachers, who lived in her dormitory, an old woman who was especially fond of her and nicknamed her *"la ravie."* It was the name for one of the figures in the traditional Provencal crêche, the god struck simple who stands with his arms raised in wonder. When the news came of her winning of the prize, *Mlle. Lanvin* was in the infirmary, where she went often with bouts of asthma.

On a spring night, Diana had walked over to see her. Inside the infirmary the air was close and overheated. Wrinkled, pale, but vigorous, *Madamoiselle* lay in her narrow bed in a tiny private room. She motioned Diana to a chair beside her and stared at her intently. Instead of speaking to her in French, she spoke in English. "So," she said, "it seems *ma petite ravie,* you are a poet. That is a wonderful and a terrible thing." Diana watching *Madamoiselle's* gnarled hands on the white sheets was embarrassed, unsure, and pleased. *Madamoiselle* kissed her on the brow and waved her off with a wheeze. Diana left the infirmary with relief.

Remembering that Diana, she remembered that she was alone, excited by her nascent sense of self, but utterly at a loss at how to proceed. Within a year and a half she was married, and the real work began, the work of moving about on land.

She stared hard at the white empty paper in front of her and thought about writing a letter to her mother. She could tell her mother everything, but what did that mean? There was no one to whom one could tell everything. How much her mother had told her, but how little. It seemed from the time she was eight years old she was her mother's confidante, indeed, she often felt like her mother's mother, for clearly her mother needed someone to care about her, to care the way a woman cares for another woman: noticing her daily struggle to fulfill the demands put upon her, wanting to help her, to keep her from being tired, and it seemed to her that her mother, despite help in the house, was always tired and breathless. Yet even though her mother would say in the same breath, "He's impossible," and "I love him," how much neither she nor any mother ever tells her daughter.

It was her mother's natural instinct to please others, and it was Diana's to please herself. As a child Diana had worshipped that power of goodness in her mother, it seemed to her that there was nothing in the world which her mother couldn't renounce, as though there were nothing she couldn't understand and forgive as corollaries of that mysterious power of renunciation of self. She deferred utterly to the least wish of Diana's father and then to her children's wishes if they could be accommodated. Diana couldn't believe that to confer happiness was her mother's power and wish: to be loved and to love. Diana thought that she was selfish and took after her father. Her mother wanted everything for her which she wanted for herself, but her mother could imagine no greater good than husband and children. To be alone was the most terrible thing which could happen to a woman, thought her mother, though she was perfectly happy in her moments of solitude, reading a book, looking out or a window – but those were the precious moments of calm in a life lived hectically at a pace other than her own.

As a child, Diana thought that her mother's lot was unfair, but her mother seemed and asserted that she was utterly happy. That was the paradox. And her mother never presented the truth as less paradoxical than it was. Diana gave up trying to write a poem and wrote a gay, cheerful letter to her mother.

* * * * * * *

Spring was arriving. There was a great deal of rain, and then one day the huge plane trees, which lined their avenue, put out delicate new wet leaves. In the markets iris were everywhere, iris of a deep blue that burned like fire with feral yellow tongues. Diana bought bunches and bunches every time she went out to do the marketing. The children talked now endlessly about vacation and Saint-Tropez. It was the ideal center for them to visit, they had finally gone into classes with French children and were busy learning French history of the Roman and medieval times. Patrice talked incessantly about the weather and the joys of Saint-Tropez, hopeful this time that the family would come. There was no mention of Michelle. Day after day he appeared to talk about the forthcoming French elections and in the evening they gathered around their TV to watch one candidate after another address their unseen audience, *Mesdames, Messieurs, Chers auditeurs....* orotund, gross, banal. Why, Diana wondered did people like Patrice find it all so fascinating, understanding as well as they did that it was all a game, and a game of lies. What difference did it make which set of liars the electorate decided upon? But then, thought Diana wryly, no one could teach a Frenchman anything about disenchantment, if anything she knew herself to be far less cynical, far more the idealist than Patrice. But then, he too had his romantic side with his admiration for a dry stuffy Protestant minister of finance, who totally lacked the bonhomie necessary for winning elections.

On the eve of Patrice's departure for Saint-Tropez, he whispered to Diana, "You don't think Tom will change his mind this time, do you?" Diana shook her head. Tom's work was going badly, he needed to get away. A week later their plane landed at Marseille, where they were all wildly excited to see palm trees. They took the winding sea road into the city and, nosing their rented car along the back streets, found a quiet restaurant where they could have a late lunch. Around them foreigners like themselves, who had found their way with the aid of guidebooks and tourist arrows, were spreading maps and asking for things in broken French. Diana contemplated the children, Nick with his dimpled radiant smile and Kit with her pansy-velvet cheeks. Wasn't this why they had come to Paris to spend a year in order to buy a sense of family that would be obvious to themselves? And yet even last night it had been too much for her, still; to tuck them in; to see two of them looking up at her, but not to see the third. "You tuck them in," she had said angrily to Tom, wondering why it was always hers, to do, or why he never wanted to share it with her. She heard again the desolate wailing of their cat who meowed in every corner, closet, and secret place, when a kitten was taken from her litter.

At this instant she saw everything through a frame of joy and pride, Tom and Nick studied the map together, deeply sweetly serious, and Kit discretely tugged at her hand and whispered, "The waiters all have a funny accent, are they French?" Like a bird on her nest Diana wanted to sit there forever absorbing them all. She sipped her wine. The sounds of the port mingled with the light coming in through the open door. She had created all of them. In their Ptolemaic world, she was the central planet: their earth, their sun, their moon. Matrix and artificer she fashioned them each second as the sun's heat is omnipresent even at night. But she was also their prisoner; "it" in the circle game; queen and captive.

Tom looked up and grinned at her, his brown eyes loving. "You're beautiful," he said. Yes; he knew, he always knew. Was it because he saw her with the eyes of love – or was she just transparent? Nick interrupted her thoughts. "Mom, we told Patrice we were coming straight to Saint-Tropez when we called him at the airport and he'll be wondering where we are,"

Obediently they concluded the meal. But driving out of the old port they read in their guidebook that there was a famous flower market nearby. Never mind, said Diana to herself, Patrice can wait. They wandered breathlessly up and down stalls filled with roses, mimosa, iris, lilies, carnations, lilacs, and then at one place, unbelievably branches and branches of plum blossoms and cherry blossoms.

"Let's bring some to Patrice for the house," suggested Diana, covetous at the sight of a long gray branch with delicate white-pink nacreous blossoms along its shiny sides.

She was holding them to herself like a bride when their car pulled up the dirt road and on to the gravel path beside the fabled house. There Patrice was talking with an wizened bent woman who must surely be the *fermière* he had described so many times to Kit.

Nick had been right, of course. "What took you so long?" Patrice reproached them. "I was getting dreadfully worried. I thought you might have had an accident." He presented them to *Madame Clement*, who grinned toothlessly and backed away.

They looked around. It was, as was usually the case, completely unlike what Diana had imagined. The house was a fairly new bungalow, on a hillside with other houses in view, on land which sloped down to the sea. Behind them, even higher on the hill, someone was in the process of constructing a house which would probably be similar to the ones around it. Next to them hidden by a clump of cypress was the house of the farmer, *Madame Clement*. In the distance the main road continued its way towards Port Grimaud. Only a few cars and an occasional motor bike were seen on it. The scene seemed both rural and suburban. It was a landscape that didn't bear looking at, jumbled and tacky like a cheap gift shop. Coming up along the coast that landscape persisted. The narrow road was crowded on both sides with gas stations, cheap cafes and restaurants, and cement pensions. "Villa" this, and "Villa" that. To be here in peace one had simply to sink into the scene and peer out of it steadfastly to the sea, or towards some notion of the sea.

Patrice helped Tom get the bags out of the car and proudly led the way into the house. "Here," said Patrice, pointing to the living room, "Here is the window I told you of, where we can see the sea." Then they were in a long low room furnished with a few rickety tables, a day bed pushed along one wall, a wicker arm chair, and four rush chairs around what appeared to be a dining room table. The large window framed the view of the hillside, houses and a bit of blue. A small hanging light swung over the table. The room had the look of summer houses all over the world, shells, whose only reason for being is to shelter one at night and, which for the most part, stand empty with their doors open while their inhabitants soak up sun and air.

To one side of this room was a tiny, narrow kitchen, where they found an old terra cotta vase big enough to hold the branches of the plum tree. There, in glory, they swept in front of the broad expanse of window, making the room come alive.

Meanwhile, the children had found and fought over the beds they were to have and were tugging to show Tom and

Diana their room. It contained two twin beds, a rattan writing desk, a dark ugly chest of drawers, and two small windows high up for greater privacy. It felt dusty. Unaired, and very much the parents' bedroom. "But where will Patrice sleep?" asked Nick. "Oh, I have my own house right over there," said Patrice and pointed to a small stone house of one room which looked much older than the bungalow. "That is where we have a library with our books and bed for guests and I have all my books there so I can study whenever I like."

To Diana's surprise, Nick seemed disappointed, but she was relieved. It was bad enough the children were directly on the other side of their room, it would have been intolerable to have Patrice stretched out on the day bed along the other wall.

When they awoke the next day, the room was black, and the house was totally silent. Outside there was a solitary bird repeating a delicate trill, and that was all. They stretched, dressed, and went out into brilliant sunshine. No sign of the children or Patrice. "He must be showing them the countryside and the farmer," said Diana. She went into the little kitchen and found things which Patrice had bought for breakfast: rolls, butter, coffee, and jam, and she and Tom sat down in front of the living room window at the table and blinked and sipped their coffee. The silence was total.

Then voices and steps and the children burst into the house followed by warning shushes from Patrice. They beamed on discovering Diana and Tom awake. "We saw the farmer and she gave us some eggs and ugh, they had stuff all over them, and she gave us twenty little tiny ones, and she had killed a rabbit and showed us," reported Kit. "It was disgusting," frowned Nick, but whether he meant everything, or just the dead rabbit, Diana wasn't sure. There was about Nick's reactions to things a fierce certainty and a finality that always put Diana at a loss. Never did he reveal hesitancy, or fears, or ask for corroboration or support from her or Tom, and she felt in particular that there was a barrier between him and her which would never allow her to come close.

One had children in the first place to love them, and then, slowly, in the second place, one wanted to be loved back. Kit needed her in a dark, nuzzling blind kitten way. Younger she would suddenly throw herself into Diana's lap, or demand to be held and hugged, and then wordlessly, rush off. When she and Nora had played games it was always Kit who climbed into their big doll cradle and sucked her thumb and was the baby. But Kit was the middle child between the splendid first who had had all of her undivided attention for two and a half years, and Nora, the baby, eighteen months younger than she. It had been Nora with whom Diana would have had the closest relationship. Nora who already at four was like a mother to her, strong, watchful, understanding everything, curious about everything, like Diana and like Tom, the best of both of them. Only Nora could have said, entering her room delicately one day when Diana was with her aunt, "Now I know Mom wants to talk poetry, but I just need her for a minute to help tie my shoe." At four Nora could see everyone, herself included as a person distinct from others. For the other two she was just Mommy, the figure-she-who-was-always. Only Nora had seen her as Diana. But who could she say these things to?

They decided to go into Saint-Tropez and do the shopping and eat lunch and drive around to places Patrice thought would interest them. The spring season was mild and warm. The tourists were French, mostly, with a sprinkling of English. It was still possible to walk around the port and sit in a cafe without being overwhelmed by numbers of people. Saint-Tropez was a place like many others. Once life had been simple, and then, by virtue of its simplicity, it had lost that quality. There were the usual tourist shops, some full of junk, others of chic, with shark-faced proprietors, who opened their jaws the moment one walked in.

There were the homosexuals very at home in their secret world, the door slammed on everyone else, and then the simple sturdy, delighted to be there wait-until-we-tell-them-back-home tourists, posting the cards and sunning themselves; happy to be getting the sun at least, for nothing. Even when the tide of strangers ebbed, the place was strange to itself.

Patrice led them on a grand tour of the little streets, showed them the local museum, the best bakery, the best fish place. After that they went into a big-chain supermarket and bought what seemed to Diana to be obscene quantities of food, then to the open air market to buy the famous custard cake, a local specialty, and returned, exhausted, from their first day. Tom had loaded up on guidebooks and more maps. That night they played Monopoly and plotted the next day's outings. They were to be there a week and then travel as far as Nimes to the west and *Fontaine de la Vaucluse* to the north before circling back to Marseilles and flying back to Paris. "Don't forget you are going to take me to see Colette's house," Diana reminded Patrice. "I haven't forgotten," he said, "but for that we have to get up very early, because, I think, there are people living in the house now."

Each day passed slowly, unburdened by noise. They woke to sun and birds. Patrice got up to cycle to town for the paper and fresh bread. Diana and Tom would get up and sit outside in the shabby faded deck chairs watching Nick and Kit and Patrice play games of ping pong on a tilting table. It made Diana feel very much the mother of a large brood, as though, by residing in the house, she had to assume the role of Patrice's mother and Tom, his father. But at night, the reverse took place. Patrice and she would do the dishes together, and, laughing and talking rapidly, she would glance out to the living room and see Tom reading with a sense of shock. Curled in corners reading madly, the children were one unit, and she and Patrice were another. Tom was a large rock that seemed to have no organic reason for being there. A man who was not working was disquieting. A man in the home, a man marking time, a man who had never reached out to his children.

Often when he was away Diana thought how natural it was for him to be gone. She with the children formed a continuous life flow, an indissoluble unit. In his absence, she always felt on holiday as though she had been excused from chores. She rose and slept at her own time, ate simply, did everything without having to check each action against his wishes or his supposed wishes. A great fatigue lifted from her, a burst of energy took its place in those times of his absence. He was a child, an unnatural child. And she, she needed mothering herself. Looking at the back of his head she felt a twinge of bad conscience that she was enjoying herself so with Patrice, and then she thought, angrily, but if we were alone he wouldn't be talking to me, he'd be sitting in the same way,   reading with his usual intensity, oblivious to my presence.

One night, the tiny house seemed maddeningly small, locking them in like a prison. Outside, the stars lavished themselves on the sky. Patrice, feeling their restlessness, suggested a chic casino for dancing, and they piled into the car and drove to town; only to find that it opened only during the summer. Diana felt frustrated. She wondered what it would be like to dance with Patrice. And at the same time she was relieved. She was the one who became self-conscious in public places and refused to do things she wanted to do which Tom naturally did.

During the day they drove all over to neighboring towns where there were ruins of old chateaux forts. Once they went up into the hills to view a splendid Benedictine monastery. They lunched at all the recommended and starred restaurants in the countryside. The sight of Kit, slumped over her truffle in a pastry case, face smudged from travel, white school blouse a bit grimy, and an expression of discontent, as she moaned that all she wanted were French fries, sent Patrice into spasms of discrete laughter. He looked fondly at her and whispered to Diana, *"Elle n'est guère sortable."*

In *Bormes les Mimosas* they discovered an ancient settlement where small stone houses nestled close to the old chateau. Walking up the ancient cobbles, they could imagine themselves the humble dependents of the great powers who maintained the castle. They walked under the portcullis almost whispering. Nearby a cock crow, guttural and hoarse, was heard.

They sat in the shadow of the old castle. The earth had piled up around the exposed stone passageways. Grass seamed the scarred skull of the tower. Thyme, rosemary, purple and white clover, were underfoot. Butterflies of the most delicate lavender-white fluttered like paper or falling ash. Something grim – as grim as death – was cracked open now to sun and rain and winds that blew like god voices through the fallen stones, and the earth threw over them a living shroud, took them to herself, and transformed them, planted life along the scar tissue of the past.

Diana plaited necklaces of clover for Kit, thin wiry stalks looped around the globes of white and purple. Nick, at the top of the steep, worn steps, peered over the plain which unfolded beneath the castle. Tom studied a diagram in the Michelin and pointed out the points that were visible from this vantage point. Kit meanwhile became very excited. She had found a cat obviously pregnant. Breathlessly, she described it to Diana, "Grey with black stripes and a white nose, and it looked very fierce and wild and hissed at me." There was a pause. "Do you think it will have its babies now?" she wondered – she ran off again to see if such a miracle might have occurred.

The heat of the stone warmed Diana's back. The aroma of the earth rose around her. She fell into the heavy drowse which follows love. When she opened her eyes, Patrice was standing in front of her, smiling down affectionately. She smiled back, embarrassed to have been looked at unawares. "So," he said with satisfaction, "the family is enjoying itself, and you, Diana, you're getting a rest, are you not?" He rubbed his hands in that strange way he had. She nodded.

She was grateful to him. He had worked so much good for them during their time in Paris. She wondered if he wasn't the agent of some mysterious good luck. Who could understand the forces which were at work in a life? Why they had turned back after leaving the apartment where they had found him, rubbing his hands, when they returned. He had gotten them all to Cluny, and now, to Saint-Tropez. Perhaps he was crazy, but it worked out for them. Yesterday, when he had taken the children off to the beach to search for driftwood each one had clung affectionately to a hand, And surely children could tell about a person's essential trustworthiness?

The night before they were to leave, Diana reminded Patrice about the excursion to Colette's house. "Can you do it? We'll have to get up by six o'clock." He had been impressed by how late she and Tom slept every morning, she thought. "Of course," she said.

That morning she woke with a start at six, exactly. She could always wake herself at any time she needed to. But there was a sharp sadness in thinking that this would be the last morning to wake in that place. Why did they want to leave, she wondered? It was so pleasant here. And then she thought that Tom was really bored, and she was too. There was too much time. She started to move, and Tom turned over and threw his arm around her sleepily.

"Where are you going?" he murmured. "Let's make love."

She wiggled off. "I have to get up. Patrice has promised to take me to Colette's house." Tom shrugged, "Why now?"

and turned over again.

Diana dressed quickly in the little bathroom where the ants were busy tracking up and down the blue tiles. She was sure Patrice would be waiting impatiently outside, and she smiled in anticipation as she slipped quietly out the front door. The last veils of predawn were being burnt away by the sun, ascending to a sky of purest blue. Diana shivered in the dewy chill and moved across the wet grass to the little studio where Patrice slept.

She knocked on the door; calling his name, surprised that he, who always lectured her on the joys of early morning rising, was not visible. There was a long silence and then a slow, *"Quoi?"* from Patrice. You said you'd take me to Colette's house today," called Diana laughing. Everything seemed rather ridiculous. There was a movement from inside, and the door opened a crack. Behind Patrice's sleepy face, she caught a glimpse of a very damp booklined room in great disorder. There was a wood stove in one corner and an unmade daybed along the wall with sheets on it of an ancient gray color. Diana felt astonished and dismayed that Patrice had been living there like that, and they had not known it.

Patrice was frowning slightly, his face swollen with sleep, his eyes very naked without his glasses. At the sight of him, so different from the way she had imagined Diana felt put out and embarrassed "Patrice," she laughed. "You told me you were always up at this hour...." "O. K.", he said shortly, "I'm coming, I forgot." Diana hesitated. Perhaps she should tell him to forget it? But it was too late, the morning light possessed her whole body. The birds had begun to sing madly. She was opening, opening. Patrice slammed the door in her face. What kind of dreams did he have in that place? Fantasies of Michelle, worries about his exams, money, Isabelle?

After a pause he reappeared, a dirty pullover over his shirt.

"We will go this way," he announced curtly, still in a bad temper. They walked down the small road which led to the main road, crossed it, and then began to track right through a farmer's field. To the right of them, the farmhouse was shut up tight, shutters fastened, nothing stirred. Nothing but the occasional rasp of a cock's cry. Diana had the curious sensation of being totally exposed and vulnerable as though at any moment someone was going to shout "Stop, you are not allowed to do this!" Was it because she was doing something unobserved? Suddenly it came to her that that was why Patrice lied. He lied for power, like Prometheus, he had to acquire that power by stealth. Sleeping people were people one could rob.

They tread carefully, avoiding the cow pats. The red tiles of the scattered houses gleamed in the sun, the air was a mixture of sea and pines and dew rising from the thick grass. They left the field, crossed another main road, and took a path through a stand of dark pines. On the sandy path a snail, like a doughty warrior, horns alert, moved slowly off on some quest, on his back, the round shining ramparts of his little castle, brown with delicate white marking.

"In my grandfather's time," Patrice said, "there were practically no homes around here, certainly not all these villas. My grandfather was a brilliant man, but his wife was a terrible woman. Her family got control of everything, and they sold the land off, the land that was ours." He shook his head. "He was brilliant but very weak when it came to money and women. Perhaps that's the way it always is? By the way, what did you think about what I told you last night, about Henri de Pelerin?"

Diana laughed to herself. How was she to answer that? Patrice's idol, the only honest man in the cabinet, irreproachable, Protestant, saintly, Henri had recently been revealed to Patrice as a man who had had a mistress for eighteen years. Patrice was crushed. He had been told that by the wife of a government official, he said, *"une femme qui a beaucoup d'indulgence pour moi."* The words were pronounced rather smugly. They had been in the midst of washing up the dishes and laughing madly at stories, and suddenly that phrase hung there, a sour note, for Diana. Was she to be so described with such satisfaction as "a woman who's been awfully good to me?" She pushed the thought out of her head.

"I don't know, Patrice," she answered, "but at least no one can accuse Henri of being unfaithful to his mistress."

Patrice laughed, turning to give Diana a sharp look. Just then her foot slipped on the soft pine needles underfoot, and she went down, sprawling, on her hands and knees, at his feet. Looking up she saw an expression on his face of naked disgust, and she felt a hot flush pass through her. A voice said, you should not be here, he does not want to be here. Then instantly Patrice was reaching down to pull her up saying, "Are you all right, you didn't hurt yourself, did you?" You are older, you have no business being here, said the voice.

Diana waved off his hand. "How much further is it?" He pointed, "Not very far, see, there is the main road." Now out of the pines they felt the heat of the sun, but all around them the countryside lay still sleeping.

They reached the house. It had a low cement wall around it and an arched green wooden gate in front directly off the macadam road. Gingerly, Patrice pushed the gate open. Underfoot was a child's red tricycle and blocks; on a line some diapers and undershirts hung motionless. Ahead of them the house was a bright flamingo pink. It had three windows on the second floor and two in the front, and a brown door entrance narrow and unwelcoming. Diana stared at the windows with apprehension. Quickly she followed Patrice around to the right side of the house, past a small garden to the back.

"You'll see," whispered Patrice, "the patio is lovely, and you can just see the sea through the pines."

Diana glanced tensely at the shuttered windows of the second floor. At the same time she tried to conjure up the ghost of Colette; lunching on the simple back terrace. This was the house, which she described living in after an unhappy love affair. Here she lunched day after day with a new lover, whom in the end she sent away knowing that her peace of mind, her need to work, could never be stretched to include him. Colette, she prayed, patron saint of women writers, not of the lunar female world of Virginia Woolf, but of the noonday world of senses and sensibilities, spelling out on the flesh the braille of the spirit.

She closed her eyes and imagined for an instant being the woman who sent the man away, accepting human loneliness as a condition for that solitude, that communion with herself out of which her writing could come. And opened her eyes and shivered in the shadow of the house. There was an air of shabby lower middle class dishevelment about it, which depressed her. Through the ragged pines she caught a thumbnail of blue sea. Where was the cypress Patrice had spoken of? She tugged at Patrice's sleeve. "Let's go," she whispered. They stole back past the laundry and tricycle, and shut the gate behind them. When they got back to the house it was only seven-thirty. "But where are you going?" asked Patrice in surprise at seeing Diana reenter the house.

"Back to bed," she answered with a malicious satisfaction.

In the bedroom she slipped off all her clothes and, naked, crawled in beside Tom. She shivered in the chill of the room after the hot sun outside. The heat of Tom's hands on her body scalded her.

They woke from a drugged sleep at ten, packed, swept the house, stripped the beds, and decided to have lunch with

Patrice in town, before setting off to Aix and the *Fontaine de la Vaucluse*. Leaving, Diana took a last look through the big picture window in the dining room. On the table the plum blossom's long slender branches reached out to gather in the space. Like a snapshot, the window frame held the water, the pines, farmhouses, and red-tiled villas. It was silent and dusty. Something that happened a long time ago. Outside the children fought for the position of choice in the car.

The town, when they got there, was sunny and tranquil, just enough tourists to keep the shopkeepers happy. On the way to the restaurant Patrice was leading them to, at the far end of the port, they peered into every shop window as though they were seeing the town for the first time.

The restaurant overlooked a beach. They took a table with an unobstructed view and ordered. The children rushed off to explore the beach and climb an old rowboat. Tom checked maps and calculated miles. Diana let the conversations around them swim in and out of her consciousness, while the sun caressed her skin. Two currents reached her. The first was of the incessant remonstrance given to French children, remonstrations as mindless as the directions people gave dogs. "Sit up," "Don't talk with your mouth full," "Don't talk," "Eat," "Be quiet," repeated over and over in tones which dripped with righteous satisfaction. The second current was that of the English tourists. There were the skinny twiggy girls with huge doe eyes accompanied by stud males from a twilight zone.

"Where are you going this summer?" asked a girl, whose "poor girl" sweater outlined her ribs and nipples, of a young man, shirt open to the navel, who wore dark pilot glasses with lenses that reflected the viewer back to herself.

"Dunno, maybe Mykonos. Did you hear the story Don brought back? It seems there were these birds, six of them, and they had rented a place to stay, they thought...." His voice dropped.

Poor birds, thought Diana. She opened her eyes to find the waiter approaching their table and went in search of the children. Kit, as usual, had found a dog with whom she had fallen in love, it was a miniature poodle energetically getting its white curls dirty in the sand. "Look how it loves me, Mom," Kit whispered in ecstasy, as it followed her up the steps to the restaurant terrace. She said that about every dog.

Nick sat down and finished his chicken and French fries in five minutes and asked for a sandwich jambon. Kit picked at her ham, pickles, and French fries, and finally pushed the ham away. "I'm not very hungry," she said, looking around for the dog. Patrice looked at her fondly. The sun was making Diana sleepy. "Why don't you finish her ham," Diana said, passing the plate to Patrice.

"Ah no," he said, "you take it."

"Oh, I couldn't," said Diana. "You love ham so much." It was an old joke between them.

"Yes, but I love you more," said Patrice very quietly.

A shock of exhilaration passed through her. She looked quickly at him, he was looking at his plate rather sadly. Of course, she thought. I knew, of course, he loves me, and I love him. That's what it had been about from the first time cousin Sylvia had said, "Well, that young man doesn't take his eyes off you for a second," to the incident at the kitchen window at the Drouots. The pleasure was electric, as though she were getting spanked to life: love, the universal midwife. She wanted that moment to be repeated over and over and over.... She locked it away to hug it to herself in private. With a melancholy air, Patrice was now eating the ham. On the other side of Diana at the table, Tom had heard nothing. He finished his coffee and yawned.

"I think we'd better be going now," he said. "We want to get to Aix and then Vaucluse by tonight."

The bill was paid. Patrice walked them to the car. "Are you sure you won't come with us," asked Tom again. They had offered over the last few days to take him along, of course. But he seemed embarrassed at having lived off of them so well. He shook his head. Diana was relieved. He smiled down lovingly at all of them. "Drive carefully," he said and waved them off.

¤

Chapter IX

Back in Paris after the sun of the south, the spring seemed doubly cold. Despite the chill, the sky at moments filled with Napoleonic grandeur, bombast of clouds and bits of blue: the soft romantic blue of Hussars' eyes. Now when the children returned home it was light. It was hard to remember the swift irrevocable fall of the winter dusk.

Tom had left for the States soon after their return, glad to be getting away. His stomach continued to hurt, but a checkup with the doctor at the American Hospital had produced nothing beyond the comforting observation that most visiting American academics suffered one way or another from their year of cultural deprivation, and the only remedy he knew was to prescribe frequent trips home. In fact, he reported to Tom, he had known one scientist who had spent a week out of every month back in his lab.

Diana and Tom had laughed about that, while Tom packed a small bag cheerily. From home, news had reached them about commotion at the university, building takeovers, something called "Black Studies." The war in Vietnam was beginning to ooze like a lanced boil.

"I'll call you and tell you what's happening," Tom promised. He hugged her hard at the door, and kissing him, in his arms, she felt the mass of his body come for her, collect her, absorb her. Or was that her wish? To be absorbed into him?

Now more than ever she needed him to go, to leave her

alone so she could explore without interruption the new sensations of energy which she felt. Not to love Patrice, not to share their common love in a tender exchange (she imagined him on her, in her, calling her name – and she his) was wrong. It would be a perversion of love's natural instinct. What she was overwhelmed by had nothing to do with Tom. Surely people could love, did love more than one person at a time? She wanted Patrice, desired him. Everything was fated so that she would give to Patrice that special love she had for him. This was what the world was for. Deprived of the medium of love the world was dreary numb and cold.

And it would be a pure love, she promised herself. There had to be a way things like this could happen in one's life and enrich one, not leave one feeling bitter and disillusioned. She didn't want to leave Tom and the children or even, to change her life. What she wanted she imagined was what men want when they fall in love with an innocent young girl. Young men were supple and pliant, full of panache and freshness, because as yet they carried no load, they were innocent of experience. For a bit she wished to jettison her cargo of death and family and responsibility. She desired to give herself, she who had always been given to by Tom. She had never trusted herself to give for fear it would be refused. She would do this thing, and years later she would have and cherish the memory of it.

In the silence of the apartment after Tom's departure, she was imprisoned in a block of crystal, imbedded in an airless timelessness. Her body was being consumed, like that of an addict, wasted, by the secret joy she carried within. She had lost the need to eat and sleep, although she slept to complement the pleasure of waking, but her waking was dreaming, and Rilke's words, "the unlived life of which one can die" alternated in her mind with his words, echoing "but I love you more, you more, you."

The hundred year's sleep of marriage and motherhood had

lifted, and she existed once more, restored to herself, put down at the brink, the edge, the moment when the rose opens, a voice prophecies from the cave, ship's sails belly in the wind. And so she waited for what she knew would happen because the world was once more possible.

A week ago, Nick had pulled her down to kiss him when she tucked him in. "Do you love me, Mommy?" he asked.

"Do you love me?" What storms could be shaking his sturdy little soul she wondered. It was not like him, the first born, the word made flesh, to question that given. But he continued and asked her frequently in the daytime, at all sorts of odd moments, in a brisk and enquiring voice. "Of course," she would answer. "Of course I do."

It troubled her. Did he sense in the depths of his clear soul that she was betraying him, did he assign blame to himself for something being amiss? Her imagination dwelt on Patrice, seeing him, Nick's age, watching his mother's actions with all the intensity of a small boy helpless, hungry, jealous, possessive. The mother, eternal betrayer frustrating son and daughter alike.

Diana was staring at the storm clouds gathering overhead when the phone rang shrilly. A woman's voice, high, polite, French, "Was this *Mme. Field?* This was *Mme. Givret*. She hoped she was in no way disturbing her, but she wondered if she had perhaps seen recently the young Patrice Montcheval....?"

Diana was taken aback. "Yes," she answered slowly wondering what the question was leading to.

"Was he alright, that is, in good health?" the voice continued, "because his grandmother was a bit worried, he had not appeared for an appointment with her that morning...." the voice faded off tactfully.

"But I saw him last night, *Madame* and he was in good health," affirmed Diana, feeling herself grow hot at being the one to be questioned.

"Ah well, then," the voice went on, "You see, we had not heard from him since Saint-Tropez, a little card saying that he wasn't going to be able to come to a little reception we were giving, and I said I perfectly well understand, but if you change your mind we'd love to see you."

"Well," said Diana, torn between her loyalty to Patrice and a desire to ask questions: what is the real situation between your daughter and Patrice? Why are you calling me, when you know perfectly well he was at the Ball on Saturday night?

"Oh, I'm glad to hear everything is fine," the voice rushed on. "I hope you will forgive me *Madame* if I have disturbed you."

When she hung up, her hands trembling, the apartment had grown as dark as night, a loose shutter banged in a sudden gust of wind, and thick large drops of rain began to fall slantwise across the French windows. You were in your darkness hidden, but outside others were looking in, finding you, although you couldn't see them. That's why as a child she had hated to play hide and seek, the moment of being discovered, being about to be discovered and having to reach safety, was too fearful, too deadly with tension. "Ollie ollie oxen, all in free." There were some who could play those games, and some who couldn't.

Thunder pealed overhead, thick and furry. She went to the kitchen and started to warm some café-au-lait. Who talked to whom? What did they say? *"La femme americaine" "Elle a beaucoup d'indulgence pour moi."* "He is always there." "What does she want with him?" "The concierge says they are always together." "What does she want with him?" "What kind of' a person is she?"

Another crack of thunder, and then the sound of the canaries in the apartment below trilling unconcernedly. She cursed herself for not having spoken; in two minutes she could have gotten the whole story from Michelle's mother. What had Patrice done to alarm them all? Could he have threatened suicide? Why were there endless mysteries about him?

Her thoughts went back to Saturday night. He had just returned from Saint-Tropez, and Diana had been standing there, in the kitchen, when she had heard a rap on the glass of the kitchen door. There he stood grinning at her as she let him in. She was wearing her favorite black nylon shirt and maroon pants, and she knew she looked very, very well, and that he was looking at her admiringly. Nick and Kit rushed to greet him and recount all of the adventures they had had since they left him. It seemed perfectly natural for Diana to offer him dinner, and perfectly natural for him to accept after first politely refusing.

They sat and smiled at each other across the wide oak table. They exchanged notes and gossip and stories. Diana told him that Tom was off in the States for a few weeks. Everything felt right to her about her feelings for him; it seemed as though all things had been said, that all barriers were down, there was no need to force or push things to what would be their inevitable conclusion. Her hair, just washed, fell to her shoulders, soft silky a light brown shot through with red. She could pass easily as a woman ten years younger.

She was surprised, because it was already almost nine thirty when Patrice said with a slight sigh, "I must go now." And then, "Why don't you come with me? I have to go to a very stuffy boring reception, tuxedo and all, that Michelle's aunt is giving for all the debutantes. You would find it amusing, Diana, why not?"

She laughed half tempted. "But you know I don't even own a long dress."

"Ah come just as you are, nothing could suit you better." She laughed again. Everything was perfect, she wanted his eyes on her like that forever. "You'll be all dressed up and *très snob*," she said. "Well come and show me how you look before you go."

"Ah, but it will be so dull," he protested, "perhaps I won't go."

"Oh," she protested in her turn, "but Michelle will be counting on you." She got up from the table and started to clear, and Patrice leaped to help her. They were together again, and it was so natural, it was all she wanted really.

It grew later and later and she thought he had given up the idea of going, when, with a final sigh, he said, "I must go now. I'd much rather stay and talk with you." She waved him off, thinking that her arms looked very beautiful, her delicate shoulders caressed by the French nylon. She locked the kitchen door behind him.

The following night he appeared looking rather pale and wan.

"How was it?" she asked.

"Oh it was marvelous, there was a rock and roll band, and Edy Mitchell sang, there were mobs of people."

"How long did it go on?"

There was a pause.

"Well, I left before it was over."

"But didn't you all go out to dance somewhere else, doesn't

everybody do that?" She tried to remember affairs of debutantes she had known. He made no answer.

"Tell me," Diana went on, trying to remember other details, "did all the girls wear gloves? Long white gloves?" He looked confused. "No," he answered slowly. Then, "There was a garden, but it was cold, but still it was one way of being alone."

He had said all that sitting awkwardly with his trench coat on. She was sitting opposite him in the armchair, acquired at long last for comfortable reading. She wondered at him, his haggard look. He was restless as if there were things he wanted to say but couldn't. The night before he had looked so handsome in his very French fashion, the defined arched eyebrows, the large blue eyes, the long lashes, triangular shaped face, well defined chin and nose. And now she was conscious of his body in its shabby chinos, his nervous hands, his drawn and youthful face.

He told her that he had seen his grandmother the morning before. She had been completely worn out from nursing her brother through the last stages of cancer of the liver. "This summer she will go back for a bit to Toulouse to rest and recuperate. She is eighty-two herself."

Diana had been afraid to ask him how things were going with Isabelle. Perhaps that was what was causing him to act so strangely. He rose, still awkward, and left. She had felt cheated.

Standing there in the dark, Diana went over every phrase of that conversation. It had sounded perfectly genuine at the time, but now she questioned whether he had gone, what his hesitations had meant. A few weeks after they had been to Cluny he had admitted that he had never made the first call to Henri which he had pretended to in the bedroom; he had tricked her into assenting first before he called. And then there was the mad lie about Michelle going to Japan. His lying was strange and pointless, and to her, unnecessary. Now that she had missed a chance to really find out what was going on she was angry with herself and determined this time to question him and elicit the truth.

He turned up two days later, bringing a new issue stamp for Kit that showed a graceful dolphin rising above a wave. After dinner in the little kitchen, a bit nervously Diana began.

"Did you know that I had a call from *Mme. Givret* yesterday morning?"

"Ah?"

"She wanted to know, of all things; how your health was," Diana tried to inject a note of lightness into her voice. "It seems you missed an appointment with your grandmother, and your grandmother was anxious.... I told her you were in good health, I thought." Here Diana paused, she couldn't think of any really subtle way of putting things. "But you must have seen *Mme. Givret* on Saturday night at the ball? Or didn't you go to the ball?" It sounded all wrong. It sounded like an accusation of guilt. She felt herself trapped in a dense heavy fluid. She was no swimmer.

Patrice looked stonily ahead, "Of course I went, but she wasn't in the receiving line, and the place was mobbed, so I never saw her. Poor old Grandmother, I think she just needs to worry about someone so she's picked me out."

"But Patrice," said Diana, determined not to be put off, "didn't you see Michelle at the dance?"

"Of course," he answered shortly.

Diana lost her courage completely. The mother of the girl he danced with twenty-four hours earlier doesn't call a stranger to find out how he is, as if he was never there that night at all. She felt immensely helpless.

Patrice looked at her sharply now, "Look, I was there. What's the matter, don't you writers love mystery? Don't keep going on about it, Diana."

And what was the use of going on about it, Diana thought. There's no way of knowing what is going on. He's lying, and he's in some dreadful situation if he has to lie. It was all unreal anyway. What she cared about was her feeling for him. Night after night, as Tom made love to her, she had already possessed Patrice, held him in her arms, felt him penetrate her, heard him call her name, murmured his. He will never make a move towards you said her voice. He thinks of you and Tom as a perfect *menage*, imagines Michelle and himself like you two. You are a middle-aged idol cum mother. You'll never get past all that, said her voice.

She woke, wearied and unrefreshed the next morning. She had been dreaming a complicated dream about Nora, one which she dreamed often, of a threat to Nora which was unlifted, but Nora was at any rate still alive. When she woke she saw Dr. Pinsky's thin intelligent face before her as though she were still dreaming. He was smiling as he gave them the diagnosis of a rapidly growing brain tumor. He leaned over the desk and, seriously, but enthusiastically, outlined treatment, if she was to stay at his hospital. Another doctor whom they had never seen would put a catheter in Nora's neck and give her immense doses of chemicals directly to the brain. It would be done in two parts, after administering the first dose the first doctor would leave on a trip to Vietnam for several months.

It was a long shot but they might "knock the tumor out." In the dirty, shabby, crowded hospital, where Nora had been rushed for a week of tests, she had been slapped by a nurse for refusing to turn over quickly enough to have her temperature taken.

"We have to work quickly," said Dr. Pinsky, "Why don't you think about it for a few hours? Then I'll put you in touch with Dr. Hauptman, who is, as I've said, getting ready to leave for Vietnam in a few weeks." Dr. Pinsky shook their hands cordially, was he taught to always smile as he told the bad news, Diana wondered, or was it some sort of medical shield that permitted only discussion of procedures of which he was so sure they had the only possible solution? They walked down green narrow corridors with small rooms, where machines whirred and clicked, and immobile people with white bandages wrapped around their heads lay like dummies.

Propped up on the pillows Diana gazed at the dome of the *École Militaire* glowing in the light. This morning it was heavy and solid and yet, at the same time, like a little toy, not to be taken seriously. Nothing can replace death but love, love the creation of that which was not there before. Love is the birth-giving, which I shall never feel again, she thought. Never feel that hammering at the base of the spine, those shuddering pangs as though the whole earth was being wrenched in two, and I the earth, earth possessed of a spirit, which must be delivered, even at the price of my death, and then at the end to receive my life back, and a new one to hold, wet, wrinkled, torn, ancient shard of the cosmos, its bones the very bones of the earth and the marrow of the stars, its elements those same as those from which the first life was composed. Small cosmic life, whose old neutered face presages its end, its cry the shrill piercing cry of despair at what has been left behind and what it must come to.

What do men substitute for that knowledge in bone and blood that women possess from giving birth? It was right, Diana knew, that Tom, not she, had slept at Nora's side when she died, for Diana was the bearer of life, and, like African kings, who are not allowed to touch the soil lest the power that flows in them destroy or be lost for their people, it would be against nature for her to preside at death, when her business was with life.

She watched a cloud scud through the sky and understood at that moment that she had tried to acquire Tom's power at one remove. Now she would have to look for power in herself. Perhaps she needed Patrice to lose the last of her virginity and dependency. She was still dependent on Tom for a sense of herself as a woman, a desirable object. For this she paid the price paid by the beloved, the price paid by those who cannot bear the precariousness of being the lover. To be the lover meant to risk self and pride and humiliation. It meant believing in one's luck, daring, and confidence. She had been handed good things, but she had not earned them. Her poetry was not yet a reality to her. What did a few poems published mean to her, already half-way in her life, come so far without a sense of herself existing alone, facing the world alone as a man must and does? At the most she could dream herself a person who would in time perform. In reality she was a figure in a tapestry. Every thread, which designated her, was wefted and warped in relation to Tom, the children, her parents. A life filled with being; empty of doing. She remembered with a shudder of distaste the older faculty wife who attended Livermore's class, who had been writing for years. Her poetry was weak and sentimental. She was a ridiculous figure, tolerated and listened to because her husband was famous. Perhaps that was all she had to look forward to.

She shut her eyes blotting out the dome and the sky, but from under the budding leaves of the plane trees she could hear the traffic, hear voices. It lulled her and she desired nothing but sleep, endless sleep, but looking at the bedside clock she saw it would soon be time to lunch with cousin Sylvia, back from one of her numerous trips to the States. It was a relief to have something to do, something for which she had to rouse herself and leave bed. There was so much time, it absorbed her like a snowstorm in which she would eventually lose consciousness and sleep to death.

In the little washroom off their bedroom, she stared at herself in the glass. When she wasn't smiling, her face fell into a tragic mask that revolted her; surely she didn't look so old, so grotesque, mouth a-droop with disapproval and despair? The comb passed quickly through her hair, came out thick with hairs, and again a paralyzing fear gripped her that she would soon be bald, totally bald, and have to wear a wig. She smiled, smiled, smiled to banish forever the other face. You must always keep a smile on your face she whispered to herself warningly. She would have to be forever on guard to prevent anyone from seeing that visage.

In a smokey, crowded, elegant restaurant on the Right Bank she and Sylvia embraced and were shown to a small table against the wall. Sylvia sat, ramrodded straight in her chair, and launched into a tirade against her old friend Jane, Diana's aunt. Much of it Diana didn't understand at all. "She's filled the girls' heads so full of that nonsensical radical women business I can't even talk to them without their eyes filling with tears. I have no patience with that sort of thing or the mad way students are carrying on now. Taking over buildings, doing away with ROTC, what nonsense. They'll be burning books next, and the liberals are so afraid of them they'll go along with it just to be young and chic."

"Jane has, I'm sorry to say, always fallen for some wacky line or other. In the old days it was Communism, all because of that fat repulsive woman whom she idolized, that awful Sadie Berkowitz. Jane always thought that crowd was god, until they dropped her, and then it was every new theory on how to raise a baby, those children of hers were little spoiled monsters, and the years of analysis and that did nothing. Oh nothing except debts, debts, debts."

She paused for breath and sipped a bit of white wine. Then fastidiously and ravenously raised a piece of her *co-*

quille St. Jacques to her mouth where the two front teeth, exactly like those of a cobra, sprang forth to fasten and enfold the morsel.

Diana looked away. She thought sadly of her adored Aunt Jane. People were beautiful, talented with the capacity for giving to others, and they died, like Arthur, Sylvia's brother, or like Jane, they lost their way and wandered forever trying to find what it seemed they were promised.

"She was so beautiful, you can't imagine how beautiful Jane was," her mother would say with a sigh, "and everyone loved her and babied her, she was grandpa's favorite. Men couldn't resist her. And everything came easily to her; she never had to work."

Diana remembered how, when she was a little girl, Jane had been fun and excitement and gaiety, not sober and what Diana called "goody, goody," like her mother, always drawing the moral lesson in things, always making you understand how you should be striving to be better. And she had adored her Uncle Ben, who was as handsome and blond as her aunt was beautiful and dark. She could remember visiting them in their apartment in the Village after her cousin George had been born. They lived in a little place on Christopher Street that you entered through the basement. Diana thought it secret and exciting and was surprised by hearing her mother say, "They live in a basement," with a look of sorrow and gentle distaste. "Imagine anyone can look into their windows and see what's going on." Cousin George had been a red-faced screaming baby yelling on the diaper table as Ida, the nursemaid, huge, fat, with a thick Jewish accent diapered and powdered him. Poor George, the wanted baby whom no one really wanted, least of all Aunt Jane, who needed a mother and not a son.

The waiters moved up and down the narrow aisles with the tight graceful steps of bullfighters. Diana noticed they were all remarkably handsome and young.

Sylvia was continuing her vehemence undiminished. "I'm surprised George has turned out as well as he has. She was no help, and of course they are sick at the things Rachel is doing, demonstrations and bombings. She could have been badly hurt or killed by those policemen in Chicago.... Now they see the consequences of some of the things they have preached. I just hope Brenda and Lyn stay away from them."

There was an awkward silence. Diana stared fascinated by Sylvia's totally white hair, which made her dark eyes and dark eyebrows more fearfully intense. Only Sylvia would take you out to lunch, she thought, and spend the time attacking your favorite aunt and uncle. She looked down at Sylvia's hands with their strangely stumpy fingers, the skin yellowing like parchment. She hadn't seen Sylvia since late December when she had come unexpectedly back to town for the last concert that her old friend Morris Ryerson would ever give. Dying of cancer, he played well that evening, a man whose pudgy dumpy Jewish face, the face of a harried counterman in a deli, had been refined to repose: an adumbration of the end. The grand piano knelt before him, a great sable butterfly, wings at mid span. He bent over the piano as a man bends over the adored body of a woman. He played with the tenderness and rapture of a last embrace and yet there was no sadness in it only irrepressible joy.

"It's Morrie's last," Sylvia had said, "I have two extra tickets. He probably doesn't have more than two months." Her voice was in a quiet rage. Tom was busy at the lab, and Diana brought Patrice. It was the century of cancer as the nineteenth century that of tuberculosis. To look day by day into the vortex of death like staring at the sun until you go blind. Cancer had been Diana's anxiety since she was fifteen. There was a blue mole on her arm. "A tinderbox," the doctor said who examined her. It was removed four years later. Now the fear had transformed itself from strange to familiar, cancer was the death of Nora. If she had to die that way, it would be a death made hallowed and cherished, because it was Nora's, she would live it out and be with Nora, their separation denied.

"You're looking very well, my dear," said Sylvia suddenly shifting gear. "You've lost a lot of weight. You were putting on a bit too much around Christmas time, but you're looking very good now."

Sylvia liked everyone to be thin. When her younger daughter was fifteen, she put her on a starvation diet because her breasts were too big, and it revolted Sylvia to see them. Until that time, Lyn had been the petted one, and the older daughter shunted aside and uncared for. But Brenda, the older one, had flourished and grown into a spectacular beauty, as luscious as a Gaughin, with Sylvia's creamy skin and masses of dark jet hair, voluptuous mouth, thick shiny black brows, and dark Chinese eyes.

None of the children, now in their late twenties, showed any desire to marry. The three of them, Arthur, Brenda, and Lyn, within four years of each other, were close for other reasons as well, they were like the survivors of some huge catastrophic event, their childhood.

Diana nodded at the compliment. Sylvia studied her very intently for a minute. It seemed to Diana that she might even guess the reason why she was looking so well, might speak of Patrice.

"You're looking very good, in fact. What will you have for dessert? I'm just going to have a little yogurt, but you go ahead and order anything you wish. This is my treat."

Diana ordered the *tarte aux mirabelles*. She loved their yellow-green lucent shapes shining in syrup, nestled together like small eggs, their tart and sweet explosion on the palate. The handsome waiter looked approvingly at

Sylvia as he brought their dessert and coffee. There was no doubt, Sylvia was a woman of the world, such a woman as Diana would never be. She felt always like a child in a world of grownups. Nor could she define what it meant to be grownup, and, if she couldn't define it, how would she know if she ever wanted it?

Sylvia signaled the waiter for the bill, extracted her reading glasses from her bag, and studied it carefully. Halfway through she looked up with a radiant smile. "Diana, my dear, I just remembered that you owe me money for the two concert tickets I got for you and that young Frenchman, what was his name? You remember in December when we went to hear Morrie play? You could pay me now, he'll pay you back won't he? So you could just give me the money for both now." She was flushed with pleasure.

Diana laughed to herself. She certainly wasn't going to get the money back from Patrice after all these months, and they had both thought the tickets a gift at the time. She opened her bag and took out a handful of francs and handed them to Sylvia, who was two francs short of making the correct change, and Diana suddenly felt that perhaps being a grownup was not saying, "Oh, never mind" as she ordinarily would have. Sylvia and Ed never said "Oh, never mind." She watched as Sylvia peered short sightedly into her change purse, pulling out half-franc pieces and holding them off to check. Finally Diana said, "Why don't you hand the purse to me?"

Thoughtfully, with exquisite slowness, she pulled out five twenty-franc pieces and then began to pick over the five and ten centime pieces left. Sylvia's voice rang out. It was torture more than she could stand. "Never mind the change," she said commandingly. For an instant Diana thought she was paying Sylvia, and then she burst out laughing remembering that it was, after all, her change.

But remembering about being grownup (resistance to another's will?) Diana said firmly, "You owe me one franc." The waiter brought Sylvia her change, and she handed over a one franc piece with a straight face, and then said, laughing almost to herself, "Did you hear how I told you to forget the change, and it was your change?"

On the way out they stood for a moment at the restaurant door, Sylvia's shoulders were thrown back, an air of satisfaction on her face as she buttoned her suede jacket. It was a proprietary look that she gave Paris, her Paris. The traffic made its characteristic wave noise, a rise and fall that pulsed with the lights, the smell of spring mixed with sunshine and the musky scent of French perfumes, the bitter coffee aroma, the burned-grass scent of the Gauloises, rose around them, caressed them, lapped them in memories of past springs. A cloud passed over the sun and threw them into the shadows, then reconsidered and withdrew, granting them the sun once more.

"Let's do a bit of shopping," said Sylvia. "I have an invitation for the big spring sale at *Maggie Rouff.* We might find something there for you." They sauntered down the broad avenue until they came to the bland elegance of the salon, its summer awning gaily proclaiming emblazoned initials *MR* in gold on white. It was a temple, a temple where Diana would never have dared to set foot without the supporting presence of one who worshipped the god within.

The door swung open, and Sylvia was greeted with warm approval by the head *vendeuse*. Swanlike she inclined her head and neck, *"Mme. Field,"* she cooed. The *vendeuse's* lips and eyebrows were penciled in, making her flat face even more like a fashion drawing in a magazine. The average French woman, Diana had noticed, had a most ungenerous unsensual mouth. She thought of the French face like the French garden: lines drawn, paths raked, no grass; everything to be as formal and man-made as possible. Ideally perhaps, the French wanted a tabula rasa for a face, leaving each woman to create what she thought uniquely appropriate to herself.

Sylvia smiled with just the right degree of warmth. She knows her smiles down to the last centime, observed Diana enviously, following her down the aisle, thickly carpeted and crowded with well-dressed women. The women moved from rack to rack, in and out of the dressing rooms, considering themselves in the glass like sleepwalkers. For the most part they all had excellent figures, and they all wore the same face, the disconcerting mask of the middle-aged, middle-class woman. Their tanned skin was starting to flake around the eyes and forehead, starting to droop along the chin, fall in folds around the neck. Their eyes smoldered, acquisitive and chaotic. Hands reached out to feel, stroke, touch, stroke the fabrics. But the clothes were as boring as the women. Predictable good taste, classic lines, darts, tucks, hems, the fabrics linen, cottons, a few silks, and everything cut like a suit of armor, a package, a container. Up and down the racks they went, looking, looking.

Diana dared to try on a dress. It was made of purple linen, and purple was Tom's favorite color. But the dress would have nothing to do with her or her body. It stood away from her, and she saw revealed the drop of her upper arms, the full heaviness of her breasts, her stocky legs where the flesh met below the triangle at her thighs. The yellow of the florescent lights in the dressing room sallowed her flesh. The airless cubicle mocked her, held her like a mummy case, and she felt the fear and loathing of the body, the enemy, the ultimate betrayer. She remembered the smell of her cunt as she bent over it in various yoga positions, the Turtle, or confronted it in the Shoulder Stand. She thought of her fleshy labia, a color for which there was no name between pink and brown and purple, and encircled by hairs, grown back after three birth preps, sparse and bristly. That he could kiss her and lick her and love her there, filled her with admiration, and envy, for she could not love herself. She left the booth.

Sylvia was in front of a mirror in a sleeveless red dress with a slight mandarin collar. She stared at herself the way she would another woman. She looked stunning, like a Chinese carving. The *vendeuse* appreciated her as a work of art. "That dress is made for *Madame*," she murmured. "*Madame* is admirable in that red." Diana looked with envy. What would it be like to be in that body, that head?. And she saw Sylvia suddenly opening her mouth, bending over a man, englobing his penis, her yellow body curved, quivering. A hungry woman.

Three women peered into the mirrors, where a fourth woman moved, turned, stopped, turned, tilted a head with a crest of white hair, ignoring them. Surely seeing oneself was the beginning of evil, the fall from the grace of oneness. Would the image in the mirror speak?

"If *Madame* is undecided," murmured the vendeuse, "I can put this aside for *Madame, Madame* can telephone me later."

Sylvia made a noncommittal sound and disappeared into the fitting room. Diana followed her in and watched her inspect the dress after she had taken it off. She went over it seam by seam. In two places it was slightly ripped, but nothing that couldn't be easily fixed. They left the fitting room.

"Mettez ça a coté pour quelques heures, je vous telephonerai," she murmured to the vendeuse whose weary middle-aged face creased into smiles. *"Bon, Madame,"* she bowed.

They left and walked on to another shop, a tiny boutique very elegantly furnished in gold, black and white. There two salesgirls, young and sexy, with high pointed breasts, and rounded buttocks set on long skinny legs, were exchanging gossip about their boyfriends and were totally uninterested in them. It was a shop devoted to hair accessories and stockings. "The best place to come," advised Sylvia. "Their stockings are famous, they never run." After great deliberation, she bought two pairs of slightly different shades of gray. "So much better than the awful American stuff," she sniffed contemptuously.

The afternoon was wearing on. They strolled back to Sylvia's place, past the beautiful shop windows, and arrived at the building off the little *Place.* It seemed an instant since the moment they had arrived in France, but eight months had gone by. "I'm very proud of myself," Sylvia was saying, "I've put locks on all the windows and doors now. We were broken into again. They didn't take my mink or the amethyst, anything, they only wanted money or checks. But they made such a mess. It would be easier if I left a note saying, come in, look around, take what you want but don't make a mess."

They climbed the stairs to the apartments. Everything seemed dark and unfamiliar, and, when they opened the big doors, it was like entering a grotto, or a cave, one needed to switch on the lights immediately. Diana wished she were back with her windows and sky. But following Sylvia into the petit salon she recovered some of her former feeling for the place. "Look," said Sylvia commandingly. And she presented her with her latest acquisition, a Venus Comb, perfect with its long delicate spines and its nacreous turban. There was also a new fish fossil, its body in the stone piece of archaic calligraphy. The huge block of amethyst lay in its pride of place on one of the shelves. Earth hoards laid by like the treasures amassed by Anglo-Saxon kings. *Edmund Atheling and his brother Eac* – giver of rings, leader of earls. The old Anglo-Saxon lines rang in her head. Beowulf, the long dirge for things passed away, days spent living, acquiring, desiring, at the end a handful of shells and some rags. She looked down at Sylvia's stubby fingers holding the Venus Comb and a need to sleep overcame her so strong that she felt as if she were drugged. She kissed Sylvia goodbye and fled out into the light, fled back to her thoughts of Patrice, like someone called away from table in the midst of a feast. In a dream, she took the bus, got off, walked two blocks, entered the apartment, crawled into bed. There, shutting her eyes against the warm spring sunlight that flooded the bedroom, she called him to her, made herself come, and fell instantly into a dead sleep.

She awoke to hear the doorbell ringing and wondered what time it was, dismayed at the thought the children might find her in bed, but her watch said it was only four. The bell rang once, then twice. It must be Patrice she thought and turned over wearily, expecting that he would leave. But as she turned over to go back to sleep, she heard an odd sound, rather like that of a key in the lock. She listened intently. Silence. Could it be the concierge in an emergency, she wondered? There was nothing. She closed her eyes. But suddenly there was a sound, a sound as though someone were dialing. Diana froze, in another moment she felt that she would be made party to something she didn't want.

"Qui est la?" she shouted. Could it be a thief she wondered, remembering Sylvia's stories earlier? Then *"Patrice?"* And to her amazement his voice answered, very, very slow and very smooth, the voice of one feeling his way in the dark.

"Ah," he said, "I wanted to find out if you got the phone message the other evening. They said it was urgent."

"Yes," said Diana, with controlled rage, wanting to scream. "I did."

"Ah, bon, bon," he replied in the manner of one who wishes to sooth, and behind him she heard the door close very gently, indeed.

Now she was wide awake and trembling. She rushed to

the door and made sure it was shut. Tears of rage were in her eyes, her body shivered uncontrollably. Did he have a key to the apartment, had he come here often to use the phone, to read her diaries? He had entered secretly, he had lied to her, to her. She sat down at the desk and wrote the first thing which came to her.

"Dear Patrice," she scribbled, "I've known for some time that you are in obvious emotional confusion. I think you need desperately to talk to someone about the things that are bothering you, and to begin to try to understand why you act the way you do. In any event you had no business entering our place if you thought no one was here, and I shall expect an explanation and an apology."

She folded the note up, wrote his name on the outside and stuck it in a little, empty, metal name-card holder on their front door. In her head Henri's words kept repeating. *"Patrice, c'est un grand malade."* She remembered at home a neighbor of theirs who had had a nervous breakdown, and who had appeared one snowy afternoon saying that she was looking for her children, white-faced and rigid, only to be followed by her husband several hours later, who explained that she was ill and having to be hospitalized as the result of a severe anxiety attack. Perhaps this was the onset of something similar for Patrice. But she felt no pity for him, nothing but the most intense hatred, as if he had insulted or violated her, and nothing could make up for that, not her desire to kill him, certainly. What she wanted was to humiliate him and hear him beg for forgiveness. Hear him admit that he had behaved foully.

Two days passed then the note disappeared and another was put in its place. He had written in English,

"Dear Diana, I came by to see if you had gotten the message the other night, and while I leaned against the door, it opened. You must not have shut it properly, and then I remembered a phone call I had to make. I'm sorry that I woke you up. Don't try to be my mother figure; I've got one too many of those already. *Amicalement*, Patrice." Again, tears of impotence and shame came to her eyes. She had been slapped. She was helpless and weak, he could mock her with impunity.

It was five o'clock; time for the children to return from school. She ripped the note into tiny pieces. The bell rang, and, expecting Kit, she walked over to open it. There he was, grinning broadly. She stared white with rage, and, suddenly behind him, Kit's little head could be seen, as she diligently plodded up the stairs.

"Did you find my note?" asked Patrice pleasantly.

Diana's voice was gone. She nodded.

"Ah," he went on, "do you accept *mes excuses*?"

Just barely able to speak, she whispered with fury, "Not those." His face darkened a bit. *"Alors?" "Alors, au revoir."* Diana pointed to the open door, and as he turned on his heel and left, she wanted to scream, whoever else you lie to and deceive; you're not going to lie to me. And she wanted to die, shaking with desolation.

* * * * * *

The next day she began to get herself and the children ready for the trip they were taking to England, where they were to meet Tom in London on his way back from the States. They had planned a few days there and then to go up to Cambridge to see old friends. There was much to do. She went to the bank, washed clothes at their tiny laundromat around the corner, threw things out of the refrigerator, left notes for Agnes about doing a big cleaning of the apartment. The reality of seeing Tom was part of the grayness she had entered on. But the thought of Patrice caused her to writhe in frustration. He had escaped her; the rebuke "don't try to be a mother figure," throbbed like a burn. He had shamed her, and she was in his power.

The following morning they got into a taxi and headed for the airport, the children each tugging a small bag and she, a larger one. Both children looked apprehensive, and Diana realized with a shock that this was the first time that she had ever taken them anywhere by herself. Or gone anywhere by herself. Anxiously she checked passports, worried about gate numbers, and staggered under the weight of the bag, which had suddenly become filled with iron books. She cursed herself for the way in which she had always let Tom look out for everything, she wasn't even sure how to read the notations on the plane tickets. But once inside the plane, they all drew a deep breath. Feeling the plane rear up, leaving the airport behind, leaving Paris behind was a foretaste of the final departure. Bitter, cheated, now she knew nothing of what she had imagined would happen. He was despicable. She looked out at the towers of clouds around them uneasy. To be away from the earth, to be locked inside a metal bullet, and surrounded on all sides by air, chilled and repelled her; it was arid like the North Pole, beautiful the way diamonds were, cold and empty. She was a daughter of earth. When the plane set down at Heathrow, she shuddered and pulled herself together. The children clutched at her, and they were swept out with the others, only to find themselves in that interminable crush of people designated as "aliens." With meticulous maddeningly masked hostility of the British, they were slowly processed through the queue. By a miracle neither of the children had to go to the bathroom.

She changed some money, and they all ran for the bus, which was to take them to the central London tube station. They lurched upstairs, the children breathless with the wonder of their first double-decker bus, and off they went through the ugly neat urbanized countryside of "villas" cheek by jowl, the flat red-brick dreariness and slatternly alleys laid end to end in English exurbia.

At the bus station they discovered they would have to walk several blocks to the Tube. Diana marshalled the children like an implacable leader, and they staggered off, Kit bringing up the rear, crimson with the exertion of her bag. Finally at the Tube they plunged down, down, down into the bowels of the filthiest dankest station Diana could ever remember encountering. Used to the cheery toy aspect of the Metro, the children were repelled. On and on the train plunged giving Nick plenty of time to read the tube map, which he loved. And Kit could take in, to her eyes content, a row of Sikhs sitting opposite like exotic birds with their snowy white turbans piled like gossamer snail shells on their dark brows. The air was thick and stale with cigarette smoke. The people were heavy, dirty, lumpy in shapeless tweeds and woolens and thick shoes.

By the time they got off and went up to the light, they were all three exhausted. "Please can't we take a taxi," Kit moaned, "I can't carry this any longer." Nick was, of course, pressing his lips together and saying nothing. Diana relented. It couldn't be too expensive by now, and so they drove up in style to the bed and breakfast place which had been recommended by friends – one of fifty identical looking places, red brick fronts shining in the sun, neat white steps leading to doors with brass knockers, near Bloomsbury Square and the British Museum.

They clambered out of the taxi and were greeted by a stern looking proprietor who said, "Your husband's here, got in last night," in a reproachful way, and showed them down a long dark carpeted corridor to a back room. Triumphantly they knocked on the door. "It's us," they called. Tom, unshaven and small-eyed, opened the door in his familiar blue bathrobe and gave them all hugs. Diana felt embarrassed, as though she were kissing a stranger.

"I'll settle in the children," she said, in a businesslike manner, and led them off in the direction of their room, like someone playing for time. The room turned out to be light and sunny, facing on to the street. Its ceiling was immensely high, and in the room were four beds neatly arranged around the room, where flowered wallpaper like a disease climbed upwards.

The children fell on their beds and opened their books. "I'll be back in a while," said Diana, "and we'll go and get something to eat." They didn't even look up as she left. She trudged slowly back down the corridor and let herself into Tom's room. He was under the sheets. There was no window in the room. His underwear, pants, socks and papers were strewn around the room. It was like the room of a derelict. "Come on," he said, "come here. God, I missed you."

She took off her clothes, bare of desire, stripped of her dreams. There was no thought in her head of refusing, no possible protest that she didn't want it, didn't feel like it. No, this was her assignment, her lot, her end: his arms, the bed, the sour smell, the disruption; the intrusion, the inevitable. Oh, the inevitability, the regularity, never her wanting, always his wanting. She had never been allowed to know hunger for an instant. A memory of Cambridge returned. Her confusion then, first married, always the two selves, the one that wept for joy to be together with him, reading in the evening, sleeping together warm arms around each other in bed at night, and the other self who wept in exasperation, "You don't love me, you only want me for sex," harried and made frantic by the pressure of a masculine sexuality, which took her, consumed her, and then happily withdrew to its own silent, satisfied realms. He was the most loving of lovers, she was never unsatisfied, but sensually she was a child. Each time she tried to construct a web, that web was taken out of her hands. The fragile web of herself, trying to find its own pattern and articulations, undergoing the inevitable destruction that marriage brings to a woman. There she learned to live on someone else's time. In the morning lying next to him, her stomach cramped with nervousness, she longed to get up early, but he liked to sleep late, and sleep with his arms around her, and make love when he arose. Not that he obliged her to, it was only that she knew no other way. She had taken on the responsibility of another, presence and pulse, because she had not wanted the responsibility for herself. But who was there, then, to explain that to her?

To gain time she pretended to be interested in his news. "What's happening back home?" she asked," "Tell me." And slowly, stroking her breasts and stomach, kissing her between each word, he described the unprecedented agitation and unrest at the school. But like a child with a hurt, she could think of nothing but what had happened with Patrice. She was so frightened, so unhappy that she would never see him again. She rehearsed different ways of bringing it up. But Tom was clever, he understood her so well, if she even mentioned what had happened, he would know everything. He was telling her now about the demand for Black Studies programs, about the faculty's division into two camps on the issue of Vietnam. It was interesting, but it had no power to touch her. Politics never had, there was no reality in it for her. Just a lot of men talking theory, splitting hairs. Real things were simple, but they were made complicated by the over-nice minds which inhabited the university.

Inside her Patrice's name was waiting like a scream to tear out of her throat; she had to tell him, she couldn't wait another minute. Even if Tom guessed everything by her outrage. She wanted to hear him say angrily, we must never talk to him again. She had to be right, then it would all be worth it. "So I wrote him a note," she heard herself talking, "he really is sick, just as Henri said...." she waited. She freed herself slightly from his arms and looked up. Tommy was grinning down at her. "Umm," he agreed. He kissed her, held her sideways, and penetrated her; she was burning, melting, "But you don't have to get so angry, just forget it when you see him again, he's just a bit crazy."

She felt a rush of gratitude, the joy, that secret joy, was hers again. She could see him again. She had been the one to be foolish, in fact, she understood now he was right to defend himself. He didn't want her to be his mother, he felt differently about her than that. It was her fault for interfering and prying; people simply didn't want others to pry in their affairs. She closed her eyes. She would write him a note, maybe, and take the matter lightly, maybe. Her body was moving in the old rhythm. She belonged with Tom. There was no other place for her than here, here in this clammy dark and disorder, the "lav" in the hall, flushing dismally nearby. It was over with Patrice. She had learned her lesson. Shuddering, she began to moan and let herself fall from the top of the wave.

Back in Cambridge nothing had changed. They rented a punt and glided, with the children, on the dark narrow little Cam. Along the backs, the colleges rose in stillness against the delicate sky. At Trinity the cherry trees bent down to the tulips sown in the high silky grasses. Everything was laid out with the lavish unpremeditated thought of the English gardener. There were the spires of Kings, Lawrence's "old sow on her back." The quiet laughter and voices of the men and women punting by drifted on the soft air. For lunch they took the children to the little pub by the river near the bridge. Fitzbillies still sold sticky buns, the marketplace had the same stalls, stall keepers, the same hearty rough browned faces. What had changed? Time was a Ferris wheel, bringing you up at certain moments, showing you where you had been, then plunging you back to a space where there was no perspective.

Thirteen years had gone by since they left Cambridge, after their first two years of marriage. Franz and Gerte, the older couple, German refugees, who had befriended them, seemed younger if anything. The flats they had lived in, one out on Castle Hill, one in the center of town over a coffee shop, were unchanged. In the little kitchens of those flats she had tried to write, but there was nothing to say. Her life seemed to her to be a blank. She knew nothing. She lived. She went to lectures, walked, shopped for food in the market, cooked, hung on Tom's arm at night as they walked through the town. They always had people coming to see them, they were a focus, their flats a magnet for friends, who felt their love for each other, love which spilled over into food, warmth, gaiety. Being back in Cambridge was like having a sponge erase all the confusion of Paris. She wondered if Patrice had cast a spell on her. To want to make love to a young man one didn't even like, seemed impossible to conceive, as they sat in the tranquil well-remembered domesticity of the chilly parlor at Franz and Gerte's. Franz offered, as was his custom, a fat big Dutch cigar to Tom, and the two of them, so alike in their warm teddy bear completeness, sat puffing contentedly, while Gerte darned and mended, and Diana amused them with stories about life in France, as she had done so many years before after their frequent vacations on the continent.

The few days passed with their litanies of memories. "Daddy and I went here, Daddy and I did this, did that." She was continually stopping the children to point out a place; to remark on a scene. It was less, much less to them than their own little grains which they were storing away.

But when it was time to leave Diana became frightened at having to face Patrice. It was a war between them, and she had lost a major battle, but it was also a marriage with too much common property to dispose of, too much doing for one another to be relinquished, too much intimacy to be jettisoned overnight.

They returned home, the children clutched sackfuls of books from Heffer's, the heavy entrance door banged behind them, the concierge, taking water from the tap in the courtyard, smiled her sly smile at them, and they ascended by the iron cage and creaking rope to their door. At the sound of their voices the birds set up a racket of welcome. In their absence. Agnes had waxed and polished their glass cage so it sparkled in the sun. The children threw open the windows onto the balcony and, taking their books outside, sat at the small round white table on the bright plastic chairs. Tom took himself off to the lab to see what was happening. Diana stood, heavy and lost. Nothing had any meaning if Patrice was not to be a part of it. But of course he couldn't be any longer. "Let's have early dinner, and go to the movies," said Tom. She agreed without desire. Without Patrice, without the possibility of Patrice, she could not exist. Where her life touched that of Tom and the children it disappeared.

As the door shut behind Tom she went to the desk and wrote a note in French. "Drop in and hear the news of the 'revolution'" and, by way of speaking lightly about the incident, "I suppose it wasn't very Zen of me to get so angry." She put it in the desk drawer, and she prayed that he wouldn't come by.

Making dinner, she listened for the elevator to stop at their floor, for the bell to ring. She dropped things; her hands were cold. The last scene between them flashed uncontrollably on and off in her mind. At dinner they all gathered about the long wooden table. "Seems funny without Patrice," Nick suddenly remarked, "bet he doesn't know we're back yet." Diana could feel her cheeks flush.

"Getting to the end of school vacation is like getting to the end of your grapefruit," said Kit, looking down at hers. They burst out laughing.

"Only two more months to go and school's over," said Nick cheerfully.

"I hate *Meudon* and that stupid gym and making those dumb drawings," moaned Kit.

"How were things at the lab?" asked Diana of Tom.

"Just the same," he replied, noncommittally.

Inwardly she shrugged. There was never any way to talk about that aspect of things, then, reproachfully, she told herself it wasn't his fault that experiments took years and then often didn't work. Why would he want to talk about it especially since the technical aspects, which he willingly explained if she asked, went in one ear and out the other?

But it is all so dull she wanted to scream, never anything to say to me, never bringing anyone home, never any interesting things happening to them. Everything was his fault. He ate everything in two seconds, before she had a chance to sit down, especially since she always forgot things and had to go back to the kitchen for them. They sat quietly. If Patrice had been there, they would all have been laughing and joking, and they would have felt like a family. Now they were four bodies isolated from each other, depressed.

Tom got up and went to the hall closet they jokingly referred to as their "cave." "Better remember to order more Bordeaux from *Nicholas*," he said when he returned to the table. "And get some Meursault, too; hmm?" She nodded. It maddened her, this never ending list of things to be attended to. It seemed that all their conversation was simply that, his telling her what to do.

How she hated and loathed the repetitive, the mechanics of living. She admired Carole Bridges, an American acquaintance from whom she was taking Yoga lessons, because she worked at everything regularly: so much time for piano, French, Yoga, and she improved at all of them. As for herself, she knew she spent so much time hating the things she had to be that she had little energy left over. Sometimes she thought of herself as a person in flight, but in flight from what she couldn't say. She wanted to bear children, but she didn't particularly want to rear them, beyond the age of five they seemed to have little need of her or she of them. What did she want? What had seemed substantial things faded to shadows now. Had she been asleep then? Or was she asleep now?

Dinner was over. One more of a million dinners was over. She got up quickly and cleared the table. No one helped. And she set about washing things as quickly as she could, so there would be nothing, or very little, when they returned from the movies. It was very light still. They kissed the children, and on the way out Diana put the note for Patrice in the little metal card holder. Self-consciously she said, "Well, I wonder what's happening with *le grand malade*?" Tom smiled inscrutably. Her heart was beating for fear that they'd meet him in the lobby or coming in the door.

When they returned, the note was missing. Again her heart began to pound. They had no sooner settled in, Tom in the big black reading chair, she in the smaller one; when there was a knock at the door. Her palms went cold then hot. Nick ran and opened the door. "I knew it would be you," he said, and he kissed Patrice affectionately. Kit skipped up to him; "Patrice," she said, "I have a new Asterix." She clung affectionately to his hand. He came forward circumspectly. Tom rose and shook his hand. Diana gave him a cold smile, but extended her hand also. Scattered on the floor were piles of books, underground manifestoes, and handbills put out by the students, which Tom had brought back to show her. Diana determined to say as little as possible. Tom began to describe the events at home. Diana read Fansheen, and Tom and Patrice looked over the other papers. Several times Diana caught Patrice looking at her sharply. He's wondering if I told Tom everything that happened; she thought with satisfaction; and he wants to know just how I feel towards him. But that thought was painful.

She excused herself and went out to finish the dishes, refusing his eager offer to help as coldly as she dared. A few minutes later she heard the murmur of voices, and the front door slammed. She remained in the kitchen, imprisoned in an icy block of misery. Tom came into the kitchen, laughing quietly to himself. "He's such a conservative kid," Tom said, "or rather he's too cynical to believe that anything can change." She was surprised. It was rare that Tom ever commented on politics. She knew his heart was in the right place, but that was the extent of it. But now that it had entered his own little bailiwick things were different. As it was finally making a difference to the middle-class families whose sons were being taken off to the war. The French proverb *"il ne faut jamais dire Fontaine, je ne boirai pas de ton eau,"* flashed through her mind. She thought bitterly of herself and Patrice. Nothing can ever be ruled out, except death, but always people are doing just that, saying this is not for me, this I will never do, until they wake to find themselves doing that very thing. She smiled at Tom. He was always surprising her.

A few days later, returned from a large shopping at the marché, dragging her little shopping cart behind her, she was stopped in the entrance by the concierge. "*Madame* is back," she announced by way of preliminary. Diana nodded an acknowledgement. "Everything was in order when you returned?" Diana nodded again, wondering what was coming. *"Ah bon,"* she said and, staring intently at Diana, she added, "Patrice asked me for the keys to your apartment twice, he told me once a fuse had blown. *Votre Agnes* told me that on Friday, when she came to clean, the place was reeking of cigarette smoke, and all the ashtrays were full, *Madame*, but of course *Madame* probably knows this."

Diana tried to stare back, expressionless. She would have given anything to have been able to lie, but she was unable to give the lie direct. She knew, somewhere in her, that it was because Patrice lied that he had power over her, the power of wanting to force him to admit it and to surrender the truth to her, only to her. She longed to be permitted to enter his conspiracy against the world. The silence between her and *Mme. Guillemin* persisted one second too long. Diana turned her head to avoid the triumphant gaze of the concierge. *"Patrice, c' est un bon enfant, enfin,"* said *Mme. Guillemin* with a shrug, generous in her victory. Diana lugged the shopping cart into the elevator. The stolid black form of the concierge moved off, a spider heavy with eggs, back into her lair. A shiver went through Diana. It was really too much. He could have gone through every paper, every drawer in the apartment. It is hopeless, she thought, stalemated. And realized how far she had retreated to earlier feelings by the wrench this gave her. She tried to look at it philosophically once more. It was all to the good, her burning fantasies needed to be *douched*.

But what difference did it make? She wanted to look at him. She wanted the experience for whatever it represented. She wanted that veil of unsatisfied desire, which, laid across the quotidian, informed it with joy, excitement, anticipation, not the satisfaction, no, but the always about to be satisfied, the potential, the possible.

Putting things away, the kitchen was cramped, still, the world around her darker, more sober, without the possibility of encounter. He was the key to that, and now, for the third time, she was being shown that she should throw the key away. What did she want with such a bogus experience? Could she, would she really betray Tom? But no one talked about honor anymore, any more than one could dare speak of patriotism. Narrow, stupid words that poisoned people, finally. "The unlived life of which one can die." She was afraid merely afraid to get hurt, and by that token she knew she would be hurt.

¤

Chapter X

It was the third week in May. Tom was leaving in the afternoon for Berlin. That morning she lay beside him in the dark, feeling a new energy rise in her. He was going away for a week to Germany. Lines began to rise and fall in her head. Maybe this morning she could get to work. She left bed and pulled her clothes from the chair holding her breath, a fugitive.

Suddenly he opened one eye. "Where are you going?" he asked. With false carelessness she answered, "Just going to get dressed and get breakfast. I thought you'd want to sleep longer."

She knew he wanted to make love.

"I have an earache," he said.

"Darling," she said, "Are you sure? Maybe it's because of a stuffy nose. You need some nose spray and," she considered, "some warm oil."

It was a sop. Taking care of him, she felt the lines disappear. She wanted to cry with vexation.

"I'll warm the oil."

The kitchen shimmered in a blue light, which was growing into a morning gray. She fumbled for some small container, finally found a small metal measuring cup, and poured some salad oil in, turned the flame under it, and wondered where to find some cotton. Children in pain, children crying, Nora screaming in the hospital, "My ear hurts!" She hurried to the little bathroom in their room, checked, heaved a sigh of relief, of course, in the aspirin bottle. Rushed back to the kitchen, grabbed the cup from the stove, burning herself. Every few seconds she tested it on her wrist. When it feels comfortable on the wrist, she mouthed to herself. After an eternity it felt lukewarm.

He turned over to present her with the ear, when she returned to the bedside.

"Did you test it on your wrist?" he demanded.

"Yes, of course I did."

"And is it alright?"

"Of course."

Why did he question everything, she wondered?

She began to soak up a few drops of the oil with the cotton. Gently she let them drip into his ear.

"Ow," he almost yelled. "That's burning."

She recoiled in fear. "I'm sorry, really I tested it."

"Well, how did it feel, could you feel it?"

"It was lukewarm."

"That's too hot, don't you see, it's supposed to have no temperature at all, body temperature."

Look, she started to say, I've given a million bottles. I know all about testing on wrists.... "I'm sorry," she said, "it felt alright to me."

"Test it again."

She tested, she felt nothing.

Drip, drip, the outer-ear glistened, the cartilage and skin was pearled with drops of oil. With firmness his fingers massaged the ear to help the oil sink in. Utter discouragement invaded her body, she felt herself sinking with weariness. How could she have burned him? Taking care of people was what she knew about, not he. She stared at the wall behind the bed. He smiled good naturedly. "You're dangerous," he said with a grin.

"Yes," she said bitterly. "I'm no good; I'm incompetent." If you're so great, why don't you just leave, she thought.... She hunched in her bathrobe. "You think I'm no good," she added for emphasis.

"Nonsense," he laughed, "I love you, I think you're wonderful."

"Do you feel better?"

"I'm convincing myself it's going away."

She rubbed his back. He smiled. His head on the pillow always reminded her of Nora. She went on rubbing but turned her head away. He kissed her hand gently.

"I'll make us some breakfast now. Would you like an omelette?"

"Oh, that would be wonderful," he said. He so loved her to take care of him.

In the late afternoon, Diana sat outside on the balcony, a notebook open on the table, trying to write a poem. Ahead of her the Eiffel Tower rose like a giant piece of Erector Set.

Like two straight hedges, the trees which lined the *Champs Elysees* stood thick and green leading to the toy grandeur of the *École Militaire*. If she shifted slightly the flags at one end of the gardens of the UNESCO whipped in the wind or drooped like rags when the air was still. Directly below the trees on the avenue, her trees were luxuriant now, and like a green drape they muffled the sound of traffic, which rose and fell like a giantess humming to herself.

Time was turning, a wheel, which was taking them into summer, taking them away from Paris, away from this voyage where they were always a speck on the horizon, taking them back to land. The sun and the clouds were playing cache-cache and down below young mothers were walking what Diana called their "twos" the toddler on foot, the baby in the carriage. Seen from this vantage point they appeared like humble foot soldiers in an army from which death had discharged her. Or rather, she had been demobilized after the last birth. Nature had no more need of her, the sealed orders, to bear, had been obeyed. She was now set adrift to do as she would, to live off the land, as unwelcome as most veterans are returning to an indifferent society.

It's unfair to say that it is death which has brought me here, she thought. Nora has only taught me that there is an end to everything at last, to the most exquisite torture, to the most ecstatic pleasure, to innocence. But without her death I should be at the same place on the road. She had brought with her to Paris her old journals, journals that went back to her school year in Paris up to the present. All afternoon she had been descending, bringing up pieces of herself, herself a lost continent. A form was taking shape, but of what woman she couldn't be sure. At times the voice that spoke was the predictable one she "would have remembered," naive, sentimental, romantic, practical, gossipy. But there was another voice. In the earliest diaries, it was ambitious, almost driven, nourishing itself on dreams of writing, publishing, being a writer, but that note was quickly lost and replaced with an exile's cry, a cry that could be heard only infrequently over the following years. It was a voice which remembered, as did the Jew, that a promise had been made, a covenant entered into. Now it was visionary, now it was ironic, telling her that so much motherhood, so much wifeliness was unnecessary, demanded by neither Tom nor the children, merely an excuse for what she feared to face. It was the voice which remembered poetry and wrote of poems which she never knew she had read in those years. It seemed she was two people, one of whom had gotten the upper hand and subdued, but never entirely subjugated, the other.

There was too much in the journals to grasp. They inspired no poetry. She had been dreaming the hours away, feeling the sun and air on her skin, absorbing light and color like a restoring liquid. Only one thought repeated itself over and over in her mind, not ready to leave, not ready, and she didn't hear the children return until they appeared behind her, slipping their warm rosy arms around her neck and kissing her.

That night she had a dream She was in a dusty tea shop; the light was the light at five o'clock on a spring day, golden and syrupy. A woman was sitting with her at the table, which was in the far corner of the place, so they were both able to look out at the empty streets. But the woman was staring at her with huge dark-brown doe eyes rimmed with thick dark lashes. She was uncomfortable because the rest of the woman's face was skull like, with sunken cheeks and ugly large yellowed teeth with tobacco stains. The woman's hands and arms were thin as a skeleton's, and her collar bone protruded – two large knobs above a boat-neck blouse, which concealed her with some sort of a denial. The woman said nothing in the dream but clasped and unclasped her long bony tobacco-stained fingers, and Diana felt herself grow embarrassed and uncomfortable, but she knew she should be friendly, and all she could think of was deadly dead a lie, and she knew that the tea she was drinking was making her sick. When she woke the next morning, she could remember every detail. She was sure she knew the woman. Dead a lie she repeated to herself. "Dadelus," she remembered in a rush. The Portrait of an Artist, the woman was her English teacher freshman year, she had given her a low mark on her first paper and then come to treat her as a favorite. At the end of the year she had taken her out to tea. She was leaving the college. Bitterly she had said, "Very few of us are chosen, though many are called." What had she tried to tell Diana, about herself, about Diana? Nothing came back. Her name was Miss Hughes. Diana felt a strange pang, thinking of it. She had missed a chance then to learn what it was all about, that pain of Miss Hughes, and her unspoken message.

Patrice had resumed his old place in the household. He slipped in and out bringing flowers, stamps, books, and newspapers. Once more he was pressed to stay to dinner, and he washed up and chatted in the kitchen. Sylvia, coming unexpectedly to the apartment and finding him there, said, sniffing haughtily after the door closed behind him, "Well, Tommy is certainly very patient. I can tell you Ed wouldn't put up with it." But what the "it" was she never specified. And after all, thought Diana defensively, it isn't as though Ed doesn't put up with plenty from her. And what about her young men? For Sylvia was currently presenting to all her friends a young Polish refugee, with whom she went everywhere. Ed was of course in Basel. Diana had her own notions about Sylvia, but, of course, that's why she was so quick to see the point about Patrice. Or maybe she just thought him an unforgivable expense.

The days were disappearing; the end was coming closer. And, as in the last days of Nora's life, Diana's hope grew stronger. Somehow, she told herself, she and Patrice must be destined to come together briefly and beautifully.

The news from his family was bad. Isabelle had had to return to the hospital. She was immobile, and another operation was performed. Diana and he sat under the hemispheres of umbrella trees on a park bench at the Champs de Mars. In the distance the bell tinkled to call the children to the puppet show in one corner, it sounded like the Host. Diana tried to avoid Patrice's anxious eyes. "My mother never leaves her side," he said, "and she, Isabelle, she is so good, she jokes and laughs and tries to cheer my mother. She is so much better than I am. But she is young and strong, she had a bad time before, and then she got better." He swallowed and said in a low voice, "My mother writes she has a tube in her head." Then, as to an authority, "What do you think, Diana?"

Diana made a sound. Sturdy laughing children were passing before them on the humble donkeys that went up and down a little track guided by a shabby Algerian teenager. Patrice's hands clenched on his knees. On that terrible day after Christmas, when Nora had started to grow worse again, they had had to bring her back to the hospital for a new series of radiation. In the bed next to hers, surprising among all the young children, there had been an eighteen year old girl, dying of leukemia. Day after day her mother sat there knitting, talking to her in a cheerful ordinary voice. Often a priest came to talk to the mother and address some hearty remarks to the air above the girl's head. She was hooked into IV's and bags in every possible direction and was heavily doped on morphine. Night after night, when Diana and Tom left the hospital after kissing Nora, the girl's breathing grew more labored, the mother's smile more rigid. "It's a disgrace," Diana heard one nurse whisper to another. "They shouldn't have anyone in that condition with the others." The other nurse shrugged, "There's no way to get her a room alone, yet." Nora whispered to Diana, "She makes a lot of noise." And then one night the bed was gone from that corner. Leaving Nora, through a half opened door they saw the mother in a room, her head leaning against the bedside. Diana looked quickly away, but as they waited for the elevator to go down, the woman appeared, supported by a man and the fat jolly priest. Only then did Diana understand the girl had been dying. She saw, without wanting to, the mother's face, a face too terrible to look at, being no face at all, but a mirror of what she had just looked upon. A voice said is that what I will look like? They drew back, and let her go down in the elevator alone, with the two men.

"But she will rally again, I know," Patrice was saying softly, staring at Diana intently from behind his glasses. "She did once before and she is young and strong."

Diana looked at him silently. What did it matter how strange and crazy he was, he had nobody but her to comfort him. She had imagined the scene a million times in her head, how Isabelle would die before he reached the States, and how she would be the one he would turn to. All she wanted was to give to him, to comfort him, to love him, because everything was so short and painful in this life. And she would always remember it, and have it to cherish when she got old. It would be, something. She stared at his profile, as he watching the children running up and down without really seeing them. She found him so handsome. Young men were so handsome. They were lit from within with a kind of exaltation and unrest. Nothing was sure for them, nothing decided, nothing, then, had hardened; they were supple, green. There was a song, *"Il Avait Vingt Ans"* sung by *Barbara* about a summer romance between an older woman and a twenty year old. Her voice, that was warm and lighthearted vibrant and sensual, celebrated the desire of a woman, no different than a man's, for a beautiful object.

That night she dreamed that Nick was on top of her, making love to her. His tongue was in her mouth, and she thought, to herself, he tastes saltier, meaning, than Tom. There was a black servant in the house, who knew they were married, but she was wondering about their relations, because she knew it wasn't "right" although it seemed so natural. Nick seemed to enjoy it, but she tried to imagine him telling people, "I'm married to my mother." How did that happen they'd want to know, and there's no real answer he can give them. But she also imagined in the dream that their relationship would probably stop, and how he would say, "My first woman was my mother." She didn't even particularly want them to go on being married and, still in the dream, she got out of bed, still puzzled by the way the odd thing was going on in their house.

The dream was still real when she woke that morning, struck by the naturalness of it. She remembered Jocasta's words of comfort to Oedipus about the vision of Tiresias: "but many a man has slept with his mother in dreams and in prophecies." Wasn't Jocasta's voice that of an older time, when all men were consorts, merely?

That evening Patrice popped in and invited her to go to the movies. "It's an old *Gerald Phillipe* movie, *M. Reboux*. It's very witty Diana, you'll like it. And you just can't stay in the apartment all the time Tom's gone."

"But I've gone out three times this week," protested Diana, annoyed by what she felt was condescension and pity. As if she had no life of her own. And he knew she had, because the children had told her that he had come by each time and played with them. "He pretended he was our babysitter," Nick said with disgust. "He needs one more than we do!"

"But if we want to make it we have to go quickly."

Diana left the children their dinner, and they set off, the sun beginning to cast long golden rays over the horizon. Downstairs the concierge looked reprovingly at them as they rushed out into the velvety light, laughing.

But the movie was depressing and tawdry, and Diana felt uneasy that Patrice had thought it "witty." It was about a man who lives off women, making love to them, taking their money, destroying them by his charm and good looks. When they left the theatre it was dark and there, in the corners of the doorways in that shabby neighborhood, were the prostitutes. Their hair was piled high, their faces were painted into careful nothingness. They wore plain raincoats, and their legs were solidly calved in their teetering high heeled shoes. Business women, secretaries one would have said. She glanced at Patrice to see what effect their presence had on him, remembering Henri's remarks about the need for licensed bordellos. Had Patrice ever been with a woman she wondered? She thought not. He was making a casual reference to the women, "*Couve de Murville* wanted them off the streets, but the other députés just laughed in his face."

The night, which had fallen, was a late spring night, freighted with the scent of human desire, restlessness, hunger. Night in the city was Greek ritual drama; something in which every citizen took part, participant or spectator, re-enacting, watching the ancient story unfold. The odor of the cars, the bodies pushing along the sidewalks, the smell of wine, beer, the bitter chicory of the coffee, the musky scent of the women's perfumes, the ammonia reek of the pissoirs, all of it contained in those little puffs of warm cool spring night air, an immense heady aphrodisiac.

Diana longed to stay out but was afraid to speak. Patrice, reading her mind said, "Let's go have something to eat at *Le Drugstore*." They turned and walked up towards *St. Germain*. When they got to the *Drugstor*e, they had to push their way in through the crowds, which thronged the entryway and stairs. People were milling about, looking for friends, or just looking, smiling, talking, smoking. Every table upstairs seemed taken, but at last they found one, back near the kitchen, piled high with dirty dishes and lipstick stained glasses. Triumphantly they dived for it, just ahead of another couple, and looked up to see that they were sitting under the hands of *Gerard Philippe*. It must be a sign, Diana thought to herself, and she remembered the young avid face of *Philippe* ordering the wine in the famous eating scene of "Devil In The Flesh," *Roman Radiguet's* story of a young man's first love for an "older" woman, the wife of a soldier at the front in the First World War. She laughed, remembering that in the story the "older" woman was no more than twenty-five, the boy still a *lycéen*.

They ordered, talking and joking, but Diana was only conscious of Patrice's eyes burning on her face. He said suddenly, seriously, *"Tu a bonne mine, Diana,"* (it seemed like years ago she had arranged that they would *tutoie* one another for the pleasure of hearing that syllable from him to her.) He pointed to the sign of *Philippe* and said, "That's our sign." Her heart skipped, she tried to pretend she didn't know what he was referring to.

"It's mine," she said, trying to sound nonchalant.

"No, it's ours."

She had no appetite and willingly passed him everything on her plate. After eating, they went below and browsed in the bookstore, leafing through the latest American periodicals as well as the new French books. It was one o'clock when they left. All public transportation had stopped. It was beautiful, clear, and starry. They began to walk; looking for a taxi and Diana suggested that they go towards the river.

They crossed *St. Germain,* stared down the *Rue Bonaparte*, crossed the *Rue Jacob* passing the open bistros and bars. The many little hotels were lit up, and sounds of voices and laughter carried on the air. But then they arrived at the quiet of the Seine. There before them, with the sound of their footsteps over the gravel to be heard as they approached, was the *Pont des Arts*, its lights arching over the river. It was so unbearably beautiful, it seemed it would disappear as they walked to it. They stood on the bridge alone in silence. For them alone the balls of light balanced on their dark candelabra. For them Paris rose up on either side of her banks, for them the river flowed darkly, proudly, threading its way back to the time when Paris was a rude group of huts, no, further, back to the time when there was only the river, the river needing nothing but itself. They were outward bound on that river. I will never stand here again, said Diana to herself, loving someone so madly, so ridiculously. Reluctantly they turned their backs and crossed over to the Right Bank.

"I will show you how to tear *Pompidou*," said Patrice with a grin. "That's what we do at night you know." He went up to one of the thousand pre-election posters plastered to a wall and ripped it. Only the bottom half came off and *Pompidou*, beetle-browed, heavy crafty jowls, his lips pursed in a smile of false *bonhommerie*, simpered on. A taxi passed and they hailed it.

Inside it felt close and intimate, contained in such a small space together. Patrice's eyes gleamed out of the dark. "I like to be with the rich," he said unexpectedly. "I know how to maneuver them and get their money from them." Bitterly he added, "I hate them."

Diana was taken aback, revolted by the boast. He had paid for dinner and the movies. Was she the rich one he wanted to manipulate? She frowned. "There are more admirable ways to spend your time," she said sarcastically. He laughed. "You are so virtuous, but I am not." The taxi rushed through the dark deserted street.

It was two o'clock when they arrived home and crept quietly up the stairs in the dark. Diana invited him in for the customary drink of mineral water, for which he had a passion. She was wide awake. There were so many things unspoken, unexplored. They went out on the dining room balcony and stood looking out at the night.

"Sometimes I have heard a nightingale," said Patrice, "from my room upstairs." They listened straining. Their voices murmured in the dark. Not even a footstep in this *bourgeois* and bedded quartier. She leaned against one corner of the balcony, her back to the gritty cement wall. Patrice was standing so close to her. If he turned and kissed her? She tried to imagine what she would do, say. He turned his face towards her and smiled. Then suddenly he made a fearful grimace of pain. His face was drawn. Slowly he rubbed his forehead with the palm of his hand. Diana was frightened. He really has problems she reminded herself. Then, whatever it was, passed. He brightened.

The night extended itself in waves of fragrance, the moon climbed higher and higher. How could people sleep, Diana wondered, as she stared at the dark curtained windows opposite them and imagined the people lying in those close rooms like mummies swaddled in sheets. What a strange thing sleep was anyway. At a certain time, as in an enchantment, people all fall down, become still, lie dreaming their dreams of beauties, of cooks, of coachmen. They tunneled into those dreams like moles and brought back strange stuffs, pieces of them, like merchants risking death on the high seas to bring back something rare and valuable. All over Paris everyone slept except her and Patrice. They moved from one side of the balcony to the other.

What was the matter with her, she wondered, that she couldn't get him to kiss her?

Her old sense of sexual inadequacy came back. She thought of her two best friends at school, they would have had no problem. Inside herself she felt something frightening. There was a terrible purity to her, she knew it, something of the eternal virgin, like her namesake, queen of the night chaste and fair. Yes, she had loved Diana the most of all the goddesses, when, as a little girl, she first read Bulfinch's Mythology. She loved her for her freedom and independence from all relationships, loved her because she was One, whole, intact. And yet she was the protectress of all living things that lived in her forest domain. A little girl she wanted to be strong and free.

The sky was growing clearer. The moon had sunk, the stars long gone. It was four o'clock. They were both as pale as harlequins. Tiptoeing through the dining room and kitchen, she unlocked the back door and let him out. As if a spell had been broken, she suddenly felt exhausted and fell into bed naked, her clothes in a heap on the floor.

She dreamed she was holding Nora, or a form for which she felt the tenderness she felt for Nora, and in it was sorrow and guilt as well. But the shadowy Nora melted, and she saw that Patrice was there, lying on top of her, his eyes wide and strained – and at the same instant she felt something touch her naked thigh. It was soft and limp like a broken thumb, and a voice in her head said, or it was suddenly Patrice's grandmother's voice, "He is of course, impotent," and she woke with a beating shame, her body burning.

The telephone was ringing shrilly. She opened her eyes to morning. Grabbing Tom's blue bathrobe hastily she ran barefoot to the hall to silence the noise.

"*Madame Field?*" It was an old woman's voice, careful, precise. "You will forgive me, I hope, for disturbing you at this hour, but I must get in touch with Patrice. Our poor dear good Isabelle, *elle s'est endormie à jamais.* Would you be so kind as to ask Patrice to call me, but please mention no word of this to him. It is better that I tell him when he comes to me. Thank you, *Madame*, I hope that someday we shall meet. Patrice has told me much about you."

Diana began to shake all over uncontrollably. She went into the children's room. They were lying on their beds. Nick was reading, Kitty was practicing her knitting, casting off and on as Agnes had recently taught her. "Nick," she said, trying to keep any emotion out of her voice. "It's very important. Could you go upstairs and knock on Patrice's door and tell him he's to come here and call his grandmother?"

It was surfacing, the moment of death, the wait at the door for the children that day to come home from school. The unbelievable, unpronounceable words, "Nora is dead." Nora, whom you saw last night alive in her bed, but dying and you couldn't or wouldn't know that, now you must live forever with her death. It was once more that moment when no human being should be alone to bear the news of what we- live with all our lives.

"But how will I know which is his door?" Nick asked anxiously. He was afraid to go up to that floor and knock on a strange door, she saw that. But she couldn't go, no.

"His door is right over our dining room," she said, hoping that was true. "But you went up there with him once, when he took you to the top of the roof. Just call Patrice, and he'll hear you, so you won't have to worry about getting the wrong door." That seemed to work. Nick went up.

Diana rushed to the bedroom and threw on some clothes. Then she went to the kitchen and tried to make herself a cup of coffee, listening all the time for Nick and Patrice. After what seemed like a long time they appeared. Patrice had on a pair of chinos, a tee shirt, and was barefooted. His eyes blinked sleepily behind his glasses, and his skin looked sallow in the morning light. Diana nodded, not daring to speak.

He began to make apologies for his grandmother having awakened her so early, but his voice trailed away. At the phone she heard his voice, unnaturally high and childlike, *"Grandmere?"* he began. It was too much. She loved him, and he was suffering. The phone was set back in its cradle. Slowly he walked into the dining room where Diana was hugging herself to stop the shaking of her body. Everything was too much, it was bursting out of her. Patrice looked very confused and stood still for a moment.

She drew closer. She cared, she didn't care about anything. "Patrice," she murmured, throwing her arms around him, feeling his body, it was completely rigid. *"Je t' aime."* There, it was over, it was out, it was acknowledged.

"Mon dieu, qu'est que je vais faire?"

Did he say that a moment before or after Diana kissed him, lopsidedly on his ear? She went crimson. But she said to herself, that was not a kiss of love. That was love of one's fellow human, love that needed to comfort someone in pain. He is all alone. She drew back quickly, turned, and went into the kitchen, and handed him a drink of water. He was still dazed, it appeared, looking at her so strangely as if he had heard or felt nothing of what she had done or said.

"Why did she call, my grandmother? She says she wants me to come over there. Did she tell you something about Isabelle?" he asked, suddenly suspicious.

Diana said nothing. She held her breath. She had imagined that the grandmother had told him because of the odd way he stood in the dining room, because he had said, "My God, what am I going to do?" before she had kissed him, hadn't he?

"Oh, no," Diana lied.

"No, it couldn't be that," he said and went out.

Desire and pain, her dream of him, the grandmother's voice and then the phone call and the sight of him. It was impossible to believe anything had happened which had happened. She was glad she had kissed him, glad she had spoken. What did it matter? But she was relieved just the same that he could always interpret her emotion as that of pity and sympathy for the suffering he was about to undergo. Yes, that would give them both a way out of embarrassment.

The children departed gaily for school. It was their last day, there would be a party and chocolate and games. They hugged her for joy as they left, and she came out onto their balcony to watch and to wave to them. She could see them almost to the school gates, two small figures dressed in gray and white. Her shivering dissolved in the sun.

She looked at her watch – almost eleven – the part of the day she detested; the sun was officious, the day cluttered, and people all locked into their tasks, for most, the simple ones of getting through until five o'clock. She took out the shopping cart to buy dinner, because she was going to lunch, and the stores might be closed when she returned.

She went down in the elevator praying that she would not meet *Mme. Guillemin.*

When she got back the door to the apartment was open, and there was Patrice, like an apparition, dressed in a sober dark grey suit, sitting at the head of the dining room table, pale and grim.

"It is all over," he said, not looking at her. "My grandmother told you? She was in a coma for two weeks. My mother never left her, sat with her, and held her hand."

Patrice, Patrice she cried out in her head, but no sound came. She couldn't reach him. He was alone, as she was with pain and confusion.

"Eh bien," he said, and walked out through the front door, turning to look at her once, his mouth a tight thin line.

She put away the food, changed her shoes, combed her hair, and went out again, closing the door firmly behind her. Old friends of her family were in town and were taking her to lunch. She had arranged to meet them at their hotel and to bring them to *Le Pavillion du Lac* because the park was so beautiful now. As she passed the florist where she so often bought flowers she saw in the window a fuchsia. It stood like a miniature tree, willow shaped in grief, each white blossom a mute bell, each bell of white, ruffled in crimson, hanging its head down, the long slender stamens tiny veins of blood. Behind the glass she caught sight of the florist, a bizarre shovel-faced woman, gaunt and upright as a soldier, who lived in her shop like the ruler of an empire. She had bad breath and fingers that were crippled with arthritis, yet every time Diana came in she was making intricate and beautiful flower arrangements. Diana ordered the plant sent to Patrice's grandmother. Then she ran and caught the bus just as it was pulling away from the curb. Gallantly beaming, the conductor and a passenger who were standing leaning over the back helped pull her in.

It was full summer. The chestnut trees were arching over the old paving stones. A woman walking about was breasts, hips, thighs, and a warm wet desirable tunnel. Diana folded herself against a corner of the platform and gazed at the dappled streets, the shops, the strollers, admired the solipsistic driving of the French. It was the commonest of sights to see them pull up at lights and begin to scream insults at each other. Lights flashed in the trees, the sun cast gold coins on the streets. June was a Midas. Now the bus turned to cross the *Alexander the Third* bridge with its splendid rearing horses. Pomp, pomp, and she remembered the French word for funerals, *les pompes funèbres*. Death in broad daylight walking with her the bells of the fuchsia down hanging, death and the maiden. A *bateau mouche* passed under the bridge, crammed full of tourists, over-ocularized, with cameras and binoculars hanging around necks and dangling from shoulders. She felt the complacent amusement of one who inhabited the town.

But when she got off the bus and walked the few blocks to the hotel, where the Simons were staying behind the *Champs Elysées*, she marveled at all the little streets she had not yet explored, each neighborhood with its complement of *tenturie, boulangerie, pharmacie, mercerie.* Here suddenly a tiny fish store displayed in the shadows the bright colors of mullet, mackerel, dorado, ray, sole, and the real scallops, which the children loved so much, with their gay, orange tongues. She was already making her goodbyes. Death made itself real to you, and then it was unreal. Now she would see Adele Simon, operated on two months ago for breast cancer. It seemed as if the whole world were being eaten up in that one trochée. And yet no one had the power to reach her beyond Nora. She could comprehend other deaths but she could not feel them.

Coming in from the bright sunshine, the small expensive-looking lobby of the hotel was very dark and drab. She was instructed to go to the Simons' room, when she asked for them at the desk. It was a large suite with *Louis Quinze* decor and heavy brocaded curtains going from floor to ceiling. There were twin beds in pale creamy wood with green satin counterpanes which were slipping to the floor. Adele greeted her with a hearty hug. Tall, energetic, dark-haired in her late fifties, she always spoke in a harsh voice at breakneck speed. Behind glasses, whose lens were so impossibly thick that her eyes were magnified a thousand times, her gaze swam dizzily towards you like dazed fish. She seemed exactly as she had always been, lively and bright, the same except that she shared her body now with her death.

"Dan's gone out for a minute to get the paper. I'll just finish dressing. You sit on the bed. How are the children? Where is Tom? What has it been like, the year, for you?"

Now that she had stopped moving, Diana felt how exhausted she was from the events of the morning. She started to tell a story about the children and their school, watching how Adele smoothed her stockings, with a special lovingness around her long elegant legs, and slipped into a pair of expensive leather shoes. She touched herself Diana saw in a new way, a way meant to reassure. But she might live for years, Diana reminded herself, and I might be killed tomorrow crossing the street.

She was relieved when the door opened and Dan appeared. Diana's heart went out to him. She could understand what he was going through, could feel as one human being does for another, not as it was between her and Adele, already distanced by the dread and guilt one felt for the dying.

"We're ready, we're ready," proclaimed Adele, as if Dan had somehow reproached them, and, snatching up a large leather matching purse, she regally led the way through the door, while Dan following quietly gave Diana a loving firm kiss on her cheek.

All the way there in the taxi Adele told long complicated stories, filled with the digressions, subplots, explanations of who the characters were, which alone could take hours in that tightly interwoven New York world of arts and money in which they lived. But the stories were usually worth it, and they were laughing drunkenly as the taxi left them at *Le Pavillion*.

They sat outside under the leafy trees and ordered the fish, which was the specialty of the house. Beyond the tables one could see people strolling through the park, over the tiny bridges, which spanned the little stream that ran through the grounds, a stream which was inhabited by swans and ducks.

Sitting between Adele and Dan, Diana felt like a daughter. They had both been dear to her when she was an adolescent. Adele had always encouraged her to think of herself as a writer, and Dan had paid her that flattering loving attention which a young girl needs from an older man if she feels herself unpopular with boys her own age. They both loved Tom as well. Looking at them as a couple Diana felt how strongly she and Tom resembled them; she, Diana, so voluble and animated in company, and Tom, like Dan, content to sit back and listen and love. When Adele dies Dan will marry in six months, she thought. He has the habit of loving, but if anything ever happened to Tom I would never remarry.

For dessert they ordered *fraises des bois* and buried the tiny ruby hearts in gobs of yellowy *crême fraiche* served from an old brown country crock. She had first tasted them with Caroline Richardson in a posh restaurant off the *Champs Elysées*. That was how one could know oneself to be "old," when the innocence of events happening for the first time was refracted through events happening for a second time. So she had found herself a few days ago, "old" as she sat on a park bench not far from where they were eating. She had brought the children there for an outing and was sitting by herself dreaming of her poems. She could see the children in the distance talking to someone on another bench. After a bit they came running back, faces flushed with excitement "Mother, mother," they called as they came, filled with their adventures. Startled she looked down and saw herself with a handbag and shoes that matched. But surely it was her mother sitting there, a quiet person who waited with no life of her own, who was there to be filled up with one's adventures, happenings, thoughts, dreams. A mother was someone whose dimensions were fixed and unchanging. Someone who turned her face like the sunflower to gaze at one with steadfast love. But she, was she that "mother"? And she reached out, baffled, to embrace, as they leaned around her, recounting their conversation.

The sun beat down. How could she ever leave Paris, where to sit like this in the sun, and stare into the black of the coffee in its white eggshell cup, to take a square of sugar, and let it soak up the coffee and suck it slowly in one's mouth, was to be utterly in control of time looking neither forwards nor back. She was feeling giddy from the wine.

"I'm taking Adele back and putting her in for a nap," said Dan firmly, "and then I'm going to the *Jeu de Paume*. Want to come Diana?"

She shook her head. "I'll take a lift back to your place." Adele, as if she hadn't heard what Dan had said, began a long story about an amateur theatre group she belonged to in New York, and once more they were gasping and laughing as they taxied through the crowded afternoon streets. They all got out, embraced on the corner, people walking around them. Diana left them reluctantly. She was a little girl, and they loved her.

At home, the morning became real again. While she had been laughing and drinking and thinking of people and places where he had never been, Patrice had been living with his news. She remembered the snapshot of the sweet frail face of the adolescent on the beach at Saint-Tropez. Did Patrice think at all of her *"je t'aime?"* When she thought of it she felt defiant.

It doesn't matter, it doesn't matter, she repeated over and over, staring at the lettuce she was washing for dinner. She now followed the system of Agnes. *Pour tuer les petites bêtes,* you placed the lettuce in a pot with a few drops of vinegar, and swished it gently and the dirt and the slugs precipitated out. She went out on the back steps to shake the lettuce dry, something which amused the children at the beginning of the year, but which now bored them. Then she hung the *saladier* on the window latch and stared down into the back street for a long time. She could see into the kitchen window of the other apartment on their floor There a woman, whom she had never spoken to, moved slowly back and forth, preparing her evening meal. She lives alone, so that must be very simple, Diana thought. And she felt thankful that she didn't live alone.

Down below, *Mme. Guillemin*, silver haired and dwarfish from this perspective, was beating a rug. Little puffs of dust arose under the strokes of her wicker beater. She had come to work in this building as a girl, and here she was at eighty, neither good, nor clever, nor talented, just lucky and viable. She got one week of vacation a year, which she spent visiting her daughter in the provinces.

It was almost five o'clock. The sky was growing unexpectedly dark. The children burst through the door shrieking, "School's over," and "A storm, a storm's coming!" They all rushed to the front balcony. The trees began to sway and bend in the gusting wind, the sky turned the color of bruises, and lightning began to rip the clouds at briefer and briefer intervals. Suddenly Patrice appeared behind them. "We always had storms like this when we lived in Hong Kong. But the lightning was even better there." They leaned together with the children, staring out into the sky as people do on shipboard and waited for the rain to come and relieve the sultry breathlessness. Like a woman in false labor, nothing happened beyond the panting of the wind and the striking of the lightning. Behind them the back door slammed violently back and forth. They went into the kitchen, she and Patrice, and watched the sky from the long sagging rectangle of the kitchen window, Diana leaning over the sill and Patrice standing close behind her.

"Do you remember last night?" he asked. "I suddenly felt terribly ill, there was an awful pain in my head. Don't you see, I knew Isabelle was dying, I knew it."

Diana remembered, his look of pain, his putting his hand to his head. Yes, all those things were true, the invisible reticulations of the cosmic net in which all things were contained and related. So near to him, she felt the perfect happiness that comes from the mere presence of the loved one. The end result of desire was eternal begetting, and that was defined as love. But surely love had nothing to do with the possessing, the bodily joining of two people, which in the end only made them objects to each other. Wasn't love that which took sustenance from closeness without acquisition? If only he would speak and say that he felt what she was feeling, too. But it was enough.

"My grandmother thanks you for the flowers, she will write to you herself to say so." Diana turned to look at him. With a great crash, almost a shudder, the rain began. Huge flat pelting drops. *"À tout à l'heure,"* he said and rushed upstairs. She went to help the children close the windows.

The children were asleep and Diana was reading, when Patrice reappeared later that night. He was in his trench coat and sat down behind a part of the folding glass doors, so that Diana saw him as through a window.

"You look as though you're on the Transcontinental Express," she said with a laugh suddenly recalling a conversation they had had earlier in the week when he was telling her about a movie written by *Robbe-Grillet*, his literary hero.

"Yes," he said abruptly, "that's what I came for, to take you there."

As they walked down the street to the Metro he said, "Diana, I know you must be criticizing me, but you must understand that I'm in a very delicate situation."

At last, she thought, but didn't dare think further out of pride. "What is that?" she asked.

There was a long pause from Patrice. She said gently, finally, "I just think that you're very unhappy...."

"Ah," he replied, shrugging. "It's perhaps just as well if you don't understand." There was another long pause. She cursed herself for having spoken.

"I'm finding it very difficult to remember Isabelle," he said.

As they came out of the Metro and walked towards the movie, it began to rain again. He held an umbrella over Diana, and, almost defiantly, she took his arm. Why not, she said to herself, we are friends. At the box office he said with a grin, "I'm broke, could you pay for you?" She thought guiltily about the last evening they had had together and handed him the money.

Once again they were in the dark together. The movie was a funny spoof of a murder mystery, and she could look over without his noticing, she hoped, and watch his profile. Things had come about as she had known, in part, they would. She was with him, she was the one he turned to. He had made no mention of Michelle for months. He was not with her now.

They went back to the apartment. It was midnight, when they returned, and, shortly afterwards as they were sitting talking, Tommy phoned from the States. They had a long consultation about the estimates of movers' fees she had been getting; he got furious at the prices, and she, at him. Fortunately, Patrice had moved off discretely to the balcony. Then Tom calmed down. He missed her, he loved her. She felt him wanting some warmth, which she was unable to give. Afterward, when she hung up, she was overwhelmed with guilt at denying him. She couldn't even remember if she had said she loved him. Duties, chores, doing things she didn't want to do, the mention of these things, between her and him, had put her into a blind rage that made her want to lash out the way she would if he had put his hands around her neck and tried to strangle her. She would have none of it. Life had forced her to submit to death, she would submit to nothing more.

She returned to Patrice on the balcony. And now it began, her waiting for him and her understanding that he was waiting as well, to see what she would do, testing her. They went in and sat at the dining room table with a candle burning, drinking *pruneau,* talking of death, holding a wake, while the candle flame flickered in the night breeze from· the open balcony doors. She spoke to him for the first time of Nora, and he talked of his memories of Isabelle. He was leaving the day after tomorrow to rejoin his family. They talked about *Robbe-Grillet*. "He is so subtle," Patrice said, "He understands how people work to conceal things from themselves and each other." They spoke of Sylvia, for whom he again expressed great admiration. They began to quote proverbs to each other, and he put out his hand and took Diana's testing for, "cold hands, warm heart," and for once her hands were warm.

They drifted to the balcony unable to separate, she would not dismiss him, he would not take leave. It was growing light. They spoke of grief. "My parents will never recover," he said, "I am not the good person she was." It was four o'clock and the sky was the color of a *Puvis de Chavannes* painting, a sickly blue-green. Once again, they slowly parted at the kitchen door. Weary, all Diana could think was that she hadn't disgraced herself. It had been a duel of some sort, but she had not disgraced herself.

The next morning, he came by to get her to go to the polls, to watch the voting, as he had promised, but she heard the children tell him she was asleep. When she got out of bed an hour later and came, barefooted in Tom's silk dressing gown, without her glasses, to say good morning to the children, there he was sitting on the bed reading the paper, grinning up at her in her blushing discomfort at seeing him. She went away, got dressed, had coffee with him.

"I am having lunch with Michelle and the family today," he said with a mock air of *hauteur,* "It will be a very white glove affair." She was taken aback to hear him mention that name. She wanted only to think how he had seen her in the dressing gown, and how beautiful she had looked.

When he left, she took a bath, washed her hair, put on a bikini, and went out on her balcony to sunbathe. Paris was asleep, everyone was out in the country for *"le weekend."* Scarcely a car moved down the avenue, and only an occasional passerby strolled with a dog or a child. The sky overhead presented one or two clouds, like beauty marks, to set off its superb blue. The children were reading, reading alongside her. Suddenly Kit looked up, "Look, Patrice is down there," she said. Glancing through the railings, Diana saw him walking briskly towards the building. Kit waved enthusiastically; Patrice waved back.

Diana wondered if she should put on a shirt and decided against it. He probably wasn't coming in anyway. And then suddenly, he was there, unannounced. She turned and saw him staring at her back. Uncomfortable, she tried to pretend that she didn't notice how naked she was for him.

She knew that her back was long and beautiful, and that her legs were short and chunky. She wished she were clothed. He described the lunch, "It was duller, than I had even expected. I left as soon as I could. I have to pack, you know."

He looked sharply at her, was it with a touch of reproach that she had shown herself, that she had shown herself clearly middle aged, and that she had known what she was doing? She tried to divine the glance he gave her as he left, but could not. Never mind, she thought, he would be back. But he didn't come, and, to her surprise, he didn't drop in for dinner. She and the children ate quietly. Slowly the light withdrew. At ten, the children were asleep, and it was dark. She played some records and read. There was a tiny; discrete knock at the door. There he stood. Her heart leaped. He will come in now, she thought. He had to do his laundry, he said, and then he was going out with a few others and join the crowds around the party headquarters where the polling was coming in. Could she lend him thirty francs for his laundry? He'd pay her back. Diana smiled and went to look for her purse. She had nothing smaller than a hundred franc note, twenty dollars. She handed it to him.

"Just drop the change in an envelope," she said "because I'm going to bed early."

But she couldn't go to bed without seeing him. It surprised her so to hear he was going to be with friends – "his own age" she whispered to herself. She had thought of him as someone without any friends, certainly not male ones. He had never mentioned anyone. She waited up until 1:00, sure that he would drop by.

The next day she waited, starting up every time the elevator creaked. The day was long and tedious. She knew he was leaving that evening. He had. no doubt, many last minute things to attend to, but then, she said to herself, twenty dollars is a considerable sum of money, he'd have to bring change. Surely he'd want to say farewell to the children?

That night came and went. She remembered that the day before Isabelle died he had looked around the apartment and said, "I'll never come back to this apartment again." She had thought it was because of his childhood memories. Now she imagined sentimentally, that he was referring to the loss of their presence, hers, that he would not wish to return.

A week passed. Suddenly she realized that he was gone. Without a word. The knowledge began to fester like a splinter, tiny but virulent. But I will get a letter; she told herself. He was after all in a state when he left. And then on arriving, his family will need him. There will be the realization of Isabelle's death all over again, naturally he will be too preoccupied to write. But every day she trembled, when *Mme. Guillemin* brought the mail. There will be a letter she told herself, with the money, and the acknowledgement of his love for her, by a word, a line.

Sullen torrential rains descended on them. It was cold, impossible to go out. She and the children huddled together in the apartment as though it were a little ark.

It wasn't the money, she tried to tell herself, to fight down the anger that rose up in her. God knew she owed him the money, for all the many things he had done for them, given them, all of them. But yes, it was the money. His remark about the rich stayed with her. *"Une femme qui a beaucoup d'indulgence pour moi,"* he had purred. So self-satisfied in the kitchen at Saint-Tropez. Her naked back, her breasts in her bikini top. His inscrutable glance. Of course, he can't write he loves you she warned herself. But he will, he will, she knew it. Out on the balcony the rain made nipples on the railings.

And then, just as suddenly as the rains had come, the sky cleared, and the brilliant June weather returned. Tom came back. And every day she waited, but the letter didn't come. She wrote to his parents with condolences and received a short note in reply from his father. It thanked her for her sympathy. "Life is nothing but a cruel joke," it ended.

They all went off on a trip through the Loire. When they returned there was still no letter. Gradually she adjusted to being a family again, to Tom. At moments, she took out a memory of Patrice, like someone looking at an old dress or a photograph, but not often, because of the anger and shame. On the fourteenth of July, a few days before they were to leave Paris, they went dancing with friends at one of the *bals de quartier*, and, suddenly, listening to the strains of a *passé double*, Tom's arms were Patrice's, his body Patrice's body, holding her close and she smiled looking over his shoulder, melting. "What thoughts of love are you having?" asked Tom, tenderly looking into her dreamy face and holding her more closely.

She hated Patrice. He had had her. *"Il ma joué un tour,"* she said bitterly to herself. It was just as well that nothing had happened. There was nothing to tell, nothing to regret, nothing to conceal. There was no word. Nothing.

In the end, she broke the silence, not daring to write directly to him, not wanting to. When they left the apartment she left him a short note, merely saying that she hoped that all was well, that she had listened, but she had never been able to hear the nightingale he had spoken of.

Later, months later, she regretted leaving the note, sure that his mother had read it, for she had left it, along with a note for the parents and payment of the last minute bills, on a slip of paper folded over with his name, Patrice.

THE END

Made in the USA
Middletown, DE
12 April 2023